GENESIS DAY

GENESIS DAY

a novel of the new world

DAVID SLOCUM

PROTOTYPE PRESS

for the ones who never gave up on their crazy dreams

TABLE OF CONTENTS

GENESIS DAY

PART ONE
THE NEW WORLD

PART ONE

THE NEW WORLD

ONE

THE COLLAPSE BEGAN mere hours before the Germany video, but those twelve seconds of footage were the first I became aware of it.

Danny texted *CHECK THIS OUT* to our hockey team's group chat, the link coming through moments later. The title immediately caught my eye: *Man attacked in Berlin streets.*

I opened it with YouTube as I walked into my first class. Finding my seat, I set my phone on the desk and fished a pencil from my backpack.

The second bell rang. Mr. Collins began taking roll. I listened with half an ear for my name, and by the time I turned back to my phone, the video was already over. I played it again, leaning forward on my elbows.

It began with two men wrestling in the middle of a packed intersection, street lamps and headlights illuminating the fight. People shouted in German. Some were cheering. The camera zoomed in and I caught a glimpse of the attacker. He might have been in his eighties, but he seemed stronger than his age allowed. A second later, he bit the other man's ear and *yanked*. The victim screamed. Bystanders rushed to help.

The video stopped. My jaw dropped a fraction. I played it again. Yes, I saw correctly. As far as I could tell, his ear was gone. I scanned the classroom, catching Montoya's eye three rows to my left. He held up his phone and mouthed *What the fuck?*

I shrugged.

"Phones away, pencils out," Mr. Collins said. "Who's ready for the test?" A few people grumbled in acknowledgment. "Trick question, you're *all* ready because I did an incredible job preparing you."

I pursed my lips and dropped my phone in my backpack as Mr. Collins handed out the midterm. I tapped my pencil on the desk, trying to get myself to focus. It was just a fight. Things like that happen all the time, right? All you had to do was look and you'd find plenty of crazy shit online.

But if I couldn't fix the problem, I didn't want to know what it was, so I locked it away and focused on the test. Upon turning in my exam, I'd mostly forgotten about the clip. The others hadn't.

A handful of friends sent the link to me over the next hour. By third period, Danny had shared another three videos. I watched those too, worry forming in my gut at the similarities—all violent attacks—and the fact they came from different cities.

Paris. Tokyo. Rio de Janeiro.

By the time I made it to the cafeteria for lunch, I'd silenced my phone so I could study for my history test. But I couldn't escape the buzz of conversation. Everyone was talking about it. Whatever *it* was.

Urgent whispers passed from group to group. People leaned over tables and gestured wildly.

Deeply unsettled, I sat next to Jamison at our table. He had sharp eyes, pale skin, and he wore a backwards hat and the black windbreaker they'd given to everyone on our hockey team at the start of the season. The number eighty-one was embroidered in red on the back of the neck and left sleeve.

I put in my headphones and closed my eyes, giving myself a moment of quiet before I dove into my notes. I absentmindedly took a bite of pizza as I turned the page.

Jamison tensed. I followed his gaze to where Taylor Owens and two of her friends—Olivia and Riley—sat at the table across from us. Riley was taller than most guys in the school and played varsity volleyball. Olivia did something with music, though I wasn't sure what. I didn't know much else about her other than her parents were from India and her family owned one of the fancy bars downtown. She had straight black hair that framed her angular face.

And then there was Taylor. We sat next to each other in personal finance and had a few mutual friends, but we didn't spend much time together outside of school. Still, there was something about her freckles and dimpled smile that made my chest flutter every time I saw them.

Taylor tucked her red hair over one shoulder and looked in our direction.

"I think she's checking me out," Jamison said, removing his hat to run a hand through his wavy hair.

Taylor's bright green eyes caught mine. Her lips turned up and everything faded as I flashed back to Friday night.

It was just a few hours after our championship hockey game. Music shook the foundations of the house. I swayed pleasantly on my feet. Taylor's silhouette pressed me against the wall, her hands on my chest. She smelled like peaches, tasted of vodka, and somehow made the world pause as we kissed for the first time.

I mirrored her half-smile as she pulled away. She kissed me on the cheek, whispered, "I need another drink," and disappeared around the corner. A week later, it was like nothing had happened. We talked in class, and our moment at the party seemed like all we'd have.

Taylor turned to her friends. I went back to studying. This hardly lasted ten minutes before Jamison nudged me with an elbow, one earbud in. "Check your phone."

Electricity shot through my body as I remembered the videos. I braced myself before tapping the screen to find I had 157 unread messages, mostly from my hockey team. I glanced at Jamison, but he was glued to his phone. I skimmed the texts, freezing at a video title: *Violent attacks break out in the streets of New York.*

DANNY: *It's happening in the US*

MONTOYA: *Stop sending this shit*

DANNY: *It's to keep us informed*

MONTOYA: *I know what's going on!*
I don't need an update every two fuck-
ing minutes

RYAN: *I'm with Montoya*

SAM: *No way this is real. Has to be a*
hoax

DANNY: *It's not a hoax. The scale's too*
big to be fake dumbass

HANSON: *It could be a terrorist at-tack or something*

The argument continued, with unfounded theories coming out of nowhere. I kept scrolling until I reached the most recent video. *LIVE STREAM: Mass panic in Tampa Bay as citizens face an unidentified threat.*

I stared for a long moment before getting up the nerve to show Jamison. He removed his earbuds, face tightening when he saw the screen. "I'll call them."

Jamison went through his contacts and put his phone to his ear. He rose from the table and started pacing. I glanced at Taylor. She and her friends huddled around one of their phones.

I didn't want to do it, but I had to know.

I clicked the video. Both reporters sat stiffly behind the desk, wearing a blue dress and plaid suit, respectively. The man adjusted his glasses as the woman continued the report.

"*...seen countless eyewitness submissions over the last hour. It forces us to ask, what's really going on?*"

"*Although we don't know specifics, it's safe to say this is occurring across the nation. We've already heard confirmation from many cities in the United States,*" the man said.

"*But what's the threat? Is this something we should be worried about?*"

The man shifted in his seat. "*The last thing we should do is panic without adequate information. We don't know the nature of these incidents...*" he trailed off. "*It looks like our producers have ground-level footage they would like to show at this time. We must warn anyone watching that these are extremely graphic images, but we feel it is impor-*"

tant to share everything we know about the situation."

The view of the newsroom changed to shaky footage of a man shouting into the camera as he ran down the street. *"They're taking over, man! I'm telling you this is some crazy shit!"*

The producers hadn't even taken the time to censor the video, but maybe language didn't matter if you'd already decided to show graphic violence. I shifted uncomfortably at the implication.

The man continued to yell as he flipped the camera to show the flooded road. People scrambled in every direction like ants after the hill had been kicked.

"There's one!" he yelled.

The camera zoomed in to show someone being tackled from behind. Primal screaming filled the air as the attacker ripped the victim's face with her mouth and hands. The psycho's head twisted in the direction of the camera, blood glistening on her chin.

"Oh shit oh shit OH SHIT!"

The man fumbled with his keys in front of a car. He dove into the driver's seat and slammed the door closed. The camera adjusted in time to show the crazy woman throwing herself against the windshield. Spiderwebs spread across the glass, blood smearing the view. The car shot forward and the attacker flew over the top.

The footage ended, leaving me dumbfounded. The video returned to the reporters. Jamison picked up his pacing as he dialed another number.

"Again, we apologize for the language and graphic content, but we want to get to the bottom of this as much as anyone," the man said, turning to his partner. *"We're hearing similar reports around the world. I hate to say it Tracey, but are these related incidents?"*

"Making assumptions is dangerous territory, but it's clear we're facing a massive, yet unknown threat." The woman straightened her

notes. *"Even now, we are getting confirmation from first responders that there are nearly three hundred documented casualties in the United States alone. That number is growing at an exponential rate and is impossible to accurately track."*

"What exactly is the threat? As we saw in the footage, people are clearly violent, but what's the cause?"

"Unfortunately, I can't answer that. Our only clue is that most of these attacks seem to start in hospitals and nursing homes. But whatever it is, there's no sign of it slowing down."

"Targeting the most vulnerable of us…" The man bowed his head. *"The more I think about it, the clearer it is to me that this isn't a natural event. Nineteen cities impacted in a matter of hours. Around the world we have Paris, London, Berlin, Beijing…"* He paused and looked directly into the camera. *"To me, this is coordinated. This is premeditated. I keep asking myself, who could possibly be responsible for something like this?"*

"Dad! Thank god you answered," Jamison said. "What's going on? We're seeing the stuff on the news. Where's mom? She didn't pick up—"

"We have word from additional impacted cities. Los Angeles, Phoenix, Denver, Minneapolis, Nashville…" The woman went down the list with a mechanical voice.

Minneapolis.

I dropped my phone on the table and massaged my temples, the video still playing. Dread coiled around my lungs. Our school was barely ten minutes south of Minneapolis. And only three blocks away? One of the biggest hospitals in the city: St. Thomas Memorial.

I had a hard time believing this was real. But there *were* facts, however insane they seemed.

Violent outbursts. Confirmed deaths. The world under siege.

A text from Danny appeared at the top of my screen. *We're screwed. They're in Minneapolis. Nice knowing you.*

I focused on the news report to keep myself from spiraling out of control.

"...for the safety of everyone at the station, we are ending our broadcast. We urge you all to find someplace safe and wait for law enforcement to provide assistance."

Both anchors stood and began removing their microphone wires. Crew members dashed through the frame. The male reporter put his phone to his ear as he disappeared from the shot. Shouts echoed in the background. Through it all, the camera stayed fixed at the desk.

Ten seconds after everyone left the frame, the feed cut out.

I turned off my phone, coming back to reality.

The cafeteria simmered like a bomb with an invisible timer. Some people paced, taking careful steps the length of a table. Others made phone calls. Tension lined every movement. Backpacks zipped up. Whispers and anxious glances passed from table to table.

I closed my eyes. The image of the crazy woman kept replaying in my mind. The way she attacked the person on the ground. The screaming. How she threw herself at the car with no regard for her safety. She looked human, but...savage, somehow.

"Mom and Dad are safe," Jamison said, squeezing back into his seat. "They locked themselves in their hotel room."

Relief flooded my body. "Do they have any idea what's going on?"

"No one does, but Dad saw a report where a police officer shot someone," Jamison said. He furtively looked around the cafeteria. "Then the person got up."

"*What?*"

"I don't want to be the one to say it, but this might be it. *The* end…" Jamison said quietly.

I almost laughed aloud, but the seriousness in Jamison's expression made me pause. He was joking, right? He had to be.

"No way," I said.

"Hear me out," Jamison said, leaning forward until he was inches away. "People are *eating* other people. Dad saw someone get shot. That same person got up again and attacked the cop. Then the cop started attacking other people. What the hell does that sound like to you? It's the *fucking apocalypse!*"

I shook my head. "No, it's not—"

"Cody," Jamison said, low enough that I barely heard him. His eyes flickered around the cafeteria. "This is it. You know that deep down, and you *can't* ignore it."

I clenched my jaw as I scanned the sea of students. These were friends—people we'd grown up with. The lump in my throat made it hard to swallow. "…Jesus…"

Jamison scanned the tables, chewing his lip before giving a faint shrug. "I probably shouldn't say this—"

"Then don't."

"—but haven't you wondered what this might be like?"

My face tightened as I understood his meaning. "The end of the world?"

Jamison offered a tiny nod. I opened my mouth. Closed it. I couldn't form a response. I jumped to my feet, mind racing. Each breath felt like it came through a hot blanket. I tugged at my shirt collar, suddenly lightheaded. I felt people's eyes on me and saw the same fear on their faces as the kind that swirled inside my body.

We needed to get out. Everyone would start panicking soon, dangerously. I started pacing again. It felt like the walls were closing in. Too many people and not enough room. I shook my hands at my side, clenching them over and over.

Jamison opened his mouth. I cut him off. "Wait."

The siren was faint. I strained my ears against the noise around me. Yes, it was getting louder. I faced the windows that lined the entire north side of the cafeteria—the windows that pointed to the hospital and the heart of the city. The siren turned into a wail. I looked around the cafeteria. Everyone stilled.

WEEEEEOOOOOWEEEEEOOOOO!

A single cop car zipped down the street, blue and red lights splashing on the buildings. It was gone in a second, leaving only nervous silence behind. Whispers slowly filled the void.

Jamison appeared at my side. "I know you've thought about it."

"Who hasn't?" I admitted, watching the windows.

"This is it," Jamison said reverently. "This is the start of the new world."

"Stop. You're not poetic."

"I thought it was good."

"It wasn't."

"So, what's the plan?"

Additional sirens blared in the distance.

I crossed my arms and bounced on the balls of my feet. "Make it home. Wait out the riots. I don't want to be here when everyone goes ape-shit," I said, surprising myself with how easily the words slipped out. I knew what to do.

It was simple.

Look after yourself. Don't panic. Don't do anything stupid or take unnecessary risks.

In that moment, something primal surged in my veins. Excitement. Terror. The perfect thrill of a future no one could predict.

"Exactly what I was thinking," Jamison said, clapping me on the back.

"We're horrible people," I said.

Jamison shrugged. "At least we don't have to worry about going to hell for it," he said, nodding toward the windows. "I have a feeling hell is about to meet us right here, right now."

"What did I *just* tell you?"

"You have to admit that was pretty good."

Two police cars whipped down the street. Another. Two more. Out of sight, I heard the thunderous *smack* of cars slamming together.

Students pressed themselves against the windows of the cafeteria, murmurs turning to panicked shouts. I stood on the bench of our table to get a better view. People sprinted by outside, flooding the lawn in front of the cafeteria. Flailing. Scattering in every direction. A few wore scrubs and hospital gowns, but I couldn't tell who was attacking and who was trying to escape.

Gunfire *popped* in the distance. A cop backpedaled on the sidewalk, firing at an attacker I couldn't see yet. A woman tripped and another dove after her, clawing at her back. The cop raced to their sides and pointed his gun at the crazy person on top. He was tackled by someone else. A flash and a crack of gunfire. The cop pushed off the body, blood covering his face and chest. He finished off the other attacker with a shot to the head, then hoisted the woman to her feet. Blood streamed from the right side of her face.

I covered my mouth and stepped off the bench. The cafeteria boiled with terror. People screamed at the carnage. Some stood frozen in place. Others surged to the windows to document everything with their phones.

"We have to get out of here," I said.

Jamison pulled his attention away from the windows, face pale.

He nodded. I slung my backpack over my shoulder and started shoving my way through the crowd. Everyone behind us pushed their way to the windows to see what was going on. I didn't stop to answer the questions leveled in our direction. We reached the cafeteria entrance as the PA system crackled to life.

"ATTENTION, STUDENTS AND FACULTY OF LANCASTER HIGH SCHOOL. FOR EVERYONE'S SAFETY, WE ARE GOING ON IMMEDIATE LOCKDOWN."

"No, no, no…" I murmured, sliding through the doorway.

There were hallways to both sides and straight ahead. I took off to the left. The closest exit was just a few turns away. From there, it was a direct shot to the parking lot, which also meant it was closest to the chaos on the street.

"STAY IN YOUR CLASSROOMS AND LOCK THE DOORS. IF YOU ARE OUTSIDE A CLASSROOM, MOVE TO THE NEAREST SAFETY ZONE—THE AUDITORIUM OR THE LIBRARY."

"We can't go this way!" Jamison called after me.

"Do you want to get out or not?" I tossed back. "We'll find another way if it's too dangerous."

"DO NOT LET ANYONE INTO THE BUILDING. PLEASE REMAIN CALM AND MOVE IN AN ORDERLY FASHION."

I sprinted down the hallway, Jamison pounding at my heels. We turned the final corner and emerged into the north foyer just as someone burst through one of the doors. The cop, holding the injured woman in his arms like a rag doll. Someone else pushed through the doors. Then another. A half dozen made their way inside before someone's booming voice cut the air.

"No one else gets in!" Principal Shirley bellowed as he came into view. The newcomers scurried away into the bowels of the school.

"We have to get people to safety! You don't know what's going on out there!" The cop rose to his feet.

I skidded to a halt twenty feet away from the group. Jamison crashed into my back, pitching us forward.

"I do! Which is why," Principal Shirley said, punctuating each following word, "NO. ONE. ELSE. GETS. IN!" He swiftly moved down the line of doors, locking them with difficulty as people tried shoving their way through.

My gaze dropped to the woman and the pool of blood forming around her head. A few more people made it inside by the time Principal Shirley locked the final door. He stepped back as stragglers pounded on the metal. He turned away, face twisted by guilt.

His eyes caught mine. "What are you doing? Get to the auditorium!" He pointed back the way we came. He turned to the cop. "How is she?"

"She's dead," he returned.

I was about to leave when the woman moved. It was just a twitch of her hand that caught my eye. Then her arm jerked.

"…oh shit…" Jamison whispered.

"What should we—" Principal Shirley broke off mid-sentence.

The cop followed his gaze to the woman as she attempted to sit up. Gurgling noises came from her throat. The cop immediately dropped to a knee to help her up, but as soon as he did, the woman lunged for his neck.

Tortured screams echoed in the foyer. Blood gushed from the wound to cover his uniform and the woman's face. She kept biting until things were quiet again. The cop's body crumbled to the ground. Principal Shirley staggered back in horror. He spared one look in our direction before taking off the other way, heels clicking on the floor.

Through it all, I couldn't move, and I fought against my churning stomach. It was happening. The worst-case scenario was right before us. The woman's jaw worked. Bits of flesh dangled from her chin. It was like a bucket of red paint had been poured over her head.

She cocked her head in our direction. My heart seized.

Maybe we shouldn't have gone this way…

TWO

"LET'S GO, LET'S go, let's go!" Jamison exploded, shoving me away from the scene.

I stumbled the first few steps before finding my stride, the woman just behind. My backpack bounced from side to side. I shrugged it off and it thumped to the ground.

"Still think it's nothing?" Jamison asked, our feet pounding the floor.

"You were right," I said.

"Ha! Always," Jamison said. "We'll need a name for them."

"You can't be serious," I said, glancing back again. The…thing… was at the end of the hallway. We were faster than them, at least.

"Can't be zombie," Jamison panted as we careened around another corner.

"Why?"

"Too obvious. What about corpse?"

"What the hell…"

We rounded the corner to the cafeteria and collided with another group. I clipped an ankle and pitched headfirst across the floor, smacking my elbow on the ground. Feet charged past my head. I stood before I could be trampled, finding myself in front of Taylor and her friends.

"Oh my god, I'm sorry, you came out of nowhere," Taylor said, touching my arm.

I grunted in response as I massaged my throbbing elbow. Even the rush of adrenaline couldn't mask the pain. Riley and Olivia flanked Taylor and threw anxious glances behind them.

"THEY BROKE THROUGH!" A cry echoed in the cafeteria.

"There's another coming from behind," I said, taking heavy breaths.

People flooded from the cafeteria down the right hallway. I faced the direction Jamison and I had come. The corpse was seconds away.

Taylor's eyes widened at the sight of the bloodied woman. "Come on." She yanked me toward the center hallway. Fewer people were going this way because it took longer to loop to the auditorium. But with little traffic, we might beat most of the crowd. Smart.

Everything blurred as we pounded down the stretch. We skidded around corners, narrowly dodging people and discarded textbooks. It became a rhythm: sprint, dodge, fly around a corner. Again and again until my heart was pounding out of my chest and the auditorium entrance came into view.

The double doors were jammed with people trying to squeeze through. I dove into the crowd, throwing my shoulder into people with little regard for who I hit. I should have felt bad, but chivalry died the moment people started eating each other. I was *not* going to be the last one in.

I caught an elbow in the ribs and one in the side of the head. It only made me push harder. I could handle this. The best lesson hockey taught me was how to get up after being blindsided at center ice, and only unconsciousness would stop me now. If that happened, it was already too late.

I tumbled through the doorway. The ground sloped toward the stage with rows of chairs lining each side of the aisle. I stopped a few rows away to wait for Jamison and Taylor. Some people slumped in chairs, numbly looking ahead. Others ran for the stage, putting distance between them and the mayhem outside.

"You have to make a break for it!" The guy next to me shouted, phone to his ear. Mark Esso. I recognized him from the rugby team. He was *large*. At least two hundred thirty pounds of bulging muscle. I think he was Samoan.

Jamison barreled through the entrance while spouting a string of curses. I flagged him down, then Taylor.

"Have you seen the others?" Taylor asked, craning her neck around the auditorium.

I shook my head. How long before the corpse caught up with us? What about the ones that broke through the cafeteria?

Someone had to shut the doors. It was the only way to keep us from being overrun. The rational part of my brain knew this had to happen, but I couldn't be the one to do it. I couldn't trap people outside to die like that.

"Hold on, I'm coming to get you," Mark said.

He vaulted the last rows and forced his way up the stream of traffic. His momentum stalled five feet from the entrance. Olivia stumbled inside and tripped over a backpack. He immediately sprang to her side and helped her up, the flow of traffic leading them away from the doors. Taylor waved them down.

"…sure you're ok?" Mark asked as they joined us, still protectively holding Olivia's arm.

"Yeah, thanks," she said.

"Good…" Mark looked over his shoulder. He checked his phone every few seconds.

"Who are you looking for?" Jamison asked.

"My sister—"

Muffled shrieks sounded outside the doors. All semblances of order vanished as people clawed their way forward, throwing fists and elbows in their fight for safety. Someone fell. The moment he hit the ground, students trampled over his back and head until he ceased to move.

I watched in disbelief. The flow of people thinned, but the ones who made it through were covered in blood from wounds on their arms and sides. Two teachers wrestled one of the doors closed. Another—tears streaming down her face—dragged the motionless student to the side.

Mark yelled into his phone. "Alright, I'm coming!"

Two corpses hobbled through the remaining doorway. Mark narrowly dodged the first but was tackled to the ground by the second. They rolled down the aisle. Mark grunted with effort as he gripped its neck, barely keeping its snapping teeth from his face.

The second door slammed shut.

"NO!" Mark howled, grip wavering.

Hoisting his backpack by the straps, Jamison sprinted forward and unloaded a swing at the corpse's head. It fell to the side, allowing Mark to scramble to his feet. Over and over, Jamison slammed his backpack into its face until it was a mess of blood and brain chunks.

"BITCH!" Jamison growled. He set off after the other corpse, which was gnawing on an unconscious person's leg.

Mark threw himself at the doors but was quickly besieged by teachers and students. They wrestled him to the ground as he shouted, "YOU HAVE TO LET HER IN!"

"We can't do that!"

"YOU HAVE TO OPEN THE DOOR!"

Pounding and desperate shouts came from the other side. In less than a minute there was relative silence. Mark moaned on the ground. The teachers slowly released their hold on him. He didn't make any effort to move as he took one shuddering breath after another.

My knees buckled. I sank into a chair. Taylor settled next to me, barely keeping the emotion off her face. I could see the pain and terror in her eyes. Olivia sobbed on the floor. I never saw Riley make it inside…

Jamison shuffled back to our position, his gore-covered backpack hanging limply in one hand. "I knew those textbooks would come in handy," he said, sitting on my other side. He wiped his face, smearing blood over his cheeks. There was a wild glint in his eyes.

Growling sounded behind us. Jamison twisted around. "For Christ's sake…"

The trampled kid rose to his feet. Jamison snagged his backpack and climbed over the rows to meet the new corpse. Someone yelled for him to stop, but it was too late. One hit and the corpse fell. I turned away but couldn't block out the sickening *thunks* of each additional swing.

"Are there any other dead people in here? Because they are *not* our friends," Jamison said to the auditorium at large. Terrified eyes watched his every move, and when he met their gaze, they turned away.

"Psychopath!" a girl said from the crowd.

Jamison turned in a circle but didn't rise to the bait. He just waved a hand in the air and climbed back into our row, sopping backpack at his feet. "I had to do it. You know that, right?" he asked, looking toward the stage. "I had to do it," he repeated quietly, to himself this time.

I didn't answer.

I don't know how long we sat there. At some point, Olivia brought Mark over, his eyes puffy and bloodshot. Taylor pulled out her phone, hands trembling. She sorted through her contacts and put her phone to her ear. I twisted my thumbs over each other, pretending not to listen. Her voice shook.

"Mom!…no, I'm safe…they broke into the school, but we're locked in the auditorium…we're going to wait it out…no, you don't need to get me…stay at home! I'll be fine…" Tears rolled down her cheeks. "…where's dad? Ok, good…don't come get me. It'll be ok… fine. Ten minutes?…ok, call me when you're close…love you too."

Taylor hung up and sank deeper into her chair. I waited for her to talk, but she just wrapped her arms around her chest and closed her eyes.

Oppressive silence hung over the room as hundreds of students and a handful of teachers milled around in various stages of shock and grief. A few of the football players carried the bodies to the back of the auditorium and covered them with jackets. Still, nothing could be done about the stained linoleum or the salt and iron scent of blood in the air.

People with injuries huddled together against the far wall as others did their best to wrap makeshift bandages where they could. I eyed that group warily. A few people slumped against the wall, barely moving. If they started to turn…

Other groups slowly came together. The remaining football players argued in front of the stage. Teachers went back and forth, making weak attempts at calming the students. A glint of metal caught my eye a dozen rows ahead: a girl, pocketing a pair of scissors.

Our eyes met.

I leaned close to Jamison. "We need to find a way out of here."

He did a quick survey of the area, head bobbing. "There should be an exit behind the stage," he said. He leaned over and caught the attention of the others. "We're getting out of here. Want to come with us?"

"Are you insane? Where are you going?" Olivia asked.

"Keep it down," Jamison hissed. "Things are about to get bad. As soon as people start asking who's in charge, or if someone else turns…"

I half listened to Jamison while keeping an eye on the injured. Four people crowded around a limp form on the ground. I could only see the legs. They kept looking at the person, then the room, then back to the person. Someone ran up the side aisle and grabbed a teacher by the arm, hauling him over to the motionless student.

"…we'll go through backstage—"

"Time to go," I cut Jamison off, standing up. "Are you coming or not?"

Olivia hesitated, looking at Taylor for direction. It wasn't right to make her choose like this, but all I could do was trust my instincts, and it didn't feel right to stay.

"I'm coming," Mark said. "I need to find my parents…"

"I'm waiting for mine," Taylor said.

"They're not coming through the front door," Jamison said. "And you're not getting out the way we came. Do what you want, but we're leaving."

"Fine," Taylor said, then added in a whisper, "…should have called me back by now…"

"I'll come too," Olivia said.

"Alright, be calm. Don't draw attention. Everything will be fine,"

Jamison said. He motioned us toward the left aisle, away from the wounded.

Taylor made another call as we walked toward the stage. Then, cursing, she tried again. No answer. We were nearly at the stage when the right side of the room burst into motion. Shouts rose in the air. I spared a glance back. The corpse rose on shaky feet.

Montoya?

My heart sank with recognition but I had no time to dwell.

We skirted a pack of freshmen and climbed the stage to enter the wings. The shouts faded as we made our way deeper backstage. Props and overflowing costume boxes piled on the floor and in dark corners. I picked my way through the maze, scanning the ceiling.

"There it is." I pointed toward the neon exit sign.

"Hold up. We'll need weapons," Jamison said. He dove into one of the boxes of props and came up with a wooden sword. He chewed his lip. "If only I could find a knight costume…"

Olivia scowled. Mark silently went through the boxes while Jamison gave his sword a few experimental swings. He tossed it from hand to hand, feeling the weight.

"Catch," Mark said, tossing me a PVC pipe. He gave one to Olivia who looked at it like it might bite her. Taylor took hers in stride, practically bouncing off the walls.

"Fuck!" she yelled.

I cut in front of her and gripped her arms. "Taylor! Hey, look at me." I worked to catch her eyes. "We have to go."

"My parents are coming—"

"It's been thirty minutes! They would have answered if…"

"If *what?*" Her eyes blazed, knuckles white from gripping her phone.

If they were alive? I couldn't say that. Something else might have happened. Maybe their phones died, or traffic was too heavy to talk. The others didn't make a sound. Even Jamison stilled.

I said the next part as calmly and honestly as I could. "I think you know they're not making it here. It's been too long. We're leaving, and I want you to come with us."

Taylor shrugged out of my grip. She looked at the stick in her hand. I thought she might hit me with it.

"The most important thing you can do right now is take care of yourself," I said. "Try your parents again. If they don't answer, leave a message that you'll meet them back home. That's all you can do. If they're out there, you'll find each other."

I turned to join the others. Jamison's brow knit together. "That was cold."

"It had to be done," I said. The world was falling apart and all we could do was change with it. We had to make the hard choices to stay alive. I examined my weapon. "Seriously, Mark…this is the best you could find? It's going to snap if I try to hit anything with it."

"Then use it to stab things," he cut back.

I pursed my lips. *That might work.*

Taylor shuffled toward us. She shook her head in response to our questioning looks. "Let's go," she said.

"Jamison, do you have the keys?" I asked.

He patted his pocket and gave a thumbs up. Mark hovered over the door handle.

"Wait, what's the plan?" Olivia asked.

"Find our car. Make it home. Wait for things to blow over," I said.

"I don't want to go to your house," Olivia said. "I want to find my family, but I don't have a car to do that."

"I left my keys in my locker," Mark added.

"You said I should wait for my parents at my place," Taylor said.

I raised my hands to their objections. "We can't do that. Jamison and I are *letting* you come along. You can come to our place and leave from there."

"We could just beat you up and take your car," Mark said quietly.

I gave a nervous laugh. "If you knew what it looked like, maybe," I said.

Mark's face remained impassive.

Jamison held up his hands. "It's fine, we'll help you out. Our parents are out of town anyway."

I threw my arms into the air. "What did we *just* talk about?"

"We have to help them," Jamison shot back.

I clenched my jaw. Mark shifted his weight from foot to foot. Olivia looked like she was going to break down again. Taylor wouldn't meet my eyes and kept checking her phone.

It hit me then. They were terrified, just like I was, and desperate to find their families. Mark had just lost a sister. Taylor's parents weren't answering.

I became aware of the void in my chest. I'd been prepared to cut these people out of my life forever. Ready to survive at any cost. That scared me. These were real people.

What was the point of survival if you lost your humanity in the process?

My shoulders slumped. Everyone looked at me, expectant. Pleading.

"Alright, we'll do whatever you need," I said, turning to Taylor. "Do you want to wait here for your parents?"

She took a deep breath, but her voice still wavered. "I don't think they're coming."

I wanted to say how sorry I was, but the words stuck in my throat. It felt like a hollow sentiment coming from me. I motioned to the door.

"Stay quiet when we get outside," Jamison said. "We're going to have to loop around to the main parking lot. Look for a green Sequoia."

I gripped my pitiful weapon in sweaty hands. Mark shoved the door open, flooding the backstage with crisp air and blinding sunlight.

One by one, we emerged into the unknown.

THREE

I DID A quick spin to check our surroundings.

We faced the southern part of the campus where the football and soccer fields sprawled into the distance. Concrete paths wound to other buildings through grass and groves of trees. We were a good distance from the main city streets, but that didn't mean we were safe.

A few corpses milled about on our right, blinking in and out of sight as they passed between trees. Another pack crossed the soccer field at a lazy pace. Both groups were too far away to notice us, and if they did, we already had a good head start.

Otherwise, it was strangely deserted.

I dropped my hands to my sides.

Part of me expected the school grounds to be crawling with the dead, but that didn't quite make sense. I didn't know how many people had been turned, but it probably wasn't as much as I originally thought. The stampedes of people made it seem like we were already surrounded by corpses. Besides, they seemed to be drawn by the panic. Why stay here when everyone was trampling through the city? They would follow the crowd, not the few.

Maybe. I didn't know how this was supposed to work.

Still, the emptiness set me on edge. It carried the tangible weight of abandonment. No one sat under the trees or on the benches. No teams practiced on the fields. Nobody walked between buildings. Everyone must have found safety inside or left the area as they were chased further into the city.

I felt the heaviness of knowing this would only continue to spread, that it would only get worse. The dead would keep coming. All we could do was stay ahead of the problem.

The corpses in the distance still hadn't noticed us, and I couldn't help but watch. They shuffled without direction. Lost, almost.

Taylor and Jamison formed up on my sides. Mark let the door close with a definitive and permanent *click*. We all shared a silent, grim look.

"Onward," Jamison said, pointing with his wooden sword.

We started to move, keeping the brick walls of the school on our left. This route would take us around to the north parking lot. Jamison plodded confidently at the front of our group, but he had enough sense to keep quiet. The only sounds we made were our feet pattering steadily on the ground. A few indistinct echoes came from the distance. It could have been shouting. Or gunshots. It could have been my imagination.

I kept looking over my shoulder, expecting to be ambushed from behind. Nothing came after us.

We reached the corner of the school. Jamison halted and peered around the edge, the rest of us bunching around him to get a glimpse of the parking lot. Corpses weaved between cars. I saw the tops of their heads bobbing in and out of sight. There couldn't have been more than eight or nine.

"Do you remember where the car is?" Jamison whispered to me.

"Now you ask?" I pursed my lips, scanning the rows of cars.

"What's wrong?" Taylor asked.

"Jamison doesn't know where the car is," I said.

"I know where it is! It's in the…back," Jamison said.

Olivia's eyes threw daggers at Jamison. Mark rubbed his forehead.

"No, he's right. We got here late, so I think it's in that corner." I pointed with the PVC pipe to the rightmost section of the parking lot. Right next to the street.

A car zoomed down the road. The corpses faced the disturbance.

"They're distracted. Let's go," Jamison motioned us forward.

We'd barely made it five steps before the car disappeared. One of the corpses turned in our direction. It shuffled from between two cars, purse still slung around its neck. It picked up its pace, trying to cut us off. Only twenty feet away. Fifteen.

Jamison sprinted past it. I dodged through a row of cars. Another corpse emerged out of nothing in front of me. I reacted on instinct, using my stick to clothesline its neck. It toppled over. I didn't bother to see if it got up again as I put distance between me and the dead.

By now, a handful of corpses closed in from every direction. I searched for a way to catch up to Jamison and the others, but the sides were cut off, so I sprinted ahead. I bounded up the hood of a car, onto the roof, and vaulted across the gap to the car behind it.

I instantly knew I had too much momentum. I hit the hood of the other car and pitched forward. My shoulder struck the concrete and I rolled across the pavement. The adrenaline coursing through my body helped me spring to my feet. My shoulder throbbed.

Stupid…

I dashed off again and skirted the edge of the parking lot as the rest of the group neared Jamison's car. Olivia frantically waved me over. Jamison stepped into a corpse, sword *cracking* against its skull. It crumbled. Jamison looked up at me as I approached, smothering a grin.

"Hold this." He tossed me the sword and went around to the driver's seat. I glanced down at the corpse, hoping I wouldn't recognize it. I didn't, which felt lucky, but other people knew this person once. The others piled in the car. I took the passenger's seat.

I fell forward as Jamison put us in reverse. Thumps sounded as he knocked corpses out of the way. He revved the engine and crunched over the one that was already on the ground. I gripped the door handle as we wheeled out of the parking lot.

I looked at the sword in my hands. Blood dripped down the edge and off the tip. Drops pooled on the mat under my feet.

We skidded onto the main road and swerved around a crash before leveling out to a safer speed. Jamison adjusted the rearview mirror. "We lost 'em."

All I could do was watch the city blur in the window. One or two bodies littered the ground. Corpses sprinkled every block, their heads turning to watch us pass. A handful of times, Jamison had to navigate around a blockade of smashed cars. People were still inside, straining against airbags and seatbelts. I didn't know if they were alive. We never stopped to check.

"We can go back to our place and figure out what to do from there. Sound good?" Jamison asked.

No one responded.

I waited another few minutes before asking, "Has anyone heard from their families?"

I twisted to look everyone in the eyes. Taylor shook her head.

Olivia fiddled with her necklace. Mark hardly moved, hands folded in his lap. I took the hint and turned around.

The city slowly transformed into narrow roads, small buildings, and towering trees. Into the suburbs. Jamison made quick turns and we were soon cruising the streets of our neighborhood. Even though I hadn't seen a corpse in this area yet, a knot of anxiety formed in my gut as we neared our place. No less than a dozen families darted in and out of their houses, depositing supplies in their cars. I didn't know what they thought this would accomplish. It would be more dangerous to leave than shelter in a house.

Other places appeared vacant, but I caught people peering at the street from their windows.

Jamison pulled into our driveway. To our right, the Larks were moving out. I caught Mr. Larks eye. Tension lined his body. Instead of greeting us, he closely watched us file out of the car and disappear into the garage.

I took a seat at the kitchen counter. Jamison tossed his keys onto the surface and opened the fridge. After a minute of muttering, he moved to the row of cabinets. He inspected each one in turn, scattering a few items on the counter. A bag of chips. Oreos. Trail mix. Then he went back to the fridge and found ingredients for a turkey sandwich.

He paused long enough to tear open the chips and stuff a handful into his mouth. My stomach rumbled. I snagged the Oreos. Mark stared at the counter while Taylor and Olivia glanced around at the walls. Nobody made a move to settle in.

"Don't just stand there," Jamison said, affronted. "Sit down. Make some food. Go to the bathroom. I don't care. Just stop…doing that." He gestured vaguely at the other three. "Stop being weird. Our house is your house."

Mark sank into a chair at the dining table. Olivia joined him. Taylor settled next to me and took an Oreo. Her hands were shaking. Mine were too, but I pretended not to notice.

"Make one for me," I said.

Jamison sighed, opening the mayonnaise.

"Please," I added.

"Does anyone else want one?" Jamison asked, pointing a butter knife in our direction. "I am, after all, a culinary expert."

"Yeah, thanks," Taylor said.

Olivia and Mark agreed, and Jamison laid the rest of the loaf on the counter. I plucked an orange from a bowl and began peeling it. Olivia sat across from Mark, and they struck up a conversation too quiet for me to hear.

"I'm going to find weapons," I said after a minute. I slipped from my chair, peeled orange in hand.

"I'll join you," Taylor said.

We went to the garage. I flipped the light switch and a murky yellow glow illuminated the two cars. I picked through the overflowing shelves.

"Do you have any guns?" Taylor asked.

I returned the hammer to its spot. "No."

"We do. One, at least," she said. "We can get it when we head to my place."

"Do you know how to use it?" I asked, looking her up and down again. She nodded. "Good."

I continued to scour the shelves.

"Can I ask you a personal question?" Taylor asked.

"Sure," I said, closing my hands around a metal baseball bat. I wiped cobwebs off the handle.

"What happened to your parents?"

How did she know about that? Who told her?

I straightened slowly, fingers running over a dent in the bat. "They died in an accident a few years ago."

Taylor's eyes softened. Tiny lines appeared at the edges.

"I've known Jamison most of my life. We met in hockey and played nearly every year together. And when it happened…" My eyes wandered the garage. "Jamison's parents adopted me."

"I'm sorry," Taylor said, putting a hand on my arm.

"It's alright."

"It's not."

"But things are good now, I guess…"

Taylor hugged me. Warmly. Comforting. Both arms wrapped around my waist. I returned the gesture, cheek against the top of her head. I took in the faint scent of peaches. Once again, I felt peace in her arms. "Thank you."

"Too bad you got stuck with Jamison," she said.

I laughed. We pulled apart. "He's good, deep down. A little rough around the edges, but he has a good heart."

The door to the house burst open. "Food is ready—" Jamison cut off. "I didn't realize you two were making out. Take your time."

The door shut, but not before I glimpsed a small frown on Jamison's face. I chuckled nervously. Taylor tucked her hair behind her ear.

"Do you want to talk about last week?" she asked.

I removed a wedge of my orange. "I don't think this is the best time. Later?"

"Sure." She brushed my arm and headed for the door.

Inside, Jamison had set five places at the table, each with a sandwich and a glass of water, with the various snacks in the center.

I leaned the bat against the wall, settling next to Taylor. It was a simple thing, but the food brought a glimmer of life to the group. Jamison and I tried to carry the conversation to keep away the oppressive weight lingering in the air.

For a few minutes, it was just Jamison and I talking about the last game of our high school career. And for a while, it felt like nothing was wrong.

Things went silent again.

"What just happened?" Taylor asked, staring at her sandwich. "At school. What the hell is going on?"

"The end of the world, I think," Jamison said.

Taylor cocked her head at him.

"I don't know how you do it, Jamison," I said, voicing the thought hovering in the back of my mind.

"Do what?"

"Act so unfazed, like nothing's happening."

"What else am I supposed to do?"

"I don't know, read the room, maybe."

"Alright, first off, *you* were the one who was ready to leave everyone behind, not me. And all I've done is save our asses."

I bristled. "I guess that makes you a saint, then. What about the heads you smashed in?"

"Those were corpses, Cody," Jamison said, meeting my eyes. "I did what no one else could."

"Corpses?" Taylor asked.

"It's what we're calling them," Jamison said, "the zombies."

"Jesus…" Taylor said, dropping her sandwich. She rubbed her hands together. "That's it, then? We kill them without question?"

"If you haven't noticed, they don't hesitate to attack," Jamison said. "We shouldn't either."

"What if they're still conscious somehow? And they're trapped in their own bodies…" Taylor said, trailing off at the implication.

Olivia let out a sob. Jamison swallowed uncomfortably. I examined my plate and found I was out of Oreos. I didn't reach for more. I'd already had too many and was on the verge of being sick.

Mark hardly seemed to notice. He'd spent the entire conversation in silence, mechanically eating his food. His eyes were unmoving and distant. He was in shock, almost like he'd gotten a really bad concussion. I knew what to look for too, after all these years of watching Jamison dish out massive open ice hits. Mark flinched. Slowly, he removed his phone from his pocket.

"It's my mom," he said quietly. He shuffled from the table and disappeared into the next room.

Taylor wrapped her arms around Olivia while I searched for a box of tissues. I soon returned, handed the box off to Taylor, and motioned Jamison over to the kitchen counter. He jumped at the opportunity to get away and leaned against the surface.

"What are we doing? What's the plan?" I asked in a low voice.

"I don't know how to deal with this," Jamison said, picking dirt from under his fingernails. "I don't know what we can *actually* do, but we have to stick together. That's our best shot."

"Always," I said, gripping his shoulder. I dropped my hand and traced the veins of marble on the countertop. "I should have thought of the others first."

"You're trying to survive, can't blame that," Jamison said. He absentmindedly tucked his hair behind his ears, jaw tight. "And it does affect me, you know. What we see out there, what I've…done. I just don't show it because someone has to take charge, and if I lose my shit too, that's one less person who's making clear decisions." Jamison rubbed his forehead and shrugged. "I don't know, maybe I act too quickly."

"No, you're right. We need that, and I'm not the natural leader here," I said.

I looked over at the girls as Olivia showed her phone to Taylor, who covered her mouth and let out a muffled, "Oh my god."

Jamison and I approached cautiously. He took the phone and held it up for both of us to read. It was a single message from Olivia's mom. *Work is overrun. We can't make it out. We love you so much.*

I gripped the back of a chair. Now, I felt well and truly sick.

Mark rounded the corner, face distraught. "We have to go. My dad is injured. They're at my place."

I didn't move.

"Give me the keys! I'll drive myself!" he shouted.

Jamison snatched them from the counter. "We'll go with you, but *I'm* driving." Jamison pulled me toward the garage. "We'll be back," he said over his shoulder.

Neither Taylor nor Olivia acknowledged our plan. Mark and Jamison disappeared into the garage. I retrieved the bat and took the middle row so Mark could give directions from the front. We roared down the street.

The Larks were gone by now.

So were many of the others.

FOUR

MARK URGED JAMISON to go faster, and Jamison responded by blowing through red lights at lawless intersections. I gripped the door handle as we careened down another road, skirting pileups and other drivers. I cursed myself for coming. This was how you ended up dead.

The entire drive, I couldn't stop thinking about the text from Olivia's mom. Just like that, her family was gone. Likely the same for Taylor's. Now, Mark's dad was injured, and his sister, dead.

The corpses appeared hours ago, and the city was already falling apart. All the cities were, all around the world.

I wondered how long we'd make it. Probably days. That's how long most people would have. But if we could get through the initial wave of destruction, we might stand a chance.

Jamison sped down a residential street. Mansions peeked from behind fences and towering oak trees. We swerved down a gravel driveway and ground to a halt in front of a stone house. A black Lexus glimmered in the afternoon light.

Mark jumped out before Jamison shut off the car. I scrambled out of my seat, bat in hand. Mark bounded up the front steps and pushed through the front door, shouting for his parents. Jamison left me behind as he followed Mark inside. I hesitated when I saw the trail of blood on the gravel, leading from the Lexus to the house.

Needing a moment, I scanned the area. Took in the trees. Felt the sun on my face and listened to the chirping birds.

Steeling myself, I went inside and closed the door. The others were out of sight, but it was an easy trail to follow. The blood glistened on the granite floor in the atrium. Mark yelled from upstairs. I took them two at a time and tried not to look at the family portraits lining the entire way. A door slammed. Jamison blocked my way, hand on my shoulder.

"What's going on?" I strained to see behind him.

"They're gone," he said curtly.

"Both of them?"

I skirted Jamison and found Mark slumped against the double doors to what I assumed was his parents' room. He was shaking. Growling, and what sounded like nails on plastic, came from the other side.

Mark pounded his fist into the ground. "Fuck!"

"What do we do?" I asked.

The door shook. Mark continued to hit the floor.

"Leave them…maybe?" Jamison said.

"We can't do that, not like this," Mark said.

His head rested against the door, looking up at the ceiling. He wiped his face. I tentatively offered him the bat. He looked at it, then at me, eyes bleary. Empty.

"No," he said.

He sat another minute before picking himself off the floor to push past Jamison and me. Back down the stairs. He didn't ask us to follow, but we did anyway. Soon, we were in an office. Mark went straight for the Rembrandt painting hanging on the wall. I shot a look at Jamison. He shrugged as Mark pulled it off its hooks.

There was a safe behind it. Silver. About the size of a microwave.

Mark punched in the number. The door swung open, and he rummaged around for a second. When he faced us again, he had a matte black pistol in hand. He pulled the slide back to make sure it was clear, then set it on the desk. Next, he removed a box of ammunition, two magazines, and proceeded to load both of them with clinical precision. Mark snapped one into the grip and pulled back the slide in a fluid motion, a *click-clack* resounding between us.

Tucking the other items in his pockets, he left the office, not bothering to close the safe or hang the painting. We followed Mark. He stalked up the stairs, gun pointed at the ground, trigger finger resting easily on the side. Jamison and I exchanged an uncomfortable look.

Mark halted in front of the bedroom and leveled the gun. "Open the door and get out of the way."

We stood still for a moment. The growling had subsided. No scratching at the door.

"Do it," Mark said.

Jamison jumped to attention and gripped the handle. "Three… two…" He shoved the door open and stepped aside. I raised my bat.

Nothing came out.

Mark slid forward with careful steps. I positioned myself at his back to get a better look. The corpses of his parents turned in our direction. They'd wandered to the other side of the bed in our absence. His dad had a makeshift tourniquet around his right leg. Blood dripped down his chin, staining his white dress shirt. His mom had a gash down the side of her neck.

Mark didn't hesitate. He fired a shot between the eyes of his dad. His mom didn't have a chance to react before a bullet took her too. The bodies thumped to the ground. My ears rang. Gunpowder drifted to my nose. Lightheaded, I leaned against the door frame, tightly closing my eyes against the image.

When I opened them again, Mark stood over the bodies and tucked the gun into his belt at the small of his back. He didn't say a word. Then he went to the next room. A bathroom or closet, maybe.

No matter how hard I tried, I couldn't stop looking at the bodies. My stomach churned. I tried to focus on anything but the scene in front of me. Jamison was pale, arms limp at his sides.

Mark returned with another pistol, ammunition, and magazines. He loaded the gun and extended it to Jamison, handle first. Jamison took it, fingers gingerly tracing the metal.

"Don't touch the safety. Just carry it for me," Mark said. When Jamison tucked it into his belt, Mark handed him the extra ammo and magazine. Mark looked us both in the eyes, horrible pain lurking deep within. "We need to bury them."

He said it, and it was final. It wasn't my place to object. I couldn't have spoken if I wanted to.

"Take my dad. I'll get her," he said, kneeling in front of his mom. He scooped up her body, her head lolling with each step. He didn't seem to notice the blood soaking into his jacket.

I dropped the bat on the ground as Jamison and I approached Mark's dad. He was big like his son. Muscled. More than six feet tall. A couple hundred pounds from the look of him.

As I bent to grasp his ankles, I took in the full scent of blood. Nausea crashed over me. I stumbled away, unable to make it five steps before I threw up on the ground. My whole body shook. I gasped for air, but every lungful was tinged with the sickly scent of gore. I heaved again.

I collapsed onto the floor, too weak to move. I wanted to cry, but it didn't come.

Mark returned soon enough. I picked myself up into a sitting position. I expected Mark to yell at me, to curse me for being unable to do a simple task. All he did was frown in my direction before bending down next to his dad.

He and Jamison carried the body out of the room. I crawled over to the bat and used it as a crutch to get to my feet. I kept my gaze straight ahead until I was out of the room, avoiding the blood stains on the carpet.

I found Mark and Jamison in the backyard, the bodies of Mark's parents lined up next to each other. Mark had a shovel in hand and was already sinking it into the ground. For the next hour, we took turns digging the grave. By the time it was done, my hands were raw, but I had regained some strength. I focused on the trees and the birds and the blisters on my palms as Mark filled in the grave and tightly packed the dirt.

"I'm sorry it had to be this way," Mark said to the mound. "I love you."

I shifted my weight. Jamison gripped my shoulder.

Mark dropped the shovel. "I need to pack my things. You can wait here. I'll be done soon."

Mark returned to the house, leaving Jamison and me on the back porch. We settled in chairs around the fire pit. Jamison removed the gun from behind his back.

"It's heavy," he said. He inspected it for a second, released the mag, counted the bullets, and put it back. He leveled the gun at the grave in a two-handed grip. "I've never fired one before…" Jamison said, lowering the gun with a pointed sigh.

"Can I see it?" I asked.

Jamison handed it over and propped his feet on the edge of the fire pit. I let my fingers run over the cold metal. I pointed it with one hand, but I couldn't hold it steady so I switched to both hands. It still wavered. I frowned. How could anyone reasonably aim with this?

"How do you think he learned to shoot?" Jamison asked.

I shrugged. "Same as anyone, I guess. Taylor's trained too."

Jamison raised an eyebrow. He twitched, then pulled his phone out of his pocket. "It's Dad." He put it on speaker for both of us to hear. "Dad, what's up?"

"Hey," I said.

"Boys, how are you doing? Are you safe?" Worry tinged his voice.

"We're good," I said, glancing at the gun and the grave in turn.

"It's a shit show out there," Jamison said, getting an affirming, yet stifled laugh from his dad.

"It is. All airports are shut down, so we're stuck here for the moment. Your mom and I are at the hotel still. It's safe…I just wanted to call and say I love you both so much, whatever happens."

There was a knowing pause, filled with all the things we didn't want to say.

"We love you too," we echoed.

"We'll find you when everything settles down. It won't be long."

"We're counting on it," Jamison said. He wrapped his arms around his knees. "Where's mom?"

"She's sleeping. Long day."

"Yeah…" Jamison said.

"I'll call tomorrow. Stay safe."

"You too," we said.

The call ended and we sat in silence. The sun dipped behind a tree, casting us in shadow. I zipped up my jacket.

"Do you think we'll see them again?" Jamison asked.

"I don't know," I said.

Mark returned before I completely lost myself to thought. He wore a large backpack and had a duffle bag in one hand. He held two long cases in the other. Guns, probably.

"Let's put this in the car and pack up the food," Mark said, eyes wandering to the grave. "I'm not coming back."

"Are you staying with us?" Jamison asked.

"If I can. At least until I set out on my own. Come on." Mark jerked his head back to the house.

I uncurled myself from my seat. Jamison tucked the gun back out of sight. We picked up a few more bags Mark had stowed by the door and piled everything in the trunk of Jamison's car. In fifteen minutes, we scavenged four bags of food, mostly cans of soup and pasta. Things that wouldn't go bad over time.

We made it back home safely, only passing a handful of other survivors on the road. I watched them go, and they watched us in return. Calculating, but content to let us be if we did the same.

As we unloaded the car, Mark pulled us aside and handed each of us a case. "You can use these. I'll teach you how to shoot soon."

I unclipped the case on the ground to reveal a mahogany hunting rifle. The wood was buffed to a warm glow. The scope glittered black. I took it reverently, fitting the stock to my shoulder to sight down the scope. The mailbox across the street jumped into clear view. I swiveled, having no trouble keeping it steady.

I took it in. The feel of the wood, the scope, the *rightness* of it all. I could get used to this. I nodded to myself, lowering the gun. Mark had already gone inside, and Jamison was fighting back a smile as he held up a large shotgun with a cameo pattern.

FIVE

THE SUN TOUCHED the horizon, bathing the street in an orange glow. Taylor greeted us at the door and informed us Olivia had fallen asleep in one of our rooms.

"Did you find your parents?" Taylor asked as we walked back to the car.

Mark took a bag in each hand, said, "They're gone," and stalked into the house.

Taylor looked at Jamison and me for an explanation.

"They turned before we got there. Mark…" I paused. "He shot them…and we buried them in the backyard. That's why it took so long."

Taylor brought a hand to her mouth.

Jamison leaned against the car, still casually holding the shotgun. "He killed them like it was nothing. Barely said a word at their grave."

"We should keep an eye on him," I said, looking down at the rifle.

Taylor nodded. Mark stomped toward us. He didn't meet our

eyes. He simply filled his arms and was on his way again.

"That's new," Taylor said, eyeing Jamison's gun.

"They had a whole armory," Jamison said. "He said he'd teach us how to use them."

"Good. You should learn. We have a pistol at my place we can get," Taylor said, back to survival mode. She gathered two bags of food and said she'd meet us inside.

The only things left were the guns Jamison and I carried, so I shut the trunk with a thud.

When prompted to eat, Mark only said he wanted to go to bed. Jamison offered up his room and soon reported back that Olivia had taken the guest bedroom. After a quick discussion, we decided Taylor would take mine, and Jamison and I would take his parents'.

Jamison busied himself in the kitchen, making dinner while Taylor and I watched from the counter.

"Helps clear my head," Jamison said to no one in particular. He soon had noodles boiling on the stove and sausage crackling in an open pan. He went so far as to put on an apron. Halfway through mixing the sauce, he put both hands on the counter, giving Taylor and me a concerned look. "I know what you need."

He rummaged in a cupboard and produced three mugs, clinking them on the counter. Unscrewing the lid of his dad's spiced rum, he splashed a generous portion into each of our mugs and pushed them forward. I took mine without complaint.

"To better days ahead," Jamison said.

We clinked the mugs and drank. I patted my chest as it went down, trying not to cough. Warmth immediately spread throughout my body. I had barely set mine down before Jamison filled them all again. I eyed this one warily. Shots never sat well with me, and I felt both physically and emotionally unwell from everything going on.

Jamison produced a bottle of Coke and filled each of our cups to the brim. He returned to the stove, muttering something about burning the sauce. Taylor watched Jamison, a thoughtful expression on her face. I sipped my drink until it was half gone, growing warmer and more relaxed as each minute passed. That was good. I didn't want to think tonight.

"…Cody…" Taylor said.

I snapped back to myself, realizing I'd been staring at Taylor.

The counter swayed under me. I steadied myself on the stool. "Want to see a magic trick?" I asked the room in general.

"Your magic tricks *aren't* magic tricks," Jamison said, pouring the sauce into a serving bowl.

I waved him off. Taylor watched with interest.

"I'm going to make this," I waved my hand mysteriously over my mug, "disappear." I downed the rest of the drink and stuffed the cup under my shirt, waving my hands. The glass slipped from my shirt and shattered on the ground.

Taylor's face froze somewhere between shock and laughter.

"*Goddamnit*, Cody! That was my mug," Jamison said.

I cleared my throat. "In my defense, magic is unpredictable and must be treated with utmost care. I am, clearly, out of practice," I said, then added for good measure, "I'm sorry about the mug."

There was a moment of silence, Jamison's mouth a thin line. Taylor burst out laughing. It was a wonderful sound. I found myself laughing too, and Jamison sighed, only faintly amused.

"Don't cut yourself cleaning it up," Jamison said.

I surveyed the shards around my feet. At least I had shoes on. Anyway, I could figure that out later.

Taylor clapped. "That was pretty good! Do another with the bottle."

It made perfect sense. I reached for the rum, but Jamison held it out of my reach. He pointed a finger at me and firmly said, "No," like he was scolding a dog.

I sprawled over the counter, trying to grab Jamison's apron. "Come *onnnnn.*"

"No! You'll just break the bottle and I'll have to clean that too."

"Please?"

Jamison tipped the bottle to his lips and took two gulps, not breaking eye contact, if only just to spite me. "Fine," he said, grimacing. "But you get it in a plastic cup. I don't care what you do with it then."

"I could do a lot of things with a plastic cup," I said, not entirely sure what that was supposed to mean, though Taylor seemed to find it amusing.

"I want another," she said.

Jamison poured us a satisfactory amount, the bottle nearly tapped. He began setting the food on the dining table. I slipped from my stool, crunching glass beneath my feet. I frowned, having completely forgotten about the mug.

I swayed pleasantly. The alcohol was hitting me faster than I thought it would, but that was a blessing. This last shot should be enough for me. Maybe one more after that.

I settled into a chair and dumped pasta onto my plate. The conversation was light but loud. Taylor tried to shut us up by practically yelling that Mark and Olivia were asleep. We laughed it off.

This whole time, I had the nagging feeling that I was ignoring something important. I tried not to think about it. I tried not to think about the fact that Taylor was here with *us,* because then I would remember everything that brought us to this point. I tried not to dwell on the ever-present anxiety swirling just below the surface.

I finished my rum, found a beer in the fridge, and sipped it until I felt like I was dreaming. Floating through the house. On the couch and not remembering how I got there.

This was the feeling I wanted because it meant I could pretend the whole day had been some terrible dream. I could ignore the voice in the back of my mind shouting about the end of the world. I told myself I would wake up tomorrow and everything would be back to normal.

At some point, we were watching a movie in the living room. There were playing cards strewn on the coffee table, remnants from a poker game that ended before we started because we didn't have chips. I think I had another shot, but that was a vague memory, so I couldn't be sure. Then I saw tally marks on my forearm. Taylor said that was the best way to keep track.

Was that eight? My vision was too shaky to count properly, and some of them bled into others. I certainly didn't remember having eight drinks, but then again, the next thing I found myself doing was stumbling up the stairs, Taylor's arms around me with no sign of Jamison.

Progress was slow. I kept pitching into the wall and almost fell backward several times. Making the smart choice, I resorted to crawling on my hands and knees. We reached the landing. I propped myself up with my elbows. I couldn't help but smile when I looked at Taylor. Her hair was in a haphazard bun, falling apart in places. Words I didn't know how to say bubbled in my chest, but before I could try, Taylor weaved her way to my room.

"Time for bed," she said over her shoulder. "See you tomorrow."

I dropped my head to the floor. "See you," I mumbled back.

I remained prone on the ground, my insides tumbling around like they were trapped in a washing machine. A few minutes later, I started crawling to my room, then remembered Taylor was using it. That was fine. I wouldn't have made it that far anyway. I slouched again. Maybe I would sleep here for the night.

A washing machine on a boat. In the middle of a storm.

In a moment of clarity, I realized I was going to throw up for the second time today. Lying on the floor wasn't helping, and I knew there was no getting around it. This was happening, one way or another. I just had to make it to the bathroom. At least my parents' room was close.

I summoned the energy to get to my feet, shove open the door, and bumble my way through the dark bedroom. Jamison's shape was faintly outlined on the bed. He didn't stir.

I somehow made it to the bathroom and flicked on the light, then collapsed on the ground, arms hugging the toilet bowl. The lid was already open. I didn't even have to gag myself to get started. In seconds, it was all coming out.

For a while, it was terrible heaving. Trying to breathe. Struggling to keep upright.

The only consolation was that being drunk made the whole experience slightly more bearable. Minimum consciousness. That was the trick.

I flushed, waited a bit longer, threw up some more, and waited fifteen more minutes. My stomach began to settle. I *did* feel much better, though I was horribly weak. My whole body trembled.

My head was still muddy, but thoughts I'd been holding back flooded my mind.

What was our next move?

How many friends had I lost?

How long would *I* make it?

It hit me like a blow to the chest how alone we were. Mark and

Olivia's families were gone. Taylor's was missing. My parents were halfway across the country. We'd likely never see them again. I didn't know how to process that fact.

Wait...

Had I really called Jamison's parents *mine?*

They were, in a way. My real parents were dead, but the Calloways were my family now. They'd adopted me. They called me son. That was more than a lot of people had. More than Mark and Taylor and Olivia.

I hadn't acted like they were my family. I was always reserved in some way. Never vulnerable. Never broken in front of them. But they were all I had. Why was I just now realizing this?

I began to cry.

I did this for a long time, just curled up on the bathroom floor. I cried until I had nothing left. Cried until the numb weight in my chest turned to grief over things that would never be the same.

I could have done better with so many things. I could have stayed with my parents instead of getting on that bus in St. Paul. I should have told them to get a hotel for the night and not try to drive home.

But the worst part was I couldn't take any of it back, and I couldn't possibly make it right. So, the guilt wrapped me like a blanket as I laid on the floor, eyes on the cracking paint of the faded bathroom walls.

This was it. Jamison and me, and a few classmates I hardly knew before this morning. If this was just the first day, I couldn't guess how to make it through the next. Or the one after that.

But the only choice I had was to try.

SIX

THERE WAS A minute of bliss when I woke up the next morning. Sunlight streamed through the window. I took it in, eyes closed and everything calm. Nothing was wrong.

A headache tugged me out of the moment. I rubbed my eyes and the room swayed as I sat up. I looked around, realizing it wasn't mine. Jamison was already gone, the covers thrown back.

Pieces of the last day fit together.

Our school being overrun. Calls from parents who would never be seen again. The burial in Mark's backyard. The drinking. I ran a finger over the tally marks on my arm.

Breaking down in the bathroom.

Had I really cried myself to sleep?

The awful pain in my chest confirmed it. There were moments last night when I almost convinced myself nothing was real. But now, all I had was a racing heart and the sick realization our lives were forever changed.

I went to the bathroom, rubbing my temples. I found some Advil and swallowed two pills. After a quick shower, I wrapped a towel around my waist and shaved with my dad's extra razor. For a few minutes, I placed both hands on the counter and surveyed myself in the mirror, though I didn't know what I was looking for. There were circles under my eyes, a detached expression I couldn't wipe away.

I filled a cup with water and took extra Advil across the hall to my room. Conscious of the towel, I knocked on the door.

"Come in," Taylor said, voice muffled.

I peered around the door. "I just need clothes. I thought you might want this, too."

Taylor pulled the blankets around her chin. I set the water and medicine on the nightstand and gathered an armful of clothes from my dresser.

"Thanks," Taylor said.

"Sure," I said.

Her eyes followed me to the door. I paused and gripped the handle. Part of me fought to tell her what happened last night, but she wouldn't be able to help, and she had enough to deal with.

"See you downstairs," I said, closing the door behind me.

Dressed and moderately hungover, I made my way to the kitchen. Fresh coffee permeated the air. Jamison held a steaming mug. Olivia munched on a bowl of cereal, and Mark laid on the living room couch, tapping his fingers against his chest. I scrounged my own breakfast of a banana and orange juice and took a seat.

Jamison came back to himself, eyes focusing on Olivia and me. "We need to stock up on supplies."

"We have plenty," I said, sipping my juice.

"For now," Jamison said. "But when we run out, it'll be too late. The stores will be picked clean. *All of them.* Food, gear, *guns*…we should have stocked up yesterday. It might already be too late."

"He's right," Mark said, shuffling to the table. He had dark circles under his eyes and an impassive frown on his lips. "It'll be chaos, but it's the only way to get what we need."

I slowly peeled the banana.

I'd been so focused on surviving each moment I hadn't considered what came after. We needed supplies, but the stores would be crawling with survivors and corpses. My face tightened at the thought of people stabbing each other over the last bag of potato chips.

I didn't want to face that, but we were already dead if we didn't try. It was a risk worth taking. Hopefully.

"What if we raid abandoned houses?" Olivia asked.

Jamison raised an eyebrow, scratching his chin. "That's not a bad idea."

"They can't take everything with them, and no one will be there," Olivia added to her point.

"Unless there *is* someone there and we get shot," Mark said. "How do we tell the difference?"

"The Larks are gone," I said. "Right next door. They were packing up when we got here. A lot of others are gone too."

"There you go. Forget the stores. Let's go straight for the houses," Olivia said. She leaned forward on the table, cereal forgotten.

Mark held up a hand. "We can't settle for other people's leftovers. Sure, maybe we'll find a can of soup. But weapons? No way. Not the ones that really matter. Not guns."

"We have four here," Jamison pointed out. "Is that enough?"

"Five," I said.

"We have four. *My* four, and only one person who knows how to use them," Mark countered.

"Actually, it's five," I said. Mark glowered at me like I was giving him a challenge. "Taylor can shoot, and her family owns a pistol."

Mark considered this information by rocking on his toes. "Still, we don't have enough ammunition, especially not to train you properly."

"Then we find more," I said.

"You don't just *find* guns, dumbass." Mark stepped forward to grip the table.

I was able to get a good look at the muscles in his arms this way. And once again, I was taken aback by his size. Maybe he'd flunked a few grades in middle school...

Mark continued. "Unless you want to steal them from someone, which will likely get someone killed, you go to a store for that. A gun store with a bunch of desperate people looking for the one thing they don't know how to use. It's a massacre waiting to happen."

"What do you suggest?" Jamison asked, swirling his coffee.

"Here's a thought," I said, raising a hand. "Let's keep arguing until we're sure all the supplies are gone, *then* we make our move. Slow and steady, right?"

Mark bristled, but Taylor wandered down the hallway before he could speak.

"What are you talking about?" Taylor asked.

"Here's the highlights," I said, ignoring the way Mark's eyes bored into my head. I paced in front of the table, ticking off points with my fingers. "We need supplies, but apparently it's too dangerous to go to the grocery store. We thought about raiding abandoned houses, but we might get shot if we pick the wrong one. And the houses aren't likely to have what we need. Not guns, anyway.

"I suggested we look for weapons, but Mark thinks the stores will be another Alamo. Which is fine, because we have guns. *Five,* to be exact," I said, looking pointedly at Mark. "The problem is, we don't have enough ammunition to train, and Mark thinks we're a bunch of good-for-nothing monkeys ready to shoot ourselves in the head the moment we touch a pistol." I paused, hands on my hips. "So, to answer your question, we're trying to figure out the best way to get fucked over and killed."

Jamison gave a slow clap. Mark shot him a vicious look, but Jamison didn't shrink back. Taylor raised an eyebrow. Olivia stirred her cereal.

"I'm just pointing out why it won't work," Mark said, voice strained. His hands had curled into fists.

"That doesn't help when it leaves us with no options," I said.

"At least I'm thinking it over! If it were up to you, you'd run off to try every stupid idea you have."

"Fuck off."

"You *fuck off!*" Mark spat, face clouded with rage. The veins in his neck pulsed. "Is this a joke to you? Because this isn't a *fucking game* for me. My parents are dead. My sister is dead. Olivia's family is gone, we haven't heard from Taylor's, and you're drinking all night, acting like this is some big fucking joke."

"…should watch your language…" Jamison whispered to his mug.

"Say another word and I'll break your arm," Mark seethed.

Jamison went quiet.

Mark faced me and shoved a finger into my chest. "This isn't a game, and you'll get us all killed if you don't get that through your head."

Mark turned on each of us, fire in his eyes. Jamison slouched in his chair. Olivia bit her lip as she examined her bowl. I crossed my arms and looked at my feet, guilt rising at the truth of his words.

He'd lost everything in a single day. They all had.

I knew what that was like, and I still hadn't spared the time to think about what they were going through.

"So," Olivia began, "what do we do?"

"We should split up," Taylor said.

"No, that's how we get picked off," I said.

"Now you're the one shooting down ideas—" Mark said.

"Shut up," Taylor snapped. "Everyone shut the hell up and listen. This isn't helping. Every minute we're not taking action decreases our chances of survival." Taylor looked around as if waiting for us to challenge her. No one did, so she continued. "One group goes out to find guns and whatever we can't get in the neighborhood. The other searches houses for blankets, perishable foods, flashlights, and other things like that. It's the only way to get what we need in a short amount of time."

I looked at Jamison. He shrugged.

"We'll need to inventory what we have and make a list of what we need," Mark said. "No aimless wandering. In and out. Minimize the risk."

Taylor nodded. "Cody, you and Jamison look for weapons around the house. We'll use the dining room table for that. Olivia, start cataloging our food. Mark and I will start gathering other gear."

No one moved. Mark looked unsure that he wanted to take orders from anyone besides himself. Olivia and Jamison slouched at the table, unwilling to get up.

"Let's go!" Taylor said.

"Yes, ma'am," Jamison said, pushing back his seat. He saluted Taylor. "At your service."

Taylor rolled her eyes. "Just find the damn weapons."

Jamison and I stalked the house, depositing every promising weapon on the dining room table. We'd hardly worked for twenty minutes before the table was overflowing. I surveyed the display.

Mark's guns and his few boxes of ammunition. A wooden baseball bat. Two hammers from the garage, a hatchet, and an eight-pound axe. A few pocket knives. Shovels. Old hockey sticks.

I rubbed my chin, frowning. Most of these would only be used in a worst-case scenario. It took another ten minutes to eliminate the poorest weapons. This left the guns, bats, hatchet, and a Gerber pocket knife.

Content with our progress, I checked on the others.

Olivia was in the middle of removing everything from the cupboards onto the island and kitchen table. She said we should organize everything by how quickly things needed to be eaten before they went bad. While Olivia took stock, I went through the fridge and threw away expired items like milk and month-old lunch meat, opening a fair amount of space inside. Jamison busied himself by snacking on an open bag of chips.

By the time I checked on Taylor and Mark, they'd amassed a large supply of survival gear on the living room floor. Tents. Blankets. A camping stove. Backpacks. Rope. Sleeping bags. A few flashlights.

"Do we actually need this?" I asked. "We're not going anywhere, right?"

Taylor looked at me, then at the surrounding gear. She ran a hand through her hair. "Yeah, I guess you're right. We can put it back."

"We can do that later," I said.

With Taylor's help, Mark showed us the basics of how to use each of his guns. How to load the magazine and clear a jam. How to pull back the slide to check the chamber. Safety on and off. How to carry the gun. Always treat it as if it's loaded. Never point it at someone unless you are willing to shoot. Not a toy. Not a toy. *Not a toy,* he emphasized.

Mark let me practice with the rifle, loading each round with the bolt action lever. He showed me how to eject the casing. Sighting down the scope. Breathing. Over and over until I was confident in my ability. I moved to the shotgun next, then the pistol.

It was a far cry from actually pulling the trigger, but I knew enough to keep myself alive. It would only be a matter of time before we put that knowledge to the test. And for the first time, things seemed to fall into place, to make sense. This was our reality. That fact didn't strike me with fear like I thought it would.

It made me confident that I would adapt and survive, and maybe see this nightmare through to the very end.

SEVEN

LISTS MADE AND an argument later, our foraging groups were decided.

Taylor, Jamison, and I would set out for the stores while Mark and Olivia scoured the neighborhood. Mark grumbled about his assignment as he wrote down the exact ammunition we needed. He stressed this point by shaking the paper in our faces, making us repeat the types until he was satisfied we wouldn't forget.

Taylor pocketed the list. "Exactly what it says—"

"—because if it's wrong, we'll blow our heads off, blah blah blah, we get it," Jamison finished.

Mark's eyes narrowed.

"We'll be fine," Taylor said. "I know what I'm doing."

"They don't." Mark pointed to Jamison and me.

"We're not stupid," I said.

Mark's silence spoke for him.

"Let's go," Taylor said.

I shouldered the rifle and pocketed the box of ammunition. Taylor and Olivia each took a pistol. Jamison reached for the shotgun, but Mark grabbed it first.

"I'm using it today," Mark said. "Each group gets two guns."

"What the hell? What am I supposed to use?" Jamison asked.

Mark tossed him the wooden bat. Jamison caught it, looking it over with disapproval. I stuck the hatchet into my belt. It was a much better weapon for close-quarters conflict, even if it was dull and rusty.

"Whatever," Jamison said, heading for the garage.

"We'll stop at my place first and pick up our pistol," Taylor said. There was hesitation in her words. Faint hope. The uncertainty of whether her parents would be there, despite the lack of contact.

It was only when we were on the road that Jamison spoke again. "I don't trust him."

I loaded a round into the rifle and sighted out the back window.

"Mark?" Taylor asked from the front seat. "I don't know. He's just…"

"Erratic?" Jamison offered. "I don't like the way he looks at us. It's like he's waiting for us to stab him in the back."

Taylor rubbed the back of her neck. "Maybe you shouldn't try to piss him off."

Jamison pursed his lips.

Except for Taylor giving directions to her place, we didn't talk. Jamison plugged his phone into the stereo.

I surveyed the city.

It was nearly abandoned. Few cars traveled on the roads, but there were countless crashes. Major cross streets were a mess of wrecked vehicles. Bumpers flung away. Shards of glass, metal, and fiberglass were strewn on the ground, glittering in the sunlight. Cars bent around light poles. Some had crashed headlong into residential fences.

Corpses wandered, giving little acknowledgment of their surroundings. But every time a car passed, they turned their heads to watch it fade into the distance.

Jamison pulled to a stop in front of a light blue house where a small tree stood in the front yard. I watched our backs as Taylor opened the garage. The street was deserted but not quite empty. Cars lined the road, and a few were in driveways.

Once inside, Taylor called for her parents. We followed her from room to room. Basement. Upstairs. The backyard.

No one was home.

"I'll get the gun…and some clothes," Taylor said, reserved. "Start packing up the food."

Jamison headed for the kitchen as Taylor disappeared up the stairs. I placed my hands on the counter, looking around. They'd decorated nicely. White and blue cabinetry. Stone tabletops. An open pantry with glass jars of rice, pasta, and flour.

Jamison ate directly from a tub of ice cream as he lazily placed items on the counter.

"Really?" I asked.

"What? It's not like we'll have room to take it with us," Jamison said. He shuffled over to a cherry wood cabinet, a few liquor bottles on top. "Want to take a shot?"

"No."

"Fine, I'll take one by myself."

"You're driving."

"I'll make you drive."

"That's not the point. You can't be drunk out there."

"What's the harm of one shot?"

"What's the *benefit* of one shot?"

Jamison considered the bottle of Grey Goose in his hand. "Good point. I need at least three to really feel it…"

"Take three shots and you'll get us killed," I said.

Jamison sighed. "I'm still bringing what they have, and you're drinking with me when we get home."

I didn't see the point in arguing, so I returned to picking through the cupboards. I'd loaded four bags by the time heavy footsteps came from the front of the house. Taylor rounded the corner with a large suitcase and a duffle bag in tow. She handed Jamison the extra pistol and he tucked it into his belt.

It didn't take long to pack the car, and we were soon speeding toward the nearest grocery store.

On the last turn, a Hummer barreled through the intersection in front of us. Jamison slammed the brakes to avoid getting hit.

"…asshole…" he muttered, wheeling us into the parking lot of the grocery store.

It bustled with activity. More than a dozen corpses chased people in and out of the store. Gunshots echoed and a corpse fell. The shooter jogged inside.

I tried in vain to quell the pit in my stomach. This was a bad idea.

Jamison skidded to a halt in a handicapped parking spot.

"Do you have the list?" Jamison asked Taylor. She patted her pocket.

"What about our stuff? Someone might break in," I said.

The other two followed my gaze to the trunk where our bags of food were in obvious sight.

"Someone could stay here," Jamison said.

"Is that more suspicious?" I asked.

"I don't know Cody!" Jamison said. "Tell me what to do and I'll do it."

"I don't think people will be looting cars," Taylor said. "Not with corpses running around. They'll want to get in and out as fast as they can."

Something thumped against the car. Jamison yelped as a corpse smacked its face into the driver's window.

"Where's my bat?" Jamison asked.

I retrieved it for him. He shoved the door open, tossing the corpse aside. I exited the other side with my rifle over my shoulder. Taylor and I rounded the car as Jamison mercilessly pounded the corpse's head into uneven chunks.

"You like that, huh?" He smacked it again even though it had long ceased moving.

He looked up. Speckles of blood dotted his face and shirt. Even more covered his hands and dripped from the end of the bat. Jamison stalked toward the store. Taylor and I flanked him, two corpses closing from our sides. A woman and her young son passed us with a half-full cart.

"Get out of here!" Jamison bellowed at them. The woman started running. One of the corpses broke off to chase her. "It's all a show," Jamison said quietly. "Let them know not to mess with you."

"She wasn't going to do anything," I said, looking back.

The corpse tackled her son. He screamed. I tore away my gaze as another came at us from the left. Jamison unloaded a swing to the bridge of its nose. Bones *cracked* and it fell into a heap. Taylor paled.

"Yeah, but that guy might," Jamison nodded to a large man toting a shotgun in his hands. He had a pistol in a holster at his right hip and a hunting knife at his back. The man looked us over as he entered the store.

Jamison had a point.

I found a cart at the entrance. Taylor kept her hand at the small of her back, ready to grab her gun at a moment's notice. Jamison seemed content with his bat. The gore trickling off the end added a level of savagery that would make anyone reconsider confronting us.

Inside, people ran down aisles, corpses chasing their heels. Scattered bodies littered the floor. Pools of blood turned into streaks and footprints. It didn't take long for me to realize most of the shelves were already picked clean. We passed through the aisles anyway, dumping anything we could use into the cart.

A few boxes of cereal. Tortillas. Canned beans. It wasn't much.

"Aisle sixteen," Jamison said, pointing ahead.

I didn't bother asking what he hoped to find on the aisle. Instead, I kept my head on a constant swivel as we made our way deeper into the store. We were nearly there when someone barreled around a corner and slammed into the cart. It tipped over with a resounding crash, scattering our precious goods on the floor. The woman scrambled to get away. Gunfire exploded next to my head and set my ears ringing. A corpse smacked the ground a foot away from our overturned cart.

I reeled, coming to my feet. Taylor sighted down the pistol, turning in a slow circle.

"Pick it up. I'll cover you," Taylor said.

I righted the cart and started dumping the food back inside. A few people sprinted by and snagged what they could.

"Leave the cart and drop the gun," a gruff voice said.

I turned to face the heavily weaponed man pointing his shotgun at my chest. I backed away. Taylor leveled her pistol at him, and he shifted his aim to Taylor.

"Drop the fucking gun," he repeated.

Taylor held the standoff, finger on the trigger. I saw movement behind the man. Jamison approached slowly, eyes wide and arms filled with bags of candy.

"Do it," I said.

Taylor clenched her jaw and lowered the pistol with exaggerated care. At that moment, Jamison dumped the candy and swung with everything he had at the back of the man's neck. Bones snapped. The man grunted, smacking his face on the ground. The shotgun skittered over the floor. Jamison stood over the body, arms shaking.

"Oh my god…" he said.

Taylor looked at Jamison in horror. I couldn't tear my eyes from the man's shattered vertebra deforming his neck. Jamison looked like he was going to throw up. And still, he bent down and gathered up the candy, face quivering. I noticed then the people watching us. Four of them. They scattered when I faced them.

I returned my gaze to the man, then his weapons. I shut down my thoughts as I bent to take the pistol from his holster. Then I removed the knife. Taylor retrieved the shotgun. We tossed it all into the cart.

Even with a broken neck, the fingers of the dead man twitched. A tiny growl came from his mouth. Jamison took the pistol from his belt, flipped the safety, and fired a single round into the corpse's head.

I looked away from the sight, steadying my hands on the cart. "We need to go," I said.

We jogged back through the store and burst into the sunlight. I threw open the trunk as two men approached. They eyed our cart and the other supplies.

"Don't try it," I spat.

Something about the words made them back off. Jamison shoved the cart away once everything was loaded. He tossed the keys to me. I steadied myself before climbing into the driver's seat. With no way to avoid it, I ran over the body of a corpse on the way out of the parking lot. There was a long, heavy silence once we emerged onto open roads.

Taylor retrieved her phone from her pocket. "Take a left at Emerson."

I followed her directions, passing fewer cars the further we went from the grocery store. I kept seeing the man fall in my mind. Kept hearing the thud of the bat against his neck. I glanced at Jamison in the mirror. All he did was look ahead, unseeing.

Taylor had me turn into a strip mall parking lot. *Marty's Guns and Ammo* was straight ahead, the sign made from glowing red letters. Several cars surrounded the store. There was movement inside, but I couldn't be sure how many people there were.

"Hand me the shotgun and pistol," Taylor said, facing Jamison. "The new ones."

Jamison bent over the seats and rummaged through our supplies, handing over the guns. Taylor took the shotgun first, keeping the barrel pointed at the floor. She pulled back the pump to eject a round into her lap. Taking one bullet from the pistol, she handed both guns back to Jamison. After examining the shell and bullet, she tucked them into her pocket and faced Jamison.

"Stay with our stuff," Taylor said. Jamison nodded, and Taylor handed me the new pistol and the list. "Find these. I'll look for the others."

Three men and two women snapped to face us as we entered the store. Each person sported a variety of weapons. They looked us over but made no move to get in our way.

"Just looking for ammo," Taylor said.

One of the men pointed to an aisle on our left. Taylor gave an appreciative nod. Mark was wrong. These were the reasonable people.

The glass that kept people from stealing the ammunition was broken. It crunched under my feet as I bent down to examine the selection. It was surprisingly well stocked, and I managed to find four or five boxes of each item on the list. Taylor stood up, arms full.

I tried not to look back as we left the store. The point between my shoulder blades itched as we approached the car. I half expected someone to come running out to challenge us. Nothing happened. I knocked on the window and Jamison unlocked the car. We dumped the ammunition into the backseat, forming a small mountain.

"Shit, how much do we need?" Jamison asked.

"I'd rather not come back unless we have to," Taylor said.

I drove away from the store, hardly realizing our direction until we'd nearly reached our high school. Cars clogged the street, forcing us to a crawl as I navigated around them. So many of them were smashed beyond recognition. Corpses lazily strained against their seatbelts. Their vacant eyes watched as we passed. I counted three cop cars among the vehicles.

"Wait!" Taylor yelled, making me jump. "Go back! Go back!"

I hit the brakes. Taylor hopped out before I could ask what was going on. I cursed, putting the car in park so I could run after her. Jamison followed as Taylor tore around random cars. I warily eyed the corpses in the vehicles but kept a sharper lookout on the surrounding area. Three of the dead lumbered toward us from the school lawn…four…five. I spun to face our car. Six.

"What are you doing?" I called after Taylor, gripping my pistol.

I found her in front of a silver pickup. Two corpses reached for her through the shattered window. I flinched as a shotgun blast echoed in the air. A body fell in front of Jamison. He pumped the grip and sighted on another. He pulled the trigger. Its head exploded and the body fell backwards.

I gripped Taylor's arm. "We have to go."

"No." She shrugged off my hand. "I can't leave them like this."

"Who…" I looked at the corpses again. Then at Taylor. Terrible realization washed over me.

"They came to get me," she said.

Another blast. I looked around anxiously. At least eight corpses had materialized by now. Taylor took out her gun.

"You don't have to do this," I said.

Taylor ignored me. She fired two quick shots, tears running down her face. The bodies slumped.

I took her arm and pulled her in the direction of our car. A corpse blocked our path. I leveled the pistol and pulled the trigger. Nothing happened.

Shit! Safety…

The corpse stretched for my shirt. Panicking, I emptied three rounds into its chest before finding its head. It bounced off the hood of a car as it fell, leaving a trail of blood behind. I sprinted for our car and dove into the driver's seat. Taylor and Jamison followed suit just as the dead surrounded us. I hit the gas, crushing two as we made our escape.

Taylor shook. I reached over and grabbed her hand. A steady click sounded from the backseat as Jamison reloaded his shotgun.

We didn't say a word on our way back to the house. I drove with one hand, the other holding Taylor's. She squeezed it back, head resting against the window.

EIGHT

I CARRIED AN armful of ammunition through the front door as Mark and Olivia came out to greet us.

"How'd it go?" Mark asked.

"We got what we needed," I said, pausing in front of him. I glanced at Taylor and Jamison, who gathered bags of food. "I'll fill you in when everything's inside."

"Sure," Mark said.

He trudged across the porch to help unload the supplies. I dumped the ammo on the dining room table and added my pistol and hatchet. Mark and Olivia's guns were here too, along with the other weapons they'd scavenged. There was a new axe and some large hunting knives.

We now had one rifle, two shotguns, four pistols, a variety of blunt objects, knives and axes…

It was a thorough collection. No doubt we'd be using it more and more. Today was just the beginning.

I thought about the man Jamison killed. I don't know what he would have done to us if Jamison hadn't stepped in. The man might have let us go, but he certainly would have taken our weapons along with the food. Jamison acted fast, and now we were safe with plenty of supplies.

I wondered how long this would last, and if more people would die at our hands. If it happened once, it might again. It was likely, even, the longer we survived.

I pushed away those thoughts and headed for the car. By the time we finished unloading everything, the kitchen counter was completely overflowing. We all stood around the island. Taylor hardly moved, face distraught, eyes red. Olivia leaned close and asked a question I couldn't hear. Taylor didn't respond, so Olivia simply held her arm.

"What was it like out there?" Mark asked.

Jamison ignored the question and dug out a bottle of vodka from one of the bags. "Anyone want some?"

Taylor raised her hand a fraction.

"You can't back out now, Cody. You promised," Jamison said, even though I hadn't. He pointed to Mark and Olivia. "You'll want a drink when you hear what I have to say."

"Fine, just tell us what happened," Mark said.

Jamison held up a finger, dragging out the confession. He set out five glasses and poured about two shots into each one. I fiddled with my shirt collar. Mark looked at me for an explanation as Jamison handed out the cups.

"Last one done has to strip," Jamison said, then forced a laugh. "I'm kidding! Don't be so serious." He downed his portion, grimacing as he set the cup down. "I killed someone today."

Taylor took this as her cue to drink. Mark and Olivia stilled, mouths half open.

"How…" Mark began.

"He was going to take our stuff. Had a shotgun pointed at them," Jamison gestured to Taylor and me, "so I snuck up behind him and, SMACK!" He clapped his hands together. Olivia jumped. "Took him out with my bat. I don't know if he was actually dead at that point. I mean, his neck was pretty messed up, and he wasn't moving, but I shot him anyway after that."

Olivia dropped her eyes to the cup in her hand. Mark hadn't touched his drink yet. Jamison selected a new bottle and poured himself another generous portion.

"He'd turned," I said. "You shot a corpse so it wouldn't come back."

"You don't know that," Jamison said. "He could have been knocked out."

"I saw him moving. As a corpse," I repeated.

"But it doesn't *fucking* matter!" Jamison slammed his palm onto the table. "That's my point! I killed someone and I can't take it back."

"I would have done the same if it meant protecting you," I said.

Jamison shook his head, face wan. "Bold words when you're not in that position. Anyone else want to share?"

There was a long pause with uncomfortable shifting.

"I found my parents," Taylor said. "We passed the school and I saw their car. They were dead. I shot their corpses."

"Shit..." Olivia whispered.

"I'm...so sorry," Mark said.

Taylor covered her eyes with a hand. Her body shook. I finished my vodka, then poured another for Taylor and myself. She looked up, tears streaking her face. Mark downed his cup and extended it to me so I could fill it again. Jamison bent over the counter, rubbing his eyes. He swirled his glass and choked the rest down. Grabbing the bottle of Grey Goose and a Sprite from the fridge, he saluted us and stalked out of the kitchen. No one else made an effort to follow.

I stood, torn between my desire to comfort Taylor and go after Jamison. Tossing back my shot, I went after who I could help the most. Jamison was already upstairs by the time I caught up.

"What do you want?" he asked as he opened the door to our parents' room.

"Jamison, *I'm here for you*. Talk to me."

"I've already said everything you need to know."

"No one blames you for what you did."

"That doesn't make it right."

"Maybe…maybe not. I don't know," I said. "The world is falling apart, and people like him are going to take advantage of that. We don't know what he would have done, to us or someone else."

"Exactly." Jamison stuck a finger in my chest. "We *don't know*. I made a choice before we found out." Jamison entered the room and turned on the light. "Do you want to know the worst part? I didn't even hesitate. I didn't stop to think. I just…did it. What kind of person does that make me?"

I searched for words that didn't sound like hollow attempts at comfort. I didn't know what to say, but it would have been worse to be silent. He needed me, even if I wasn't sure how to help.

"It means you'll do anything to protect the people you care about," I said.

Something in Jamison's expression broke. His eyes brimmed with tears. He set his jaw, and the veins in his neck stood out.

"Did you see how they looked at me?" he asked, searching my face. "They were horrified, like I was some monster. Even you looked at me that way—"

"No, I—"

"You don't know what that feels like."

"You're not a monster," I said, pulling him into a hug. "You're my best friend and my brother, and you're not a monster. I love you, ok? That's not going to change."

"I can't stop seeing him…"

"It's ok. It's over," I said. "It's over."

I PLODDED DOWNSTAIRS, holding the railing as the steps undulated below my feet. I caught a glimpse of the setting sun from our front windows.

I dreamily went through the kitchen and settled on the couch next to Taylor. She leaned her head back. Mark and Olivia were on the other couch. Olivia sank into the cushions with her arms crossed. Mark twisted his thumbs over each other.

I gently touched Taylor's shoulder. "How are you doing?"

"Phenomenal," she growled. She clutched a pillow to her chest and squeezed her eyes shut. "I'm sorry."

"It was a stupid question. I know how this feels," I said, unable to find something else to say. I wanted to hug her or hold her hand, *anything* to show I cared, but I knew none of that would make it better, not really. "I'm here if you want to talk."

She nodded once. I just sat on the couch next to her, our arms barely touching. Waiting.

"How's she doing?" I asked, nodding at Olivia.

Taylor pursed her lips. "Same as us, I guess."

"Yeah," I offered, nothing else for me to say. My phone buzzed. I dug it out of my pocket, looking at the caller ID. "I have to take this. I'll be back," I said. I pushed myself off the couch and found myself in the downstairs office. "Hi, Dad," I said, answering the call.

"Cody, how are you doing?"

"We're alive…"

"I tried calling Jamison, but he didn't pick up."

"He's rattled. We went out to find supplies today and had some run-ins with other people…" I couldn't bring myself to say the words, *Jamison killed a man.* That had to be Jamison's choice, and I didn't want to put that on our dad. Not yet. "We're back home, waiting it out."

"Good, stay put. Don't go out unless you absolutely have to."

"We won't," I said. "What's it like in Tampa?"

There was an exhausted sigh. *"Same as everywhere, I think. The city is overrun. The government is telling everyone to stay inside and wait for the military…"*

I rocked back. Watching the news had been the furthest thing from my mind over the last two days. We'd all been so caught up in gathering supplies and reeling from our losses that none of us had turned on a TV. I knew in the back of my mind that the rest of the world was going through the same thing, but I never really had the time to consider what that meant.

"…but no one's come to help yet. Local police are doing their best to set up shelters, but they're stretched too thin. Some people are taking it into their own hands to organize groups of survivors. Everyone left at the hotel is banding together because they don't have any other place to go."

"Is that working?"

"Well enough. A few people are stepping up. One woman seems to be taking charge, Evelyn Murphy. I volunteered to lead one of the groups she sent out to forage for supplies and weapons. It's dangerous. We lost a few people…"

"You don't have to do that," I said. "Stay safe, right? You can't tell us to do one thing and then do the opposite."

"It's different here. I'd rather be making decisions than following others."

"Just don't do anything stupid," I said, knowing there was nothing I could do to convince him not to get involved. "I can't lose you."

"We'll be alright," he said, but his voice lacked true conviction. *"Is it just you and Jamison at home?"*

"No, we picked up three others from school. Their families are gone, so it's just us now."

The line was quiet for a long moment. *"You're strong. I know you'll be fine."*

"Yeah," I said. "Hell of an anniversary for you, huh?"

There was a chuckle. *"I'll admit, it's not the best we've had. Hey, I have to meet with Murphy and some others about rationing. I'd have your mom talk to you, but she's been busy all day creating an inventory."*

"Sure," I said. "I'm glad we could talk."

"Me too. Cody, I want to say that whatever happens, we love you. We're so proud of you both. Don't forget that."

"I love you too," I said, biting my lip. I hated the resignation in the words. The possibility that we might not see each other again.

"I'll call back with Mom tomorrow."

"Ok."

The call ended.

I ran a hand through my hair, letting out a storm of anxious thoughts. *Please let me see them again,* I offered up the simple prayer.

Movement caught my attention, and I saw Taylor pacing outside the office. I stood up to meet her.

"Who was that?" she asked.

"My dad," I said.

Taylor bounced on her toes. She opened her mouth to say something, but no words came out. Her hands trembled as she brushed her hair out of her eyes. Without warning, she hugged me and began sobbing into my shirt. I held her, throat tightening.

"I didn't let myself believe they were gone until I saw them…and now that I did, I don't know what to do…" she said, words muffled by my clothes. "And then I shot them…and I'm never going to see them again…"

"I know," I whispered.

"I keep thinking about how I should have told them to stay home—"

"Shhh, you can't blame yourself."

"But—"

"It's not your fault," I said firmly. "I'm *so* sorry, but it's not your fault. You have to believe that, or else it will destroy you." Taylor didn't say anything else, and that was fine. "It's alright, I'm here."

NINE

THE NEXT MORNING, I told Jamison about my conversation with Dad and that we should expect another call today. He nodded grimly. I could tell he was still in shock over what he'd done, but there was a tangible grief on his face now. It tugged at the corners of his eyes as if he were barely keeping things under control. He slowly ate cereal, avoiding our gaze.

I checked in with Taylor. She was dazed but looked faintly better. I sat next to her, hoping my simple presence would help. I held her hand. She squeezed it back.

There was little talking as we lost ourselves in our food. I sipped my tea as I questioned whether any of this was real. It all seemed like some terrible nightmare. Every time I closed my eyes, I imagined life as it should be: our family laughing together at dinner, going to school, playing hockey. That shattered when I looked around the table and saw people who shouldn't be here. Remembered what brought us together.

All their families were gone, and Jamison and I would likely never see our parents again. We were each other's family now. I stopped myself.

No.

Defiance rose from deep inside. I wouldn't give up that easily. I couldn't. Jamison and my parents weren't dead. We still had hope, and I would do whatever it took to see them again, even if that meant traveling across the entire country. We had to try.

I sent a text to Dad. *We're coming to Florida to find you.*

I reread the message a few times. A tiny *delivered* appeared under the words. I leaned back in my chair and let out a small sigh of relief. It was done. They'd be expecting us. Maybe it was a stupid idea, and they'd probably try to talk us out of it, but I wasn't ready to lose my second family. I wouldn't be able to handle that.

I wondered if Jamison would agree to the trip.

Mark placed his elbows on the table. "I need to teach you guys how to shoot."

Everyone looked up, even Jamison.

"I thought we already did that," Jamison said.

"I showed you enough so you won't accidentally kill yourself, but not real shooting," Mark said. "You'll need the practice."

"I figured out how to use the shotgun pretty well…" Jamison mumbled.

"We need to be able to use whatever guns we have," Mark said.

Taylor absentmindedly tapped the table. "He's right. We can't keep putting this off."

"Where?" Olivia asked, tugging at an earring. "I'm not driving across town to find a range. Too many things could go wrong."

"What about the backyard?" I suggested.

Mark shook his head. "Not a chance, it's too open. The bullets would go straight into your neighbor's house. And it's too loud. It would attract the corpses."

"Let's do it inside," Jamison said, stirring the remaining Cheerios in his bowl. "It's just a house."

"Still too dangerous," Mark said.

"We could use the basement," I said, leaning forward. "It's pure concrete under the drywall, and it's safer than going anywhere else."

Mark considered this for a minute. Olivia shot a look at me as if we were crazy to use our basement for a shooting range. Maybe we were, but like Jamison said, it was just a house, and we needed to learn how to shoot. Besides, it would give us all something to focus on. Something tangible. Something to get us moving.

"That could work…" Mark said. "Are you sure you're ok with this?"

I shrugged. "It's the best option."

"Yeah, I don't care," Jamison said. "Let's do it."

"Alright," Mark said. He stood up and motioned to Jamison and me. "Find earplugs and eye protection and meet us downstairs."

It took a few minutes of searching the garage to find earplugs. We only had three pairs of safety glasses, so I scoured my room for sunglasses. By the time I made it to the basement, the others had set up a makeshift range by pushing aside the furniture and removing wall decorations from the common room. Jamison drew a lopsided target on the wall with a Sharpie. Olivia picked up my dad's guitar from its stand in the corner.

"Can I use this?" she asked.

"Go for it," I said.

She settled on the couch and plucked a few notes as we waited for Mark to begin the unofficial class. The first thing he did was review gun safety before letting us touch the weapons. Finally satisfied, he directed us to don our glasses and earplugs. Olivia and Jamison lounged on the couch behind the line of fire. Taylor stood nearby, and Mark hovered just behind my right side. He watched closely as I raised the pistol.

It wavered in my grip. The only other time I'd fired a gun was yesterday. It took me four shots to knock out the corpse, and it had only been a few feet away. I certainly needed the practice. I stood fifteen feet away from the target.

"Now, slowly pull the trigger," Mark said. "It has to be smooth or else you'll yank the shot wide."

I exhaled and squeezed the trigger. The pistol roared in the confined space and a bullet hole appeared two feet above the center of the target. Flakes of drywall floated to the ground.

A terrible shot. I self-consciously glanced at the others. No one laughed.

"Try again," Mark said, arms crossed. "Slower this time, and be ready for the kickback. Keep a firm but relaxed grip…yep, good…"

The pistol kicked.

"Better. Don't be scared of the recoil. Control the movement with your arms."

I nodded. Exhilaration blossomed in my chest as I finished off the magazine, leaving a wide swath of poorly placed bullet holes in the wall. Gunpowder hung in the air.

Jamison wasn't much better than I was, and by the time Olivia was done, you wouldn't have guessed we were trying to hit the target at all. There were so many rounds outside the borders of the circle it looked like we'd added the target as an afterthought.

Taylor stepped up. "Give me something small to hit so you know I can shoot."

I pushed a coffee table against the wall and placed a vase on top.

"*Now* mom would be mad," Jamison said.

He'd hardly gotten the words out before the vase exploded in a shower of blue porcelain. Taylor broke into a smile. It warmed me to see. Olivia yelled in excitement, clapping her hands. Mark regarded Taylor with quiet admiration.

"Holy shit," Jamison laughed, "you're amazing."

"Hold on, I'll be back in a minute," I said, dashing upstairs. I returned with two clinking bags of plates and cups.

Jamison hefted one of the glasses before hurling it against the wall. It smashed in a shower of glittering pieces. He let out a primal yell as he pounded his chest. I threw a second glass with everything I had, then hurled a plate like a discus thrower.

Taylor took the pistol and destroyed a row of saucers in quick succession. Mark soon got a turn. He set up six cups and shot them to pieces. I brought down another bag of mugs and we proceeded to turn them to dust with the rifle.

I felt far more confident with this gun than the pistol. Sure, it was much easier to hit the target because of the scope, but it simply felt *right* in my hands.

Sections of the wall were starting to fall apart by now, showing a glimpse of the concrete behind. Jamison tried his hand with a shotgun and proceeded to blast away the remaining chunks of drywall. He ran a hand through his hair as he set the gun aside.

We all took in what had become of our basement. Pieces of concrete, wood, insulation, and kitchenware covered the floor with a thick layer of debris. Wisps of smoke hovered near the ceiling. I couldn't help but laugh.

The weight on my chest had nearly disappeared. The dread in the back of my mind was quiet. For the moment, at least. I breathed deep for what felt like the first time since the Collapse.

Looking around, I realized the others needed this just as much as I did. Jamison stood on the coffee table, hands on his hips, observing the wreckage. Olivia relaxed on the couch as Mark inspected the shredded wall. Taylor bent down and collected a handful of casings.

"Should we clean up?" Taylor asked.

"Eh, what's the point?" Jamison said. "I think we should celebrate. Drinks…ice cream…board games…whatever you want."

We heartily agreed.

Jamison went upstairs with Taylor to prepare while the rest of us gathered the guns and ammo. We'd run through about half our bullets. Though my skill with a pistol was embarrassing, I had a feeling that wouldn't matter. The rifle was already my weapon of choice.

Jamison seemed to be taken with the destructive power of the shotgun, and Taylor and Mark could handle everything with ease. Only Olivia seemed out of her depth, but she would learn.

We all would.

Whether we liked it or not, this was our new way of life.

THANKS TO OUR zealous shooting, we made a quick run to the Larks and stole all of their remaining plates and cups. Then we sat down to a game of poker—with actual chips taken from the Larks—and whiskey and vanilla ice cream.

It didn't matter that it was the middle of the day. We had nowhere to go and nothing to do. No responsibility other than to stay alive. No one knew how long that was going to last, so we played games until the sun was down and none of us could walk without tipping over.

I propped my feet on the living room coffee table, drink in hand, Taylor at my side. Jamison bustled in the kitchen, adding pleasant background noise as he chopped and stirred and filled the house with the scent of frying chicken.

I must have dozed off because gentle music brought me back to consciousness. I looked around to find Olivia cross-legged on the floor with the guitar. She plucked the notes carefully at first, focusing on her fingers, then closed her eyes and started to sing. Her voice was clear and honest, and I'd never heard something so pure. Taylor threaded her arm through mine and rested her head on my shoulder.

Mark leaned forward in his easy chair. His stoic mask faded until his brow was drawn together and the corners of his eyes had softened in the fading light.

I let myself sink into the moment, warmth and quiet slowly overtaking the storm. And for a while, as long as Olivia played, nothing could chase that away.

TEN

I AWOKE TO the uncertain feeling of having forgotten something important.

I laid in bed as I searched my mind. I had no idea what I was looking for, so I went backward through yesterday, hoping this would spark a memory. Watching a movie. Olivia's music. Poker and ice cream and whiskey. Target practice. Breakfast, and talking to Jamison in the morning.

I paused there, frowning. That was it. We'd talked about what was going on in Tampa Bay, our parents, the call two nights ago…

The call.

Dad said he was going to call yesterday, but that never happened. I checked my phone just to make sure. Zero notifications.

Strange.

I sent a quick text to Dad saying *Is everything ok?* The message bounced, with a tiny *Not Delivered* underneath.

The previous one had gone through…

I tried again with the same result.

I sat up in bed and tried calling this time, but a mechanical voice said the number couldn't be reached. Next, I checked our Wi-Fi, and that's when my heart dropped.

The top right corner of my phone said *NO SERVICE.*

I switched to cellular and opened a webpage. It wouldn't load. Panicking slightly, I shook Jamison awake.

"What the hell?" He shoved me away.

"Check your phone."

"Why?"

I climbed over him and snagged it from the nightstand. His screen said the same thing. Not good.

"Our phones aren't working," I said, climbing out of bed. I threw on a T-shirt and rushed out of the room.

"What do you mean our phones aren't working?" Jamison called after me.

I knocked on Taylor's door. She answered with a groggy voice. "Come in."

I peeked inside. "I need to know if your phone is working. Do you have Wi-Fi or cellular?"

Taylor rubbed her eyes and picked it up. "No…"

"Shit." I closed the door and ran down the stairs.

Mark was already bustling around the kitchen. He dug a measuring cup into a bag of coffee grounds. "What's up?"

"Phones aren't working," I said.

Where was the TV remote? I overturned the couch cushions before finding it on the coffee table. I smashed the power button and turned on the satellite receiver. A grey *NO SIGNAL* box floated on the screen.

I sank to the floor.

I could have checked my computer, or Mark and Olivia's phones, but I knew I would only get the same result. This was it. We were cut off from the world. No communication.

The coffee pot gurgled. Mark approached, hands in his pockets. He glanced at the TV, then at me, understanding washing over him.

Taylor and Jamison came down the stairs within minutes of each other, the same confused expression on their faces. I told them what was going on. Taylor sat at the table, her mouth forming a tiny 'O'.

Olivia showed up and we discussed what had happened, but we couldn't agree on *how*. And, of course, we couldn't look anything up to find out the truth. But none of that mattered anymore. I had the sudden urge to watch the news. None of us had done that since the Collapse, and now there was no way to find out how far the corpses had spread. The number of casualties. How this had even happened in the first place.

This was it.

From here on out, we were truly on our own.

WE SPENT THE next handful of days adjusting to the lack of communication with the outside world. We played games, drank most nights, and watched movies from our DVD collection. Anything to keep ourselves busy and our minds off what was going on.

Still, we were restless.

I paced the house in endless circles, sometimes stopping to watch the street from our front windows. Corpses wandered past more often. I rarely saw our neighbors. I wondered if they were all dead or if they had evacuated. It had been more than a week since the Collapse, maybe two. I'd lost track of the days.

Sometimes, I sat on our back porch in the mornings, taking in the fresh air. Or at night when I could look up at the stars. It was hard to imagine a world in chaos during times like that, when everything was serene. Maybe that's why I did it.

And with little else going on, I found time to read again. I finished two books in three days. If I kept that up, I could potentially get through the dozens of books I'd bought but never started. And after that, I could start re-reading things I hadn't touched in years. It was a tangible plan, and I liked that. It kept me grounded, and at the same time, I could still escape.

Once again browsing the shelves in my room, I heard a soft knock on the open door. Olivia skirted the bed and crossed her arms, one hand touching her necklace. She nodded a few times to herself. "Nice collection."

"Thanks, it's coming together."

"Have you read them all?"

"Everything on this bookcase," I said, indicating the leftmost shelf next to the bed. "It's all organized by genre and author. Mostly fantasy, some fiction, biographies…what?"

Olivia was smiling as she removed my hardcover version of *The Hobbit*. "I wouldn't have guessed."

"That I like to read?"

"That you *can* read," she returned.

I laughed.

Olivia put *The Hobbit* back, and I tried not to hover as I made sure it went perfectly back into line. She sat on the bed and folded her hands in her lap. "What do you recommend?"

I put my hands on my hips and looked her over, glimpsing the pendant on a thin gold chain. A single music note, though I wasn't sure which one. I pulled *The Name of the Wind* down and settled next to her, handing it over with slight hesitation. It was like handing over a part of myself.

"It's my favorite book. It's fantasy, but it's essentially an autobiography. And there's these music scenes where you really *feel* the emotion...it's beautiful..." I trailed off, unable to properly describe the book. "Just read the prologue and you'll understand. I think you'll like it."

She nodded as she flipped through the pages. "That sounds good."

"Where'd you get the necklace?" I asked.

Olivia closed the book, lines forming at the corners of her eyes. "For my birthday, last month."

"Ah," I said, wishing I knew what to do. We sat for a minute, quiet. I squeezed my hands together, aware of the things she didn't say. "I know what it's like to lose your family. I'm sorry, for what it's worth."

"It doesn't feel like they're gone," Olivia said. "I want to find them, but I don't want to face what they've become. I couldn't do that, not like Mark and Taylor. They're strong—"

"You are too."

"Not like them," Olivia said, drawing back into herself. "I'm not built for this world."

"No one is. But you're here now, and we've made it this far."

"Until we don't."

"Maybe," I said, adjusting my position so I leaned back on one elbow. "I haven't said this before, but for a long time, I never thought I could make it to the next day. I couldn't sleep at night. I imagined all the things I could have changed or said, but then I'd wake up the next morning. And the one after that." I fell back and covered my eyes with both hands. "I was still here for some reason. I don't know why, but I'm here now, and I guess that's important."

Olivia didn't respond. She laid on the bed, eyes fixed on the ceiling, our arms nearly touching.

"I think that's all we have, really," I said, fingers tapping my chest. "The next day. And what I think about now is how to make my parents proud, because a part of me still hopes they can see I'm alright."

Olivia's hand found mine. She squeezed it in a way that didn't need words to convey she understood.

"You're not alone," I said, shifting so I could see her face. Tears flowed from the corner of her eyes. "But you don't have to talk to me about it. You don't have to talk at all."

She didn't, and neither did I.

LATER THAT NIGHT, I found Taylor in my room. Maybe it was hers now, but it didn't matter either way. We sat side by side, propped against the wall. For a while, all we did was exist in each other's presence.

"Remember when we made out?" Taylor asked, bringing up the subject we'd both been avoiding.

I coughed. "Yeah, I remember."

"Did it mean anything to you?" Taylor asked.

I paused, trying to gauge what she wanted me to say. "I probably wouldn't have done it if I wasn't drunk..." I began, trailing off as Taylor raised her eyebrows. I held up a hand. "Let me start over. I like you, and I have for a while—"

"How long?"

"—since last year. But I was nervous to ask you out. And then we won our game, and we were drunk, and it just…made sense."

"You shouldn't have added that last part," she said dryly.

I rubbed my forehead. "I'm messing this up, aren't I?"

"A little."

"It's the truth. I like you, I really do. I was just scared." I sighed. "Is that bad to admit?"

"It's kind of cute."

"Cute? *Great.*"

"I can't believe it took you that long to do something," Taylor said.

"I didn't think you were interested!" I defended. *"Are you?"*

"I am, lucky for you. I have been for a while," Taylor said, giving me a mysterious look.

"Really? Wow…" I ran a hand through my hair. "Besides, I always thought Jamison had a thing for you, and I didn't want to make it weird between us."

"He did?"

"*Does,* I think. We've never really talked about it."

"Do you think he'd get mad?"

"No, he'll be fine," I said, playing with the hem of my shirt. I looked at Taylor. "So…what do we do about this?"

"Us? Romantically?" She asked, pursing her lips. "I'm not sure."

"It's a weird time to start something."

"Is that bad?"

I shrugged. "No…but what if it doesn't work out?"

Taylor took a moment to consider this. "I think that's a poor excuse not to try."

"I guess I'm trying to say I don't know how to give you what you need…" I fought for the right words as unbidden emotion rose in my throat. "I can barely do that for myself…and it's hard for me to open up to people…"

"Cody, I don't need you to do anything," Taylor said, looking at me intently. I could hardly meet her eyes, afraid she might see the guilt I didn't know how to deal with. "And you think too much. I like you because of who you are. You're kind and you give."

"I don't—"

"Stop, don't doubt that," Taylor said. "I see all the ways you care. And sure, it's a crazy time, but I'm here for you, and I know you're there for me. That's what matters. It doesn't have to be a big thing, just us."

I nodded. She wrapped her hand in mine and I held on tight. "Just us."

"And Jamison."

I laughed. Taylor's dimples appeared again. We looked at each other, quiet. I traced her jaw with a gentle finger, taking in the scent of her perfume. Lavender, this time. I leaned forward and our lips met. I melted into the kiss, her hand resting on my chest. For a wonderful moment, every thought left my head.

She pulled back, a full smile now. The lump in my throat dissolved.

"Does this mean we're official?" I asked.

"I'd say so, but I think you have to ask…"

"Right, um…will you be my girlfriend?"

"Obviously," she said, kissing me again.

We leaned back against the wall, her head on my shoulder.

"Wait, how is dating supposed to work? There's nowhere to go," I said.

"I don't need to go anywhere," she said softly.

And she was right. Nothing was better than this: sitting on the floor as the sun went down in brilliant shades of red, orange, and purple, and her hand held firmly in mine.

ELEVEN

As THE DAYS slipped by, another problem tugged at the back of my mind.

My parents were still alive in Tampa Bay—as far as I knew—and I wanted to go after them. I *needed* to. Besides Jamison, they were the only family I had left.

I'd lost my real parents already. I'd lived through that pain, and I couldn't do it again. And maybe we'd never make it, or they'd already be gone by the time we got there, but I wouldn't let myself consider that possibility. I knew more than anything that I would never forgive myself if I never tried to find them.

I grew more restless with each passing day. Time was running out, I felt it deep inside. The longer we waited, the more unlikely it was Jamison and I would see them again.

Still, I hesitated to bring it up to the group. I didn't have a plan, and I didn't want to be the one to uproot our semi-stable way of life. Even worse would be to break us up if the others didn't want to go.

I eventually got up the nerve to approach Jamison as he made breakfast one morning. No one else was around.

"This might sound crazy," I began, "but I think we should find mom and dad."

Jamison paused, evaluating my face. "You're right, that is crazy."

"We have to do it," I said.

Jamison opened the fridge. He selected a carton of eggs, bread, and jam, and laid them on the counter. "I don't know."

"Why shouldn't we?" I asked.

"First, Dad told us to stay put," Jamison said, placing his hands on the counter. "Second, they're in *Florida*. Do you know how far that is? That's insane. We can't make that trip."

I pursed my lips.

"Besides," he said, "what if they decide to find *us*, and we've already left?"

It was a good point, but I had reason to believe they wouldn't do that. I showed him the text saying we were going to find them. Jamison mulled over the information.

"They'll be waiting," I said.

"They could be waiting a long time if we don't make it," Jamison said.

"Jamison, they're still out there," I said. "Taylor...Mark... Olivia...their families are gone, but ours isn't. That *means* something."

"What, that we'll eventually lose them too?" Jamison said, trying to move past me.

I gripped his arm. "Why are you afraid to do this?"

"Why are you not?"

"I *am* scared. But what scares me more is living out the rest of our lives pretending they're already gone!" I looked into Jamison's eyes, seeing pain and guilt flickering below the surface. Then it clicked. "You're scared of what they'd think of you. About what you did."

"You mean the man I killed? Yeah, call that a natural reaction."

"They don't know," I said. "I never told them. But I know they would understand. They love you."

"Can love forgive murder?" Jamison asked. He turned on the stove and cracked an egg.

"I forgive you," I said.

Jamison worked silently, adding another two eggs to the sizzling pan. His shoulders were tense, his movements reserved.

"We have to go," I said quietly. "You know we have to do this."

All Jamison did was give a slight nod. Relief washed over me.

"When should we tell the others?" I asked.

Jamison shrugged. "Doesn't matter. They're not going to join us."

He was probably right. They had no reason to go. Still, the thought of leaving them behind made me uneasy. I didn't want to leave any of them, but most of all, I didn't want to leave Taylor. I wouldn't stop her if she wanted to come, but if she didn't, I could live with that. It was her decision, not mine.

I found Taylor in her room, and she listened as I explained, eyes thoughtful.

"I'm not forcing you to do this," I said.

"Stop, I'm going with you," she said. "You can't get rid of me that easily."

"So, I'm not insane?"

"No, you definitely are, but you have to do everything you can to find them."

"Thank you," I said. "Really."

"Of course. And it's not like there's anything left for me here, anyway," she said, joking, but her face grew pensive. I squeezed her hand in sympathy.

"Come on, Jamison has the others in the kitchen," I said, leading us downstairs.

Jamison was finishing his breakfast at the round table. Mark and Olivia stood in front of the island. Taylor leaned her elbows over the back of a chair.

"Jamison and I want to find our parents," I said when I had their attention. "Taylor's coming too."

Jamison looked up. "She is?"

"Yes," I said.

"Are you serious?" Olivia asked.

"We are," I said.

"Why didn't you tell me about this?" Olivia turned on Taylor.

"He *just* asked me," Taylor said.

"They're in Florida, right?" Mark asked. I nodded. "I hate to say this, but how do you know they'll still be alive, even *if* you make it all the way there?"

"How do we know we'll live if we stay?" I countered.

"Right here is the safest place we can be. You can't deny that. We have everything we need. We can *make it,*" Mark said.

"I don't care about making it! Your families are gone, and I'm sorry. I really am," I said, looking around the group. "But mine is still out there, and I have a chance to see them again. Wouldn't you do whatever you could to make that happen?"

"I think it's stupid. We can't make a trip like that, not across the entire country," Mark said.

"I'm not saying you have to go. I want all of you to be there, but that's for you to decide."

"Cody." Mark stepped forward, hands up. "You need to think long term. The most important thing we can do is survive. I *know* we can wait this out, but only if we're smart."

"Survival doesn't matter if you have nothing to live for," I said. "Survival doesn't matter if you lose yourself along the way. I wouldn't be able to live with myself knowing I never even tried."

"I'm trying to stop you from doing something that *will* get you killed," Mark said.

"You don't know that will happen."

"Look around, Cody! Everyone we know is gone!"

"I thought you said this was the safest place."

"It is! We have a house. We're protected. There's no telling what we might run into out there."

"So what? Maybe I die! Maybe I get there and they're gone. That's a choice that *I* need to make, and I'm not convinced staying here is going to turn out any better."

Mark looked around for support, but none came. He deflated, rubbing his temples. "If that's what you want to do, go ahead and do it. I'm not going to stop you."

I rocked back on my heels, looking toward the others. They'd hardly moved since Mark and I took over the discussion. Taylor had watched the whole thing with her eyebrows pulled together. Olivia shifted uncomfortably as her eyes flickered between Mark and me. Jamison just sat with one arm on the table, swirling his glass of water.

"I want to help," Olivia said.

Mark looked at us in disbelief. "So that's it? You're abandoning me just to kill yourselves…"

"Screw off," I said.

"We're not abandoning you," Olivia said. She stood right in front of Mark, looking up at his face. She placed a hand on his arm. "You don't have to be alone. Come with us."

"That's a hell of a choice you're giving me." Mark brushed her arm away. "Maybe it's better this way. You can go where you want, and I only have to look after myself. Everyone's happy," he said, facing me, coldness boring into my eyes. "I just want you to know that if you leave, this will *not* end well for you."

"We know the risks. We can make our own decisions," I said.

Mark took a final, silent look around the room before turning on a heel and stalking upstairs. I let out the breath I'd been holding.

Taylor straightened up. "What do we do now?"

"I guess we start packing," I said.

WE SET TO work that day.

Mark watched us gather supplies with a stony face. He let us take four of the guns and half the ammunition, which was nice enough. He offered occasional help but mostly found pleasure in pointing out things we hadn't thought of, such as how we were going to find enough gas to get us to Florida.

"We'll stop at gas stations," Jamison said.

"I wouldn't count on them working, especially not long term," Mark said. "You should probably learn how to siphon. For that, you'll need a tube and a gas can, and I don't know if you have that here. Actually, you should look for a pump."

I clenched my jaw, adding the items to the list of things we had to scavenge before setting out.

"You'll need a detailed roadmap too," he called after me as I left the kitchen. "Do you have that? Your phones won't get you there."

He followed me into the garage where I searched the shelves for flashlights.

"I'd look for refillable water bottles as well. Oh, and a filter. Purifying tabs would work too," he said. "Have you thought about how you're going to cook food? You'll need a portable stove, propane, that kind of thing. Do you know how to make a fire?"

"Can you *please* shut up?" I snapped.

"Hey, I'm just trying to help," Mark said. "How far do you think you'll get without me? Besides Taylor, I'm the only one who really knows how to use a gun."

I pushed by him, two flashlights and a headlamp in my hands. "We'll be fine."

Mark shrugged. Back in the house, I grudgingly added Mark's suggestions to the list. That was when the lights flickered. My gaze went to the ceiling as the last bulb went out.

"That's…not good," I said.

Mark's unpleasant demeanor immediately fell away. I could see his mind racing as he worked the problem. He moved to the sink and tried the faucet. It ran but seemed to be at a lower pressure. Maybe I was making that up. He shut off the water.

"Hey! Everyone get down here!" Mark shouted.

Footsteps pounded from all corners of the house.

"What's going on?" Olivia asked.

"Looks like the power's out," Mark said. "We need to stock up on water before the pressure goes down and the city runs through the supply. Someone might figure out how to keep the water running and get the power back, but we shouldn't count on that. People will be too focused on saving themselves to worry about anyone else."

We looked at him with uncertainty. One more thing to worry about.

"How do you know that?" I asked.

"I know a lot of random shit," Mark said. "Come on, let's go."

Jamison and I found two five-gallon coolers in the basement. We cleaned them out in the backyard and started filling them up from the hose.

"Is this safe?" Jamison asked.

"Think of all the times you drank from a hose as a kid. We'll be fine," I said.

Jamison accepted that and we hauled the water into the house. The others returned from the Larks with two more coolers. Twenty gallons. Not bad, but I had no idea how much we would need. We certainly didn't need to fill up every container we had, as that wouldn't all fit in the car when we left. But purifying tabs would be essential so we could get water from rivers along the way.

Mark went with the rest of us to help find the remaining supplies we needed. I considered it a blessing when the streets were nearly absent of the living. Yet, corpses sprang up out of nowhere, steadily continuing their invasion of the city.

We ended up going to two hardware shops and one sporting goods store, finding nearly everything on the list. The only thing that eluded us was a siphoning pump. Mark grumbled about having to do it the old-fashioned way. He found a three-foot tube and a gas can.

Mark grew more pensive and avoided sarcastic comments as the day went on. He had us stop on an overpass at the edge of a swath of abandoned cars, then proceeded to teach us how to siphon gas. We all watched as he pried open the gas cover of a silver Camry, inserted the tube, and sealed the rag around the opening. He sucked on the end, drawing gasoline up to his mouth, then carefully pinched the tube and inserted the end into the can.

Gasoline trickled into the container.

Mark washed out his mouth with a swig from his water bottle. "The rag creates a vacuum and forces the gas out of the tube," he explained.

I rocked back in amazement. The others were all similarly impressed. Jamison raised an eyebrow and muttered something about Mark showing off. While Jamison and Olivia filled the can, Mark pointed to a Jeep with a corpse behind the wheel. It was about thirty feet away.

"Practice with the rifle," he said. "Taylor, cover the others."

She nodded, turning around to keep an eye on Jamison and Olivia. I raised an eyebrow and removed the gun from my shoulder. I loaded a bullet into the chamber and took my stance.

"Remember to breathe," he offered. "Slow in, slow out."

The corpse floated into the scope's view, swaying slightly. It looked at me with dead eyes.

I pulled the trigger, the stock bucking at my shoulder.

The corpse's head snapped back as the bullet crashed through the windshield. I ejected the casing as the shot echoed in the open air.

"What the hell?" Jamison shouted at us.

"Get back to work," Taylor returned.

For the next ten minutes, I picked targets from other corpses trapped in their cars. A few wandered freely, lurching toward our position. I sighted the closest one and dropped it through the nose. I did the same with the next and the next, falling into a destructive rhythm.

It was exhilarating.

Mark kept handing me bullets and I switched to the mass of corpses gathering on the road below. It was only when I heard gunfire to my left that I broke from the trance. Spent shells glittered at my feet in the afternoon sunlight.

"Time to go," Taylor called over her shoulder, picking off another corpse that was trying to flank us.

I backpedaled toward the car. More corpses than we could handle swarmed around the vehicles. We piled in and Jamison took off past a group of the dead. Mark gave me a fist bump.

"Good shooting," he said.

I allowed myself a small smile. It had felt strangely good. Freeing.

We arrived home twenty minutes later, and Mark pulled me aside while the others entered the house. He shifted from foot to foot, hands in his pockets.

"I'm sorry for earlier," he said. "I didn't mean to say you shouldn't go after your parents. You should, and I was wondering if I could go with you. I don't want to be alone."

My face softened. I squeezed his shoulder. "Of course you can come. We'd love to have you."

"Thanks," Mark said. "We'll make it. I know we will."

"Damn right," I said.

Everyone was visibly relieved when Mark shared the news, and Olivia hugged him.

We spent the rest of the day piling supplies into the trunk of Jamison's car. By the end, you couldn't see out the back windshield. Anything that didn't fit inside was strapped to the roof with rope.

The day after that, we drew up a plan for how to get to Tampa Bay. Mark outlined our path on a map, detailing the highways that would lead us through Indianapolis, Nashville, and Atlanta. If we were lucky, the whole trip could take less than a week. But like any plan, there were countless ways it could go wrong. It depended on how clogged the roads were, if we ran into large groups of corpses, how often we had to scavenge gas, other survivors…

Mark stressed the importance of taking as much time as we needed to get to our destination. Speed wasn't as important as safety.

No need to put ourselves in pointless danger. I agreed with him to a certain extent, but I didn't need to start another argument. The only thing that mattered was that we were going.

Throughout all our planning, excitement slowly blossomed in my chest. The promise of adventure. I knew it would be dangerous, but I looked forward to the journey. I was sick of being trapped. I was sick of waiting for the end.

I was done hiding in this house.

And no matter what we faced on the road, it was time for us to take control.

PART TWO
WHAT'S LEFT OVER

TWELVE

WE SET OUT early the next morning.

Crisp air cut underneath my sweatshirt, but the sunlight warmed my face. I stood for a while, taking in the quiet moment as the others double-checked our gear. I looked back at the house, an ache forming in my throat.

Taylor rubbed my arm and led me to the car where we took the back row of the Sequoia. Jamison drove, Mark gave directions from the passenger's seat, and Olivia had the middle to herself. She played music as we navigated the city.

The on-ramp to the highway was blocked with cars, so Jamison had to off-road to get around them, but soon enough, we were freely on our way. Trees blurred in patterns of green as the occasional corpse flashed by, shuffling through knee-high grass. I leaned my head against the window and closed my eyes.

When I awoke, the sun was much higher, I was uncomfortably warm, and I had a stabbing pain in my neck. Taylor leaned against my arm, making it hard to move. A butterfly of affection danced inside. I did my best to not wake her as I rolled up my sleeves and massaged the sore spot.

I smiled pleasantly, waiting for my brain to regain normal functioning.

Jamison glanced in the rearview mirror. "Are you done cuddling with Taylor?"

Mark twisted in his seat. "Other way around. She's holding on pretty tight."

"The funny thing is we're actually together," I said.

"Bullshit," Jamison said.

"No, it's true. Taylor told me," Olivia said, looking up from my book. She was *actually* reading it, and was maybe a hundred pages in.

Jamison's eyes narrowed in the mirror. "How long?"

"A week, maybe," I said.

"Have you had sex yet?"

"*Why* would you ask that?" I shot at him.

"It's a legitimate question! Have you?"

"No."

Jamison snorted.

"How much gas do we have?" Mark asked, flipping through the road maps again.

Jamison searched the dashboard. "Three-quarters of a tank. Can someone switch with me? It feels like I sat in warm water." He waited a long moment before saying, "It's the sweat."

"Yeah, I get that," I said.

"I think my underwear is halfway up my asshole," Jamison said.

"That's great," I said, rubbing my forehead.

"And I need to go to the bathroom," Jamison said.

Mark looked up from the map. "We can pull over at the next rest stop."

Jamison grumbled to himself. Thirty minutes later, we parked next to a gold sedan at a dilapidated rest stop. A cracked, concrete path led from the parking lot to the cinderblock bathrooms. Overgrown weeds grew at the base of a lone picnic table. Taylor and Jamison settled there while I stretched by the car and removed my hoodie.

"Cody!" Olivia waved at me from the women's restroom.

"What's up?"

"The door's locked. Can you open it?"

"How?"

"I don't know, you're the one with the bat. You could use a gun, too."

"Don't use a gun," Taylor cut in from the table. "Too loud."

I tossed my hands in the air. "Why not use the men's room?"

"Mark's in there."

"Just wait!"

"I can't."

I dropped my hands back to my sides, looking for support from Taylor and Jamison. All they did was offer patronizing smiles. Smothering my irritation, I retrieved the bat from the trunk and stomped over to the bathrooms. Olivia stepped aside as I prepared to attack the door handle.

"…isn't going to work…" I murmured to myself.

The first swing *cracked* against the metal and sent needles racing up my arms. I swung again and my hands went numb. Sparing a glance at Olivia, I brought my bat down once more, snapping the handle off with a satisfying *clink*.

I kicked the door open and a corpse lunged for my neck. Olivia screamed in my ear. I snapped the bat against its chin, stunning it long enough to bring it down with a proper swing. Two more heavy blows and it stopped moving. I looked at the body in revulsion. It used to be a woman. There wasn't much left of her face, but she had stringy hair and dirt-stained clothes.

I stepped back to avoid the expanding pool of blood. My ears still rang from Olivia's scream, and I couldn't feel my hands.

"You alright?" I asked Olivia.

She nodded, unable to take her eyes off the body. Taylor and Jamison ran over, and Mark appeared around the corner.

"What the hell are you doing?" Mark asked.

"This was her idea," I said, gesturing to Olivia. She frowned.

"She really did it, just up and died in the bathroom," Jamison said.

"Yeah, I'm not using it now," Olivia said, heading for the men's room.

"Unbelievable…" I said.

"How long do you think she'd been in there?" Jamison asked.

"I don't want to think about it," I said.

"Do you think she did it to herself?" Mark asked.

"I said I *don't* want to think about it." I turned away, jaw clenched. I looked to the sky where a flock of birds passed overhead. I watched them go from smudges to spots to nothing.

I headed for the car. Jamison followed, grabbing my arm and looking at me with doughy eyes. *"My hero."*

"Stop," I said.

"First you get Taylor. Now Olivia's making a move? Leave some for the rest of us," Jamison said.

"Mark's available," I said, opening the trunk.

Jamison tilted his head. "Don't get me wrong, he has a nice body and everything, but it's almost too much, you know? Besides, his stoic," Jamison made a vague gesture with his hand, *"darkness* isn't really my thing."

I dumped food in Jamison's arms and we hauled over a variety of snacks to the picnic table. We spent an hour at the rest stop before heading out again. I took my turn behind the wheel.

It felt good to drive. I could let my mind wander as I took in the sights. Occasional abandoned cars dotted the road. Corpses sometimes wandered in the billowing grass. Only twice did we pass other survivors, but they were heading in the opposite direction. I tensed as their cars flashed by. In a moment, they were gone, and we were alone once again.

We'd been driving for another two hours when Mark had me pull over on the outskirts of Madison, Wisconsin. On-ramps to the highway were clogged with cars. Skyscrapers broke the horizon.

I parked and hopped out of the driver's seat, stretching in the sunlight. Mark retrieved the siphoning gear from the trunk and set to work on a truck. It took the better part of an hour to fill the tank. Some cars were tapped when we tried them, and others only filled half the can. I leaned against a car and wiped sweat from my forehead. The sun wallowed in the blue expanse, taunting me with its shimmering rays.

After filling the tank, we ate a lunch of chips and sandwiches in the shade of an oak tree on the edge of the highway. I brushed the crumbs from my shirt and laid on the grass, watching the leaves shift above me.

We set out on the road again, carefully skirting the city. It was a couple of hours before Mark said we could stop for the night. The sun hadn't set yet, but I didn't mind. I could only spend so much time in a car before it started to feel like a prison.

Mark wove the car between trees to conceal it from the road. He immediately set to work building a fire, creating a ring with head-sized stones. Jamison and I gathered pine needles and branches, chopping up the larger ones with a hatchet. Once we finished, we sat on a log to watch Mark construct a teepee of kindling.

"Looks legit," Jamison said. "How did you learn this stuff?"

"Boy Scouts," Mark said, inspecting his work from his hands and knees.

"I was a Boy Scout once," Jamison said.

"Really?" Mark gave him a suspicious once over.

"My parents signed me up, but I never did all this," Jamison said, gesturing to the fire. "I just went to make fun of the weird kids."

Mark sighed, adjusting a stick. He reached for the box of matches.

"Hold on," Jamison raised a hand. "You're telling me you can't do some freaky voodoo ritual to summon fire?"

I laughed. Mark pointedly ignored Jamison as he struck a match. He shifted the flame under the pine needles. Smoke wafted from the little teepee and it burst into flame seconds later. Like an overprotective mother, Mark carefully tended the fire, adding progressively larger branches until flames leaped in the air and wrapped me in a blanket of warmth.

The others prepared food while Jamison and I found a place to pitch the tent. It was made for six people, so it took us a few minutes to find a big enough area. Then came the real trouble of setting it up. Neither of us had gone camping more than a handful of times in our lives, and we'd never been the ones to set up the tent.

I snapped the poles together while Jamison looked over the fabric, scratching his chin.

"I don't even know where to start," he said.

"Do you want to ask Mark for help?" I asked.

"No," he said.

"Well, if we keep staring at it, maybe it'll magically put itself together," I said thoughtfully.

Jamison flipped me off as I bent down to thread a pole through one of the loops of fabric. After numerous failed attempts, it finally resembled a tent. We deposited the sleeping bags inside and settled around the fire. Taylor handed out bowls of chicken noodle soup. I scooted close to her.

The light faded quickly, and wind rustled through the trees. Intermittent conversation kept us awake for the next couple of hours, but one by one, everyone except Taylor and me turned in for the night.

"Are you staying out here for a while?" she asked, standing up.

"Until the fire's out," I said.

"Alright, good night," Taylor said, kissing me before disappearing into the tent.

I pulled my blanket tighter around my shoulders as a breeze came through the camp. High above, the moon glowed through the branches. An owl hooted. Sparks floated beneath my chin, the wood popping every few minutes. My eyes drooped as the flames turned to coals.

Crack!

My eyes snapped open, senses straining in the dark. I remained perfectly still as goosebumps rose on my neck and arms.

A branch snapped behind me. I sprang to my feet, snatching my bat from the ground as a corpse tripped over the log I'd been sitting on. It plowed into the ground face first, and I pounded its head until chunks of brain slipped from its skull. I stepped back, my body tingling with adrenaline.

No sounds came from the tent. I looked over the mess with a frustrated grimace. I did my best to stuff the brain pieces back into the skull with a couple of sticks, but my efforts only squished them into smaller chunks.

Fucking hell.

Thoroughly irritated now, I hauled the body away from the fire, grunting with the effort.

"Thanks for saving us, Cody," I said to myself, depositing the corpse behind a tree.

"Oh, it's nothing," I returned.

"No, you're a real hero. You're brave *and* humble. It's a shame the others don't see it."

"That's nice of you to say."

A wolf howled. I shivered, twisting in the moonlit woods.

Returning to camp, I doused the remaining coals with a water bottle, steam billowing under my chin. I climbed into the tent, careful not to step on anyone. Curling up in my sleeping bag next to Taylor, I couldn't help but smile as the smoke on my clothes lulled me to sleep, adventure permeating the air.

THIRTEEN

MARK AND JAMISON were gone from the tent when I woke up. Taylor and Olivia still slept, oblivious to the world. I contentedly watched Taylor for a moment before climbing outside.

Errant rays of sunlight streamed through the branches, a kaleidoscope of green and yellow. I shaded my eyes with a hand, wiggling my fingers to get out the cold stiffness. Jamison straddled a log across from the fire pit, a rock raised above his head. A can of chili teetered on the log in front of him.

"What are you doing?" I asked, rubbing my arms to get some warmth back.

"I couldn't find the can opener, so," he said, lining up the rock and can, "I'm improvising."

"Why not eat something else?"

Jamison sighed. "Where's the fun in that?"

I shrugged. Jamison raised the rock again and brought it crashing down on the can. Chili exploded in every direction, coating his shirt in the process. Jamison dropped the rock and removed his shirt, then dipped a finger into the ruptured can.

"Tastes like cat food," he said.

"And you know that how?" I asked. Jamison continued to eat, ignoring my question. "Jamison, have you eaten cat food?"

"I don't want to talk about it."

I sighed. "Where's Mark?"

"He took the rifle. I think he's hunting."

"Why? We have plenty of food."

"I think he has a lot of pent-up aggression he hasn't dealt with properly," Jamison said.

I almost laughed at the joke, but there was no humor in Jamison's voice.

"Want one?" he asked, tossing me a can of chili before I could respond.

I broke open the top with a small, sharp rock, then gripped the lid between my thumb and forefinger and wrenched it up. My finger slipped but I didn't feel anything at first. Two seconds later, searing pain blazed through the meat of my thumb. I lifted my finger in shock as blood bubbled from the wound like a fountain.

Shit.

I hurriedly wrapped my thumb with the edge of my shirt. Blood immediately soaked through. I tore off my shirt and did my best to rip it into smaller pieces. It took two of these strips to staunch the flow. I clenched my teeth, finger pulsing like a second heart.

Jamison watched the whole thing with his mouth slightly open, food forgotten. "Good job," he said.

I shot him a look that quieted anything else he had to say. I poured water over my hands to wash away the blood and dried them with the rest of my shirt. Making my way to the car, I fished out the bag of utensils and selected a spoon. Right in the middle of it all was the can opener.

"What the hell, Jamison? It's right here," I said, waving it at him.

"Yeah, I lied about not finding it," Jamison said. "I just wanted to smash something."

"There's something wrong with you, you know that, right?"

"I prefer to be a free thinker," Jamison said with a smile.

I shook my head and plopped down on the log, shoveling chili into my mouth. I chewed uncomfortably. It was cold and slimy. I choked down a couple more mouthfuls before setting aside the can in disgust.

A gunshot echoed. Jamison and I twisted in the direction of the sound.

Taylor unzipped the tent. "What was that?"

"Mark's hunting," Jamison said.

Taylor rubbed her eyes and focused on us. "What happened to your shirts?"

"I cut my finger," I said, showing my bandaged thumb.

"Got food on mine," Jamison said.

Taylor gave us an amused look and disappeared again. Mark emerged from behind a clump of boulders. He weaved between trees, a rifle slung across his back. Something swayed in his hands, grey and limp. A rabbit. Its head was mangled, but the body seemed undamaged.

"I figured we could use some real food," Mark said. The rabbit flopped around like it didn't have bones. "Who wants to help skin this? Cody?"

Now, I was glad I'd cut my thumb open. I showed Mark. His gaze settled on Jamison, who vigorously shook his head. Mark didn't seem to care. A minute later, Jamison had a knife in one hand and the rabbit lying in front of him on one of the coolers.

Mark explained the basic process of skinning an animal, and

Jamison warily examined the rabbit, his face pale. The only reason I watched was to see Jamison squirm. He looked up, eyes pleading for help, and I grinned at him. His hands shook as he cut around the ankles. When he started peeling the skin away, I decided I'd had enough and busied myself with finding a new shirt.

Soon enough, the rabbit was roasting above the fire. There wasn't much meat to split between five people, but it was certainly better than cold chili. I handed out a box of granola bars to supplement the meal.

We broke camp an hour later and set out on the road. The day went by much like the previous one, and every few hours, we stopped to stretch our legs, eat, or fill up on gas.

We'd reached Central Illinois by late afternoon and halted in the middle of the highway. Restaurants made up the right side of the road. A shopping center sprawled on the left. Specks—corpses—moved in the expansive parking lot.

Straight ahead, a forest rose on both sides of the road.

I leaned forward from my seat in the back row, seeing our path completely blocked off by cars. Concrete medians split the highway in two and lined the edges of the road. Possibly a hundred cars were funneled down the stretch, packed tightly together.

Jamison set to work siphoning gas while the rest of us surveyed the problem.

"We'll have to move them," Mark said. "Just enough to squeeze through, but it'll take some effort. And time."

"How?" I asked.

"I don't know," Mark said. "Put them in neutral and push them aside? Move them with our car if that doesn't work…"

I rubbed my forehead. "Do you think any of them still run?"

Mark considered this. "Maybe. If the keys are in the ignition, the battery will be dead. Some people might have taken them out if they set out on foot. There's only one way to find out. Let's start at the front."

"Go ahead," Taylor said. "I'll cover Jamison."

"Don't use guns if you run into a corpse. We don't want to draw them over," Mark said.

Taylor nodded, tracking Jamison down and leaning against the car he was siphoning from. Mark, Olivia, and I made our way through the pack. I kept myself alert. We were too exposed and could easily be overwhelmed by corpses in the area. I carried a bat in my right hand, a knife on my hip, and the rifle slung over my back.

The first car in the pileup was overturned. Two more had crashed headlong into it, their hoods bent like accordions. Another had tried to avoid this group by skirting around it but only succeeded in smashing into the median. Behind, other cars were stopped just shy of the wreck.

I pursed my lips at the sight.

Even if we could move the undamaged cars, there was nowhere to put them, and the ones at the front weren't going anywhere. We would need a tow truck to haul them away or a tank to blaze a path through, and obviously, neither of those things were going to happen.

A corpse stretched for me through a shattered window. I stepped out of reach.

"This won't work," Mark said, echoing my thoughts. "We'll have to double back and go through the city."

We met up with Taylor and Jamison, telling them the new plan.

Jamison leaned against the car. "Should I finish this up first?"

Mark nodded. "I'll switch with you soon. I want to get back on the road, put this place behind us before we settle down for the night."

Jamison turned back to the car. A gallon later, Mark switched with him. I took out a few wandering corpses with the bat while Mark went from car to car. The sun had fallen below the horizon when I heard the unmistakable sound of an engine drawing closer. I looked up. Taylor straightened, hand falling to the gun at her belt.

A dirty white truck ground to a halt twenty feet away. People moved behind the windshield.

"Maybe they can help clear a path," Jamison said from his perch on top of a car.

"I'd rather leave," Mark said. "Come on, let's pack it up."

I agreed with Mark. The fewer interactions with other survivors, the better. He poured the rest of the gas into our car, depositing the can in the trunk.

"Hey!" The call came from the truck. A rotund man stepped out, waving. He had a full beard and a cameo hat squashed over his head. "Having trouble?"

"The road's blocked, but we're fine," Mark shouted back.

Three other people stepped out of the car. A lanky man with a few days' stubble on his cheeks, a plump, middle-aged woman, and a boy, probably a few years younger than us. The skinny man hefted an automatic rifle.

"We could help you out," the big man offered. He retrieved a shotgun from the bed of the truck. He had a pistol in a holster as well.

"Thanks, but we're heading out," Mark said.

The skinny man wandered over to our car, keeping his gun pointing at the ground. He peered into the trunk.

"Oh, shit! Look at the gear they found," he said. His beady eyes carried a dangerous glint.

"We don't want any trouble. We'll be out of your way soon," Mark said.

"The safest time to travel is during the day, and it's almost dark," the small man said. "Are you sure you want to be out now?"

"We're fine," Mark said.

"You know," the small man said casually, "survivors like us need to stick together. You should make camp with us tonight."

It was a thinly veiled threat. No one raised their guns, but they could do that in a split second. I kept my hands away from my weapons to avoid accidentally escalating things. Mark's jaw clenched.

"Or we could kill you and take your stuff," the small man said. I stilled. He held Mark's steely gaze for a moment before breaking into laughter. "But we'd rather work together. We're all friends here, right?"

"I think so," the big man said.

"Before we go any further, I'm Sullivan," the small man said, pointing to the others in turn. "The big guy is Joe. That's my wife Elizabeth, and my boy Arnold. Now you."

Mark introduced us, and Sullivan plastered on a smile that was far too wide.

"See? That wasn't so bad. We're all friends now, nothing to worry about," Sullivan said. "So, what do you say? Want to make camp with us?"

"Yeah, sure," Jamison said before the rest of us could respond.

"Perfect, we'll start setting up in those trees," Sullivan said, pointing to the forest.

Sullivan's group stalked back to their car. Mark fumed. He shoved Jamison.

"What are you *thinking?* We need to get out of here, not make friends," Mark said.

"The only way we get out of here is if someone gets *shot*," Jamison said. He recovered his footing and shoved Mark in return. "We drive off and they chase us down. They clearly want our stuff, but this way, we have time to make a plan."

"He has a point," I said.

Mark wheeled on me. "How are we going to get out of this? Do you see them letting us go tomorrow?"

"I don't know," I said.

"You never do," Mark growled. "Don't blame me when they kill us in our sleep." Mark opened the trunk, sparing a glance at Sullivan's car. Joe and Arnold watched us as they unloaded equipment. "Keep your weapons ready in case they try anything," Mark said quietly.

Jamison retrieved a pistol from the glovebox and tucked it into his belt and out of sight. He found a box of ammo and stuffed it into his pocket. He then hefted his shotgun and carried the portable stove over the concrete barrier and into the trees. I hauled the tent, the others gathered food, and both our groups met twenty yards into the small forest.

Mark built a fire while Sullivan hovered. I set up the tent with Taylor and Olivia while Jamison wandered off to gather firewood. Soon enough, our ramshackle camp was set up. The sun was gone, and the fire provided the only light, casting undulating shadows over our faces.

We ate undercooked pasta and sat in an uncomfortable circle. The tension slowly dissipated to the point where it simmered quietly under the surface. No one on either side made an effort to hide their weapons, but it was like we had reached an unspoken agreement; leave each other alone and there wouldn't be any problems.

"Where are you heading?" Sullivan asked between bites.

I shrugged vaguely.

"Come on," Sullivan prodded. "Where could a group of kids be heading in this shit storm?"

"Nowhere…just surviving," I said.

"Hell, if you don't have anywhere to go, why not join us?" Sullivan suggested.

"We could always use the help," Joe added.

"He's right. You seem resourceful," Sullivan pointed at me with his fork. "Where'd you find all that shit anyway?"

I shifted uncomfortably, looking to the others for help. No one spoke up.

"Didn't kill anyone for it, did you?" Sullivan asked, a feral glint in his eyes. His face played in and out of shadow.

"Careful," Jamison said, leaning forward, voice icy. "You might find out."

"See? That's what I'm talking about," Sullivan said, more amused than threatened. "You can't be soft in this world anymore. It's about *survival*. Do whatever it takes to keep yourselves alive, even if it means you have to kill another living, *breathing* person because he has something you need." He let the words hang in the air, his body taut. He broke into movement again, waving a hand in a dismissive gesture. "But we'd never do that to you. Not to our new friends."

His friendly demeanor did nothing to offset the dark undertones of what he said. I went back to my food.

"Why am I the only one talking?" Sullivan asked. "I know there's more to your story. The quiet ones always have something they're hiding. So, what is it? Where are you really going?"

"Florida," Mark said. He sat in the dirt and crossed his feet at his ankles, back against a tree.

Sullivan barked out a laugh. "You're crazier than I thought!

What the hell are you going to Florida for?"

"Trying to find your mommies?" Joe asked, not quite a sneer.

I dropped my plate and stomped into the trees.

"He didn't mean it!" Sullivan called after me. "*Manners*, Joe. What the hell?"

Out of nowhere, boiling anger consumed me. I picked up a branch and snapped it. I did it again and again until I had a small pile of kindling strewn at my feet.

Pine needles crunched. I twisted to find Jamison working his way toward me in the darkness.

"You can't let them get to you," he said.

"They're dangerous, and I don't like them," I hissed. "I want them gone."

Jamison rubbed his nose. "Cody, *we're* dangerous. I don't like it either, but I don't know what to do about it."

"We could—"

"Quieter."

"—knock them out or something."

"How? We can't surprise them like that. Not the two of us," Jamison said. He peeled a strip of bark from a tree and began taking it apart. "If we pull a gun on them, I don't think we can follow through. I don't think I could do that again…"

"We just have to scare them."

"What happens if they call our bluff?"

"I don't know! But I don't want to wait around for something bad to happen."

"We'll be alright. We'll figure it out," Jamison said. He gripped my arm in a comforting gesture. "We'll make it to Florida, no matter what comes against us."

"Sure," I said.

"Say it," Jamison said, meeting my eyes.

"Say what?"

"That we'll be ok."

I shifted my weight. "We'll be ok. We'll figure it out."

"Damn right," Jamison said. He looked back at the fire. "Looks like Arnold's trying to make a move on the girls…"

While we were gone, Arnold had squeezed between Taylor and Olivia. Jamison stopped in front of the kid.

"Move," Jamison said.

When Arnold didn't, Jamison shoved him backwards over the log. Arnold fumed as he picked himself up and brushed pine needles from his shirt.

Sullivan laughed. "He told you to move, didn't he?"

Jamison sat between the girls. Arnold composed himself and plopped down on Taylor's open side. I watched him out of the corner of my eye, bending down to add a branch to the fire.

"I like this shirt," Arnold said, catching Taylor's arm to feel the fabric of her flannel. "Where'd you get it?"

"Uh—"

"Anyway, I think you look really good."

I coughed, trying not to laugh. Taylor's eyes widened as Arnold scooted closer.

"Your eyes are pretty."

"Thank you?"

Arnold grasped Taylor's hand. In a blink, Arnold was picking himself up off the ground again.

"I'll beat the *fuck* out of you if you touch me again," Taylor said.

Sullivan burst into laughter, Joe joining in.

"Sit down before you embarrass yourself further," Sullivan said.

Arnold did, safely on the other side of the fire, but his angry expression never wavered. I scooted next to Taylor.

"Thanks for the help," Taylor whispered sarcastically.

"You had it handled," I returned, leaning close. "You do have beautiful eyes."

"Stop," Jamison said. "I don't want to hear that gooey shit, ok?"

"Then don't listen," I said.

"It's impossible not to! I'm a curious person," Jamison said.

For most of the night, Sullivan poked us with deliberately uncomfortable questions.

Where were you when everything happened? Where are your families? How old are you?

He settled back to watch us with his beady eyes. I couldn't stand this anymore and climbed into the tent, using a small lantern to illuminate the inside. I stripped off my clothes and changed into a T-shirt and athletic shorts. My rifle went between the edge of the tent and my sleeping bag.

The others joined me. It was a tight fit, even for a six-person tent. Taylor stowed her pistol next to her pillow. Mark tapped Jamison to get his attention.

"Do you have the keys?" Mark asked, barely audible.

Jamison fished them out of his pocket.

"Good," Mark said, taking out his phone.

I looked at him curiously, propped up by an elbow. Mark showed us his screen after a moment. A message typed in Notes.

What do we do about Sullivan?

Taylor and Jamison pulled out their phones in response. Mine was in the car, so I had to use someone else's to communicate. Olivia didn't have hers either.

What followed was a chaotic argument of wild gestures and shoving screens in other people's faces. It might have been amusing to watch if it weren't for the circumstances. Olivia fought Mark for his phone, and I borrowed Taylor's or Jamison's to get my point across.

It was thirty minutes before we had a plan. Not a good one, but one that would hopefully keep everyone alive. Mark's phone had the most battery, so he would set his alarm for 2 a.m. and wake everyone up. Then, we would make our escape before Sullivan's group knew what was happening. We would have to leave the tent and other supplies behind, but it was deemed necessary to be on our own again.

I settled down to sleep. The tent's fabric rippled in the wind. Moonlight glowed in patches.

Slowly, I drifted off to whispers outside the tent.

FOURTEEN

A GUNSHOT SHATTERED the night.

I snapped awake.

The inside of the tent was barely visible in the murky glow. I threw on my frozen shoes and reached for my gun, making sure it was loaded. The others scrambled into action. Mark snagged his phone, looking up with horror.

"It's dead, we missed our chance," he said.

Another shot.

"Hey! You better get out here!" Sullivan yelled. "We're being surrounded!"

I unzipped the tent and emerged into a world of grey. Fog undulated through the pre-dawn light, wrapping around trees and obscuring the ground. Sullivan emptied another round into the mist before turning to face me.

Something cracked against the back of my head. I collapsed and lost hold of my gun. Bright spots danced before my eyes. My ears rang. I struggled to get up, dirt spilling between my fingers.

The icy barrel of a gun pressed into my skull.

"Move and I shoot," Joe said.

I kept perfectly still, arms splayed, head facing the tent. Arnold picked up my rifle. Elizabeth stood on the other side, a shotgun held in a steady grip.

Mark dashed outside, pistol in hand. Sullivan's AR brought him to a grinding halt.

"Drop the gun," Sullivan said to Mark, who took in the scene. "Drop the fucking gun or your friend dies."

It thumped to the ground.

"The rest of you, come out with your hands up," Sullivan said. "And if you so much as look at us wrong, you'll be picking Cody's brains out of the dirt for the rest of the day."

I tried not to squirm. Taylor, Jamison, and Olivia shuffled outside. Only Taylor had a gun in her hand, and she dropped it when directed. Arnold scuttled forward to collect the discarded weapons, soon crawling into the tent. He came out with Jamison's shotgun. Jamison cursed, clearly hoping they would overlook his weapon.

"Run it up to the car," Sullivan said to Arnold. His son set off, arms overflowing with our things. Sullivan surveyed the camp and said, "Give us the keys."

Jamison reluctantly—slowly—took the keys from his pocket and tossed them to Sullivan.

"Now, back up," Sullivan said.

The others shuffled further into the mist. Joe lifted his gun from my head. Still groggy, I got to my feet to join the others. I felt the back of my head. A streak of blood glimmered on the tips of my fingers. Elizabeth packed up our stove and marched up the embankment. Sullivan and Joe dropped their aim and jogged toward the road.

"You can't leave us like this," I shouted after them.

Sullivan laughed in the distance. I scrambled after him, making it to the base of the small hill as he looked down on me from behind the concrete barrier. The cars surged to life and he disappeared from view. A moment later, he came back and waved a pistol in the air, making a show of setting it down out of sight.

"It could have been a lot worse," Sullivan said. "Consider yourselves lucky."

"Fuck you!" I yelled.

The cars roared and we were alone.

I climbed up the embankment and over the barrier, finding the pistol and a box of ammunition on the ground. I checked the magazine. It was full. Sullivan had also left us with the bat, two hunting knives, and a hatchet. He hadn't been heartless, and for that, I was thankful.

Mark paced. Olivia slumped to the ground by the fire pit. Jamison rubbed his face, muttering to himself. Taylor examined the back of my head.

"How do you feel?" she asked.

"I have a headache…so that's nice—"

Mark hurled a rock against a tree with a thud, shooting bark into the air. Yelling, he threw another. He snatched the bat and obliterated our lantern.

"Chill," Jamison said.

Mark's face tightened. He stalked toward Jamison like a predator. "This is your fault. It was your plan to make camp with them and because of that, we lost *everything*."

"*My fault?* They didn't outright shoot us because of what I did," Jamison said, standing to meet Mark. He didn't shrink against Mark's superior size. "You were the one who was supposed to wake us up, dumbass. Remind us how that worked out."

"I'm not taking the blame for this," Mark spat.

"Right, because the all-powerful Mark Esso can't make a single goddamn mistake," Jamison bellowed to the sky, arms spread wide. "My bad. I should thank you for your *boundless* wisdom and *fearless* leadership."

Mark swung. Jamison dodged the punch. He lashed out with his right hand, connecting with Mark's nose, then buried his left in Mark's stomach. Mark folded. Jamison took a step back, fists raised. Mark's charge knocked Jamison off his feet with a grunt. Jamison took two shots to the face before Taylor and I could jump on Mark and wrestle him away.

When they were far enough apart, we let Mark go. He wiped his nose. Jamison grinned, blood coating his teeth.

"Bitch," Jamison said.

Mark fumed, clenching his hands. A corpse shuffled through the mist toward our group, another behind it.

"Want to know what else I did for us?" Jamison asked, picking up the bat. He gave it a twirl and downed the first corpse with a single swing. He pointed the bloody end at Mark. "I hid a pistol *and* ammo. You're welcome."

Jamison smashed the second corpse and ran off into the mist. I called after him, but he was already gone. I looked around. Half a dozen corpses materialized out of nothing. I grabbed the hatchet and slashed one across the face. Taylor and Olivia took up the knives. Taylor stabbed one through the eye.

Pop! Pop!

A scream mingled with the gunshots.

Pop!

I took off, following the sounds of gunfire. Mark kept at my heels, dropping a corpse with a quick shot. Jamison sprinted toward us with everything he had. He waved his arms, face overcome with terror, right pant leg stained red.

Behind him, corpses poured from the trees. He barely kept ahead.

"Go!" Jamison shouted as he flew past us.

We ran back to camp, meeting Taylor and Olivia halfway. Jamison skidded to a halt in front of Taylor, giving her the gun and box of ammunition.

"You're a better shot than me," he said, keeping the bat for himself.

Mark kept the other gun as we sprinted for the highway. I hurdled a log. Ducked under a branch. Scrambled up the embankment and over the barrier. Jamison limped as he brought up the rear. I glanced at his bleeding shin and torn pant leg.

"What happened?" I asked.

"Fell off a boulder," he said, chest heaving.

"Let's go!" Mark said.

Thick fog concealed the road. I could hardly see twenty feet ahead of us. It shifted like it was alive, deceptive and mysterious. Mesmerizing. Bodies formed out of nothing behind us. Corpses tumbled over the median.

Our speed increased on the open road. My breath sent clouds into the air. My arms pumped, fingers slowly freezing as I clutched the hatchet. The road ahead faded into nothing. I dodged cars at the last moment, but there was nowhere to go. I didn't know how long I could run. A stitch blossomed in my side.

"Head to the mall!" Mark said, vaulting the barrier dividing the highway.

Of course.

We couldn't outrun the corpses forever, and we couldn't kill them all. Our only option was to find a place to hide. If that existed.

Corpses closed in from every direction. The others slipped in and out of the fog. In moments, I made it to the other side of the road. Jamison came into sight, then the others. Splatters of blood streaked their clothes. Bodies sprawled at their feet.

Mark jumped the median and streaked down the hill leading toward the mall. I followed suit. Knee-high grass whipped against my shins. I still couldn't see the buildings, but all that mattered was keeping Mark in sight.

The edges of the parking lot came into view. Abandoned cars littered the lot. Corpses headed straight for us. I jumped the short wall that contained the parking lot, feet pounding on the pavement.

The first buildings loomed above, shrouded in grey.

My fingers tingled, lungs burning. Black spots floated in my vision. I skirted around corpses, their arms scrambling for a hold on my shirt. I swung the hatchet and took off the top of one's skull. Mark and Taylor picked careful shots.

Directly ahead, Macy's beckoned. Corpses swarmed behind us.

I skidded to a halt in front of the store, legs quivering like Jello. The first door refused to budge. I tried the second. Locked. All of them were.

I collapsed against the glass, taking in the sight of a hundred corpses bearing down at once. Their growls squeezed my chest with terror.

"Cover me," Mark said.

I fell into line at his back. He shot the door to my right, sending spiderwebs racing across the glass. Two more shots and his gun clicked. Taylor dropped four corpses before she ran out of ammo too. I hacked away at the dead.

Mark kicked the glass and it burst into sparkling shards. He ducked through, followed closely by Taylor, Olivia, and Jamison. I sprang inside seconds before the corpses crashed into the storefront. There was a second set of doors, one of which sported bullet holes.

One by one, the dead squeezed through the opening. I brought my weapon down as fast as I could, but they kept coming. Jamison held his bat with his left hand so he could use his knife with the other. He jumped forward and sank his knife into temples, eyes, and throats.

Mark broke through the second door. We dashed inside. The only light came from the entrance, so we blundered our way through the first floor. I shoved over displays, shattering perfume bottles and displacing racks of clothes, purses, and shoes.

Mark paused at the entrance to the rest of the mall. He glanced above.

"Help me close this," he said, pointing to the metal gate peeking out of the ceiling.

It was too high to reach. I cast an anxious look into the store. Growling came from its bowels. Mark bent down so Jamison could put a foot into his open hand. Mark hoisted him up with a grunt. Jamison snagged the bottom of the gate, and Mark let go. The barrier crashed down under Jamison's weight.

Corpses lunged against the metal, sticking fingers through gaps and cutting their faces open on the edges. Jamison flipped them off as he got to his feet.

"Hope that holds," Mark said, backing away.

I did a quick scan of our surroundings. Benches, tables, and a directory made up the intersection. Skylights cast gloomy light. A dozen corpses turned to face us.

Taylor handed her box of ammunition to Olivia. "Give them to me one at a time," Taylor said, releasing the mag and tucking the gun into her belt.

"We need a place to hide," Mark said, "preferably one with weapons."

Taylor loaded the first bullet as we jogged to the directory. Olivia fed ammo to Mark as well. They scanned the directory while Jamison and I stood at their backs, bat and hatchet raised.

"Hurry up," I said, taking down the first corpse in line.

"There! Titan Sporting Goods," Olivia said. "To the left."

The moment we sprinted away, one corpse tripped and went headfirst into the directory. Taylor and Mark continued to load bullets as stores blurred at my sides. Some were blocked off by gates. Dread filled me when I considered the sporting goods store might be closed as well.

It came into view and my hopes crumbled. The gate was down.

Taylor replaced the mag and pulled back the slide. She popped off three shots, clearing our path ahead. We halted in front of the store. Jamison yanked on the metal, but it wouldn't budge.

"Shit!" he yelled, shaking it with fury.

"We have to try another place," Mark gasped.

I didn't think I could run any longer. My arms were too heavy to keep swinging. My head swam. In my half-delusional state, I thought I saw a light bobbing in the shadows of the store. I clutched the links and squinted in the darkness. Closer now…

It was getting closer!

A man appeared at the gate.

"Let us in!" I pleaded.

Taylor and Mark filled the air with gunfire. The man hesitated for a terrifying second, then dove at the locks at each corner. He wrenched it high enough for us to duck under. The gate crashed down again, blocking the corpses. They made gurgling sounds in the backs of their throats, eyes flashing back and forth as they pushed against the metal.

Our savior forgotten, I collapsed. Blood pounded in my ears. My lungs felt like they had been torn open. I clutched my chest, my heart threatening to explode at any moment.

Everything ached. My legs were unresponsive, and I didn't have the strength to lift a finger. It felt like I was melting into the floor.

Then, overcome by relief, I began to laugh.

I couldn't believe we'd made it.

FIFTEEN

I SLOWLY CAME back to myself.

My heart rate steadied. Sweat soaked through my shirt. I wiped my face. Soon enough, I was able to sit up, allowing me to rub the knots out of my legs.

Mark leaned against an aisle endcap. Taylor and Olivia sat upright, faces flushed. Jamison was still sprawled on the ground like a starfish, chest heaving.

The store was nearly consumed by darkness. A few skylights gave faint illumination. The warm, orange glow from the man's lantern did little to offset the gloomy atmosphere of the store. My gaze found the man. He looked to be in his late forties. Clean shaven. Short blond hair. Hard lines around his eyes. He held a pistol in his right hand and watched us in silence.

"Thanks for letting us in," I said.

He looked down at me. "I didn't want your deaths on my conscience."

"That's good," I said, more to myself than anyone else. "What's your name?"

"Elliot," he said, taking a long pause. "I don't want you here."

"We're not staying long," Mark said. "We just need to find a car and supplies, and we'll be gone."

"Good. Is he ok?" Elliot pointed at Jamison.

Jamison groaned as he made it into a sitting position. He touched his wounded leg, wincing. "I fell, but I'll be fine."

"I can clean it for you," Elliot said.

"Thanks, but I can handle it. It's not that bad. I just need a first aid kit," Jamison said.

"I have one," Elliot said.

"Do you have any water?" Jamison asked.

Elliot shifted his weight. "I can spare a bit."

My throat burned with thirst and my tongue stuck to the roof of my mouth. I could use some food too. My head swam.

"What's going on?" a woman's voice said. She approached the group, carrying another lantern. She was around Elliot's age and had her dark hair pulled up in a bun. "Elliot, who are they?"

He turned to face the woman. "They were trapped. I let them in."

"Are they leaving?"

"Soon. They just need a place to hide out for a bit," Elliot said. He gestured to the woman. "This is my wife, Rose."

Rose crossed her arms, frowning at our presence. I wouldn't have liked it either if I were in her shoes. Sullivan's group was only one example of how some people couldn't be trusted.

"I'll get the things you need," Elliot said. "You can set up wherever. Take this," he said, handing me his lantern.

"Thank you," I said. "We wouldn't have made it if you hadn't let us in."

Elliot pursed his lips, gun still at the ready. "Let me make this clear. We don't know you, and I want you gone as soon as possible."

"Sure," I said. "We'll stay out of your way. The last thing we want is to cause problems."

Elliot nodded, and he and Rose headed deeper into the store.

We settled down in the middle of the men's clothing section, moving the racks to set up makeshift walls. I helped Jamison and Taylor gather camp chairs and sleeping bags. Mark and Olivia came back with handfuls of energy bars and freeze-dried food. Two coolers formed a small table in the middle of everything.

Elliot returned and dropped off a couple of waters, extra lanterns, and a first aid kit for Jamison. I eagerly gulped down one of the waters while Jamison disappeared somewhere to clean his leg. I set up the lights around the perimeter of our little encampment, flooding the area with a warm glow. It was almost cozy.

Once Jamison returned, I borrowed the first aid kit to properly wrap my thumb. The shirt fabric I'd used this morning was long gone, and the gash was jagged and raw. A small amount of blood welled up in a constant stream. I gritted my teeth as the alcohol wipe boiled in the cut. Wrapping it tightly with gauze, I finished up by taping it in place.

Looking for something to do, I settled on browsing the racks of clothes. At first, I couldn't help but check the price tags. It was a tough habit to break. I began searching out the most expensive things on purpose.

My legs were so stiff that I fell over while pulling on new pants. I looked around self-consciously, but I was alone. By the time I was finished, I was wearing over seven hundred dollars worth of clothing. I didn't know what to do with my old clothes, so I left them under a rack of flannels and made my way back to the group.

Completely exhausted, I climbed into a sleeping bag and opened an energy bar. I got halfway through before I couldn't keep my eyes open any longer.

I don't know how long I slept. My phone was gone and the store was in perpetual darkness, but when I woke, I was mostly refreshed.

The rest of the day was slow, but a nice change of pace.

Jamison and I went to check out the hockey section. We unpacked a net and positioned it at the end of two aisles, one lantern behind the netting to light the area. It was a narrow shooting range, but that would only make things more interesting. Wide shots would wreak havoc on the aisle walls, and anything too high would destroy what was behind.

The real problem came when I tried to find a suitable stick. Most of what the store had to offer were wood or low-quality composites. The nicer ones either didn't have the right curve or flex or were the wrong height. I chose a Bauer with a Stamkos curve. It was a lighter flex than I was used to, but I'd make do. I couldn't help but smile as Jamison and I stood side-by-side, taping our sticks. Just like it used to be.

The next moment, I was back in the locker room, joking with the team as we blasted music and got dressed for the championship.

Jamison's shot rang off the post, hauling me back to the present.

I donned a pair of gloves and stickhandled for a few minutes to get used to the feeling again. My thumb protested against the pressure, but it wasn't going to stop me. Jamison and I took turns trying to hit the crossbar. Wrist shots. Slap shots. Setting each other up for one-timers. I snapped my stick an hour in.

"Damn it," I said, tossing aside the pieces.

Jamison laughed. I took off my glove to examine my thumb. It was bleeding again.

Later that night, Elliot and Rose offered to make food for everyone, but there wasn't much for them to prepare. Dinner consisted of pouring boiling water into bags of freeze-dried shepherds pie. I shoveled a spoonful into my mouth, surprised by how much I liked it.

"How did you get here?" Elliot asked.

"Another group stopped us last night," Mark said. "We camped outside the mall, and they stole everything this morning. The dead surprised us, and this was the only place to go."

Elliot rocked back. "People aren't what they used to be."

"There's nothing we could have done," Mark said. "We were screwed the moment they saw us."

"Still won't admit he messed up…" Jamison mumbled.

"Stop," I said to Jamison. He rolled his eyes.

"Where are you going?" Elliot asked.

I looked at Mark to see how much we should say. Elliot said he didn't trust us, but the fact that he saved us was important. He didn't have to do it. He could have left us to die and no one would have known. I got the feeling he wasn't an opportunist. Not like Sullivan. He was a good man, just trying to stay safe and protect his wife. At least, I hoped that was true.

"Florida. We're trying to find their parents," Mark said, motioning to Jamison and me.

"Good luck," Elliot said. It was honest, with no hint of derision in his voice. "There's a repair shop outside the mall. I can help you find a car that's still working."

"You don't need to do that," Mark said.

"I'd like to help," Elliot said. "We need to stock up on water anyway, if you wouldn't mind taking me with you."

Mark scratched his chin. "We can do that."

"And…we could use some help clearing out the mall," Elliot

said.

Mark leaned back, giving the rest of us a questioning look.

"Sure," I said, "it's the least we can do. We owe you our lives."

"I don't mean to pry," Rose interjected, "but where are the rest of your families?"

I paused, spoon halfway to my mouth.

Mark considered his food. "They're all gone."

"I'm sorry…" Rose said. She brushed a stray lock of hair behind her ear, sparing a glance at her husband. "We lost our daughters."

There was silence. Heavy looks at the floor. Shifting in chairs.

"What were their names?" Olivia asked.

"June was eight, and Katie was eleven," Rose said.

She kept her lips pursed, but the corner of her mouth twitched. Her eyes tightened. She wiped away a tear. Elliot squeezed her hand, jaw clenched.

I picked at my food.

There wasn't much conversation after that, and Elliot and Rose soon retired to their corner of the store. Full, and without a reason to stay awake, I climbed back into my sleeping bag for the night.

Fitful sleep followed.

I found myself walking the mall. My lantern flickered. Shadows closed in, engulfing me. I called out for Jamison. For Taylor. For my parents. No one heard me. Whispering came from behind. I whipped around to face a wall of corpses. Jamison and Taylor. Mark and Olivia. My parents—my real ones. My hockey team. I tried to run, but my feet sank into the ground. They circled me, whispering for me to join them. My mom reached for my arm—

I jerked awake. Cold sweat coated my back and forehead. I shivered, heart pounding. I closed my eyes again, but the dream swirled in my head.

I sat up and fumbled for a water bottle. The store was pitch black. I couldn't even see my hands. I finished off the water, unable to shake the terror of seeing everyone I'd known turned into corpses.

I wrapped my arms around myself, knowing I wasn't going to be able to fall asleep again. For a while, I lost myself in the inky blackness.

I thought I was imagining it at first, but a faint glow came from somewhere else in the store. I fumbled around again before coming into contact with a lantern. I switched it on, eyes burning from the sudden light.

Jamison mumbled something in his sleep. Mark and Olivia didn't stir. Taylor was gone.

I crawled out of my sleeping bag and wrapped myself in a blanket, setting off to find her. She was at the entrance to the store, a lantern illuminating her silhouette.

"Taylor," I whispered.

She yelped, nearly jumping out of her blanket. "What the hell?"

"Sorry," I said.

She wrapped the covering tighter around her shoulders. Her eyes narrowed as if she was trying to decide if she wanted to hit me or not.

"What are you doing up?" I asked.

"I could ask the same of you."

"Fair enough. Mind if I join you?"

She shook her head, so I sat next to her. Our lantern light glimmered on the gate. A corpse pressed itself against the metal, snapping its teeth at us. My skin prickled. I felt trapped. Claustrophobic.

"I couldn't sleep," Taylor said.

"Neither could I."

Taylor watched the corpse. I studied her face. I could see the fear she kept at bay by hugging her legs close to her body. The pain—a weight behind her eyes. She shuddered. I shrugged off my blanket and hugged her against my chest. My chin rested on the top of her head.

"Sometimes I don't believe my parents are gone," Taylor said. "I keep imagining I'll wake up and everything will be back to normal."

"I know," I said. "I still think about mine…"

"How did you get through it?"

"Time makes it hurt less, but it doesn't go away. Not really."

"How did we get here?" she asked, voice barely a whisper.

I didn't have an answer for that, so I said, "We'll be ok. We'll make it." The words were little more than a distant hope.

"How do you know that?" she asked.

"Because we have to."

"What if we don't? What if this is it, and the world never recovers?"

Anxieties nagged at the back of my mind. All the possibilities of failure—of death, of being left alone—threatened to strangle me. Taylor pressed her hand above my heart, bringing me back.

"We have to keep going. We have to keep fighting," I said.

"I'm scared," she said. "I'm scared nothing we do will be enough."

Her words echoed inside me. All we could do was hold each other, but it didn't feel like enough. Such a weak gesture for a terrible fear. A lump formed in my throat. All I wanted was to make her feel safe, to let her know that everything was going to be alright.

Yet, I couldn't guarantee it. I couldn't promise that any of us would make it through the next day.

"Me too," I said, closing my eyes and taking in her calming scent. "I'm scared too."

SIXTEEN

I WOKE UP disoriented. It felt like morning, but only a glimmer of light came from the skylights. Jamison munched on an energy bar in a camp chair, a lantern at his feet.

"We're clearing the mall soon," Jamison said.

I nodded and crawled out of my sleeping bag. My back was sore from the unforgiving ground. I stretched before shaking Taylor awake.

"This better be important," she grumbled.

"Want to help clear the mall?" I asked.

Taylor yawned, blinking away sleep. Her hair stuck up in places, making me smile.

"How could I miss out on that?" she asked.

"Exactly, it's classic entertainment," I said. "How are you feeling?"

"About what?"

"I thought I'd check in after last night."

Taylor squeezed my hand. "I'm good, thanks."

"Alright," I said.

I didn't know what else to say, so I kissed her and went to find some food. Thirty minutes later and loaded down with weapons, our entire group gathered at the front of the store. Considering the circumstances, the store was surprisingly well-stocked with guns and other accessories. I carried a pistol in a holster, two extra magazines on a belt, and my hatchet and a rifle in my hands.

Jamison toted a shotgun in a relaxed grip. Mark and Olivia talked. Elliot had outfitted Rose with the proper weaponry. I wouldn't have guessed she would participate in this, but she didn't shy away from the pistol in her hands. She held herself with a casual air, unworried. Maybe it was her soft face that threw me off. Then again, Taylor surprised me too. Who would have guessed she could pick off a corpse at twenty yards?

Taylor only had a pistol and a Bowie knife, and she raised an eyebrow when she saw me. I surveyed my gear, realizing I might be over prepared. Still, I kept it all. I could move, aim, and fire without difficulty. I didn't know how many corpses were out there, and I'd rather have too much firepower than not enough.

Our plan was to systematically exterminate the dead while sealing off any breach leading outside. It would be like a big game of cat and mouse, one where we were purposely closing off our exits.

We traveled as a pack, covering every angle so nothing could surprise us from behind. The mall was gloomy, but there were enough windows on the ceiling to see by. We'd hardly made it twenty feet before corpses materialized from the shadows. I snapped the rifle to my shoulder and squeezed the trigger. A corpse fell with a hole through its eye.

We halted as the dead surged to meet us.

Taylor opened up with her pistol, dropping one body after another. Jamison pumped his shotgun. Heads and chests exploded in showers of gore. The others relentlessly poured fire into the mass of corpses. They fell, and still continued to come.

Elliot and I worked on opposite sides of the circle, picking off bodies with long shots. I sank into the rhythm of destruction. The cacophony faded into the background. Smoke curled before me, but I hardly noticed. Gunpowder tingled in the back of my throat.

Track a head with the scope. Exhale. Squeeze the trigger. Move to the next.

Aim. Exhale. Fire.

Reload.

Aim. Exhale. Fire.

Again and again.

I didn't think. Time slowed. I hardly noticed the bodies crumbling. Didn't see the pools of blood. Never thought about who these corpses used to be. I just pulled the trigger, and I'd never felt so calm, so in control. Untouchable.

"…Cody…"

The voice came from far away.

"Cody."

My senses returned and I came back to myself. The calm shattered. My ears rang. Smoke stung my eyes.

"It's over," Taylor said. "You can lower your gun."

I relaxed, taking in the carnage. Countless bodies surrounded our circle, piled feet in the air. Some were only a step away. My shoes sloshed in blood. The sickly odor of gore assaulted my nose and stomach.

Still, I wondered how it could be over. We'd hardly begun. At that moment, I realized I didn't want to be finished. A part of me reveled in the fight. Craved it. Looked forward to it. It was intoxicating, and I wanted more.

I didn't know if I should be revolted or not.

"Are you alright?" Taylor asked. She gently turned my chin so I'd look her in the face. Her eyes searched mine.

"Yeah," I said, rubbing my forehead.

"Are you sure? You're a little pale."

"I'm fine."

Taylor chewed her lip but backed off. I didn't know how to explain this, and maybe I didn't want to.

"What should we do with the bodies?" Mark asked with a scowl, both hands on his hips.

"Can't leave 'em here," Elliot said. "I'm not walking past this every time I go out. And they're only going to keep rotting."

"Yeah, makes sense. It'll be a bitch to move…" Mark trailed off, looking around at the shops. "We'll stash them in there," he said, pointing to an electronics store that wasn't blocked off from the mall.

It was only thirty feet away, but we had at least a hundred bodies to transport. This wasn't going to be pretty.

Grimacing, I took one of the corpses by the ankles and began dragging it away. A wide streak of blood seeped from its mangled head. I dumped the body and went back for another, passing Mark and Jamison who had a corpse swaying between them. Olivia cursed to herself as she and Taylor hoisted a body. Disgust covered both of their faces, but Olivia looked physically sick.

I took another. And another. On and on.

I breathed through my mouth in a futile attempt to avoid the stench of decaying flesh. The problem was, I could taste it. It lingered in the back of my throat like I'd thrown up and couldn't wash it away. On my fifth trip, my feet slid out from under me. I landed on my back, the legs of the corpse dropping on my chest. I shoved it off and rolled over.

No one laughed. Mark helped me up. My back was wet with blood, but I tried not to think about it. The floor itself was a treacherous strip of gore by now. I resolved to go slower from now on and worked to shut off my mind.

I'd lost count of how many bodies I'd carried, but my hands were streaked with blood. I had to pause to collect myself.

"Do you think we can get infected this way?" I asked, holding up my hands to Jamison, bandaged thumb in plain view.

"If you can, you're already dead," Jamison said.

I frowned, wiping my hands on my pants. He was probably right. No turning back now.

By the time we finished, all I wanted was a hot shower and a case of beer.

Jamison leaned heavily against a directory.

"You ok?" I asked.

"I just…don't feel good," he said.

Even with the lack of light, I could see the dark circles under his eyes, and there was no color to his skin.

I patted him on the back. "I don't either."

"I mean it…" Jamison said. "I'm going back. You'll have to find a car without me."

"What's wrong?"

"I just need some rest…" Jamison said. "…really tired."

I watched him shuffle off, unease forming inside. Olivia approached, brow furrowed.

"Is he ok?" she asked.

"No…but I don't know what's going on."

"I can stay back with him."

I gave her a warm look. "Thanks. See if you can get him to talk."

"Don't worry, I'm very disarming," she said. She gave my arm a reassuring squeeze, said, "he'll be fine," and jogged after Jamison.

Rose went with her, leaving Taylor, Mark, Elliot, and me to find a car and go on the supply run. We checked our ammunition and decided it would be best to stock up again before we headed out. Mark and Taylor walked ahead, and Elliot and I brought up the rear.

"What do we need when we go out?" Mark asked.

"Water, food—" Elliot said.

"Alcohol," I added.

Taylor shook her head. Elliot looked me over, his expression split between amusement and concern. "Is that the best thing you can do right now?"

"Thanks, *Dad*, but it's not up to you," I said.

I immediately regretted my words. Elliot's shoulders tensed. He opened his mouth and closed it again, giving me a sidelong glance.

"I'm sorry," I said.

"Just be smart about it," Elliot said.

Back at our headquarters, Taylor, Mark, and Elliot loaded the weapons. I searched the racks of clothes to find something that wasn't covered in blood. Feeling slightly better, I did my best to wash my hands with one of the remaining water bottles. Dried blood still clung under my fingernails.

Setting out again, we made a long pass through the entire mall to make sure it was truly clear and to seal off any breaches leading outside. Besides the corpses trapped in Macy's, we didn't find any others. The whole place was eerily empty, making my skin crawl as we walked.

Now, it was time to steal a car.

Elliot led the group through the food court, halting at the double doors. Corpses lingered in the parking lot. Sunlight streamed through the glass. I basked in the warmth for a wonderful moment.

Elliot pointed straight ahead. "The shop is across the street."

I squinted, barely seeing *Ted's Auto Repair* between a row of trees.

"Ready?" Elliot asked.

We nodded. He pushed open the door. Cool air rustled under my shirt. It felt amazing to be outside again.

With fewer corpses on this side of the mall, we made it halfway across the parking lot before they noticed our presence. No one engaged them with guns, and we skirted around them instead of fighting.

I crossed a strip of grass. The street. The lot in front of the repair shop.

Six cars were parked outside and looked to be in good condition. Mark tried the shop door, but it wouldn't budge. He stepped back and took aim at the lock, blasting it open with a single shot. We filed into the store. Mark and I dashed behind the service counter as the first corpses threw themselves against the glass. Taylor and Elliot stood guard in case any of them broke through.

I rifled through drawers. Some were locked. I cast an anxious glance at the front of the store, willing the glass to hold. There had to be twenty of the dead outside, desperately trying to break in.

Mark systematically destroyed the locks of the drawers and opened one that contained several clear plastic folders.

"Found it," Mark announced to the others.

He dumped the folders onto the counter as Taylor and Elliot circled around. Each one had sheets of paperwork inside and a key shifting around at the bottom. We quickly narrowed it down to the only options that would fit everyone: a Suburban and a twelve-passenger van. Jamison would have fought tooth and nail for the van, but we selected the Suburban instead.

Mark slipped the key into his pocket and we faced the front of the store. Corpses lined every inch of the glass. Hands and faces banged against the glass. A crack spread on one of the panes.

"We need another way out," Taylor said.

No shit.

"I have an idea," Mark said. "Elliot, follow me."

Mark and Elliot entered the workshop. Taylor and I watched as they jogged to the furthest garage door, all of which were closed. Tools were strewn on the ground. A single car was still suspended on a lift.

They bent down and wrenched open the garage. Light poured into the workshop. Mark and Elliot brought their weapons to bear, spraying fire at unseen corpses. The reaction was immediate. The bodies at the glass jerked at the sound and lumbered away. Within moments, the entire storefront was clear.

Mark and Elliot sprinted for the reception area as corpses flooded the workshop. We charged through the front entrance and into the open parking lot. Mark pointed toward a white Suburban. We piled in. He threw it in gear and tore out of the parking lot. The tires squealed as we rounded corners, soon emerging onto uncontested roads.

For the next two hours, we went from store to store, searching for anything we needed on our journey, and whatever Elliot and Rose wanted for their stay at the mall.

It wasn't easy to find supplies. Every store was thoroughly picked over, so we had to make do with the leftovers.

There were enough canned foods to keep us alive for the foreseeable future, though the selection was grim. Lots of beans and odd flavors of soup. I came across two cans of sliced pineapple, which would make a nice dessert after dinner tonight.

At Target, I found toothbrushes and toothpaste. Deodorant and shampoo. A razor. Mark brimmed with excitement when he found a siphoning pump. I went down the game aisle, adding Risk and Monopoly to the cart. Taylor met up with me and dumped in an armful of candy.

"Good thinking," I said.

She kissed my cheek as we found the alcohol section. Only mildly guilty, I added to the cart. Vodka and whiskey. Rum. A few bottles of wine. Beer and hard cider. No doubt it would keep us supplied for the next few weeks.

Taylor looked it over, then at me. She scratched her nose.

"Yeah," I said, reading her mind, "it's probably too much…"

After a bit of deliberation, we cut the selection in half.

Throughout the entire supply run, we didn't find a single bottle of water, so we decided to take coolers and fill them up in a stream. Our base had plenty of filters, so doing this was an inconvenience but not a problem.

It was late afternoon by the time we made it back to the mall. Mark parked right in front of the food court entrance and we hastily unloaded the supplies inside. It took two trips each to transport everything the long distance to our base.

I felt an odd mixture of emotions as I realized we had no other reason to delay our departure. On one hand, it was the faint sadness of leaving behind a safe location, leaving Elliot and Rose, who were kind and helpful. On the other, I was anxious to get back on the road. Every passing day meant more things could go wrong.

We had to make it to Florida before it was too late.

SEVENTEEN

JAMISON WAS AWAKE by the time we returned, but he didn't look much better. He had bloodshot eyes and clammy skin. Still no color to his face. When I asked him how he was feeling, all he did was give me a hug and a weak smile. He dug into the bag of drinks and selected a beer.

Now, I was truly concerned.

I pulled Olivia aside and asked if he said anything.

She shook her head. "I don't know what's going on. He just said he's sick."

"Alright," I said. There wasn't anything we could do about it if he didn't want to talk.

Olivia went back to preparing dinner with Rose. I relaxed in a camp chair between Taylor and Jamison, sipping a warm cider. Mark dumped purifying tabs into a cooler of water and informed us it would be safe to drink in an hour. Rose looked at the drink in my hand with disapproval.

"Thanks for the help today," Elliot said, sitting down.

"Thanks for saving us," I said, raising my can.

Elliot nodded towards the drinks. "Mind if I have one?"

"Have all you want."

He cracked open a beer. "Are you sure you want to leave so soon? We just made this place livable."

"It's nice to have people around," Rose said.

"It's up to Cody and Jamison," Mark said. "I'm just along for the ride."

"It's not that I want to go, but I want to find my parents more," I said.

"What if we left the day after tomorrow?" Mark asked. "It gives us time to relax and make a plan."

Jamison shrugged. Everyone looked to me for an answer.

"Sounds good," I said.

We lapsed into easy conversation as the food was served. I opened another cider, and my head was buzzing fifteen minutes later. We soon broke out Risk and set it up on the floor. Because only six people could play at once, Elliot and Rose would be a team, and everyone else would play by themselves.

Two hours in, Elliot and Rose were eliminated by Mark's ruthless campaign. They packed it up for the night, heading for their section of the store. Mark's red pieces covered all of North and South America now. Olivia hunkered down in Australia, and Taylor and I fought over Europe. Jamison was the next one gone, but he contentedly sat back to watch.

Thirty minutes later, only Taylor and Mark remained. I whispered strategies in Taylor's ear, and Olivia did the same with Mark. Neither of them listened. I leaned back, finding Jamison staring intently at the ceiling.

"I keep thinking about what we could have done better," he said to me, contemplative.

"What do you mean?" I asked.

"The choices we made. Why did we do one thing and not another?" He tapped a finger on his chest. "What would have happened if we stayed at school? Or if we got to Mark's place before his parents died? Could we have helped them?"

"We can't second guess ourselves," I said. There were too many possibilities. Too many *what-if* situations that would drive me crazy if I let them. "All we can do is the next right thing."

"You sound like a motivational book."

"Am I wrong?"

The others yelled over a roll of the dice.

"No…but things could have been so different…" Jamison said. "What if we never met Sullivan's group? We could have taken another route, or left earlier, or *something*. What if I never hid the gun?"

I sipped water from a Nalgene. It tasted faintly metallic.

Jamison squeezed his eyes shut, pressing his hands against his temples. "I still think about the man I killed."

I paused, glancing at the others. They still hadn't noticed us talking.

"There's nothing you could have done," I said. I tried to imagine what he was going through. The more I thought about it, the more unsettled it made me. What if *I'd* been in that situation?

"I still can't believe I did it." Jamison sat up. He fumbled with a bottle of whiskey, hands shaking. "What if we went to another store? We could have done a hundred different things and it never would have happened."

I gripped Jamison's arm and forced him to look at me. "Stop. What's done is done. You have to let it go."

"I can't. I see him when I sleep…"

It made sense now—almost—why he was looking so ill. It was

like his actions were eating him from the inside out. Guilt and shame and fear, all taking their toll. I wrapped an arm around his shoulder. Emotion stormed behind his eyes.

"It's ok. You have to let it go," I said. There was nothing else I could think to tell him.

"I know," Jamison returned. He wiped his nose.

Soon enough, Mark had won the game and we lounged in a circle. Jamison slipped back into his usual self, joking and telling stories with only a glimmer of his troubles under the surface. Taylor's eyes drooped despite her efforts to stay awake. Olivia huddled close to Mark, and his arm found its way around her shoulders. I wondered if that meant anything, and I spent the next few minutes watching them to see what I was missing. Now that I was comfortably drunk, I felt my observational skills were better than ever.

Mark cracked a smile at her jokes, which was a pleasant change from his stony nature. He also didn't talk much with the rest of us, but he kept whispering to Olivia, to which she would respond a few seconds later. And Olivia looked at him with the type of gaze that saw through his walls. She was soft and understanding, with a sincere way of pursing her lips as she waited for Mark to respond. They both seemed at ease.

Maybe it did make sense after all.

I tuned into the conversation.

"…you seem like the kind of person who got in trouble a lot," Taylor said.

At first, I thought she was talking to me, but Jamison laughed. He gave a somewhat guilty shrug. "The trick is not getting caught. But sure, I've had my fair share of incidents."

"You have to tell us," Taylor said.

"It's really not that bad," Jamison said.

"Which time?" I chimed in. "When you streaked at a football game or slashed Mr. Anderson's tires?"

Jamison dismissively waved a hand. Taylor's eyebrows shot up. Olivia sat forward, interest plastered on her face.

"That was you?" Taylor asked incredulously.

Jamison sighed but gave a knowing smirk. "You know he deserved it. Besides, no one proved it was me."

"But everyone knew," I said.

"I didn't," Taylor said.

"Doesn't matter. Listen to me," Jamison leaned forward. "Mr. Anderson was a prick—"

"Yeah, I remember," Taylor said. "I turned something in *two* hours late and he gave me a zero."

"*Exactly,*" Jamison said. "He gave me a D in his class because of a single paper. I should have gotten an A."

"That's because you argued amature porn was an enlightened form of modern art," I interjected. "This dumbass actually thought it would work."

"*It was a satirical essay!*" Jamison defended. "Anyone could have seen that. It was well written, too."

"What about the time you superglued Mrs. Jenkin's desk closed?" I asked, cutting in. "And when she tried to open it, he got the whole class to make fun of her."

Jamison rubbed his face, smiling. "Again, she deserved it."

"How old were you?" Olivia asked.

"Ten? I don't know," Jamison said. "Cody, tell them about the kid in the cafeteria. You know the one."

I couldn't help but laugh as the memory surfaced. "There was this guy, Dustin. He was a bit strange—"

"You're one to talk," Jamison said.

"—so I dared him to drink his sandwich for a dollar."

"Drink?" Taylor asked.

"It wasn't a dare," Jamison said. "Cody stuffed Dustin's entire turkey sandwich into his lemonade, shook it up, and forced him to drink it. Lots of chunks. The dollar was only a formality…"

"Hey, he got most of it down," I said.

"And then he threw up on the table."

"It *was* kind of funny."

"You're still a horrible person," Jamison said, "which is probably why we get along so well."

Taylor was laughing so hard she'd doubled over. Olivia's mouth hung open. Mark shook with amusement.

"Come on, we can't be the only ones who did stuff like that," Jamison said, looking around the group.

"I used to be a clepto," Olivia offered. "I stole the weirdest things, too. I had to take a pack of gum every time I was in a store. At one point, I had an entire drawer filled with bubblegum." She fiddled with a button on her shirt. "Lots of other stuff, too. Pens… candy…underwear…"

Jamison looked at Olivia with newfound admiration.

"Mark?" I asked.

He shook his head. "Nothing crazy, but I broke someone's femur once, playing rugby."

Jamison leaned back. "I was at that game. Still can't forget the way he screamed…"

"It wasn't pretty," Mark said. "Earned me a reputation, though."

"Jamison sent someone through the glass," I said. Jamison bowed his head with mild humility. "I mean, the kid wasn't paying attention, so he deserved it. He went to the ER, right?"

"I don't know, but he could hardly skate afterwards," Jamison said. "You're thinking of the tournament in Detroit. I *destroyed* someone with his head down at center ice. They took him off on a stretcher, but the benches cleared after the hit. I broke my hand fighting and got suspended the next four games, not that I could play…"

"That's right," I said. "You're an animal…"

"I miss that," Jamison said, observing the ceiling with melancholy in his voice. "Best times of my life…"

I sobered for a moment. Those were some of my best memories, and we'd never get it again. No more hockey or high school antics. No college. No foreseeable future besides the next day…

Taylor shook her head. "You guys are insane."

"The best ones are," Jamison said.

"What about you?" I nudged Taylor, once again pushing away the strangling thoughts. "What's the craziest thing you've done?"

"I went skydiving once," she said.

Mark and Olivia perked up at that.

"Are you serious?" Jamison sat up.

"It was terrifying," Taylor laughed, "but I liked it. Not a lot of people can say they've done something like that."

"Where?" I asked.

"My family went to Costa Rica last year, and my dad really wanted to skydive, so I joined him. Why not?" Taylor sighed, fumbling with her necklace. "We went zip lining and hiking too…it was the last time we went on vacation."

Taylor chewed her lip, falling silent. I reached over and took her hand. She held on tight. The others remained quiet, no more stories to share. The moment was taut with things unsaid as we became lost in our own reflections. Jamison cracked open one of the remaining beers.

"I'm glad I got to know you guys," Jamison said. "Thanks for everything you've done. I couldn't have asked for better friends through all of this."

I squeezed Jamison's shoulder.

"Me too," Mark said. "I know I haven't been easy, and I'm sorry…It's like I broke, somehow…but you're still here and that means more to me than you know."

Olivia looked up at him sweetly. Both of her hands were wrapped around his left arm like she would never let go. She kissed him on the cheek. "We'll always be here."

Mark wiped his eyes and nodded, and the hardness in his expression wasn't quite so strong.

"To best friends," I raised my drink.

"Until the very end," Jamison finished.

We drank.

I sat back, wishing I could make this moment last, but I could no more do that than make the destruction fade or wash away the pain.

And so, the night ended.

We climbed into our respective sleeping bags. Mark turned out the lanterns. I laid next to Taylor, fingers brushing over her cheek and running through her hair. I gave her a long kiss, warmth flooding my body and mind. We pulled apart and I kissed her forehead.

Swaying like I was at the top of a tree in a gentle breeze, I drifted off to sleep.

EIGHTEEN

DESPITE THE HANGOVER, I was awake before everyone else. Head pounding, I unsteadily rose to my feet and drank some water, then sat in a chair while I ate a granola bar.

Still foggy, I went back to sleep until I was mostly functional. Again, no one else was awake yet. I passed the time by tossing the discarded cans and bottles into a trash bag. Next, I took it upon myself to begin exploring the mall, a lantern in hand. Scanning the directory, I made note of a bookstore and a toy store.

In the bookstore, I browsed the shelves, fingers brushing the spines. Regret formed in my throat as I thumbed through books I used to own. I'd left my entire collection at home when we set out. There wasn't enough room in the car to take more than three or four. Now, those books belonged to Sullivan and would likely be used as fire starter. To help cope with the loss and begin restoring my library, I selected eight titles and hauled them to the toy store in a bag.

Countless games and puzzles lined the shelves. I sat down between aisles, brainteasers strewn around me on the floor. After short deliberation, I selected a Rubik's Cube along with a few others and headed back to our base.

Everyone except Jamison was up by now. Taylor sipped water with a dazed expression. Mark was out of sight. Olivia crouched over the small camp stove, boiling water.

I proudly showed off my findings. Olivia broke away from the stove to look through my books, smiling as she picked up *The Name of the Wind*.

"I got that for you," I said.

"Thanks, I'm loving it so far," she said, sitting down to find where she'd left off. She folded the corner of a page and went back to the stove to pour water into bags of freeze-dried food. "This'll be ready soon. Wake up Jamison."

I pushed myself to my feet as Mark appeared from the other end of the store. He plopped down in a chair. "I think Elliot and Rose went for a walk."

I grunted and made the short trek to where we slept, seeing that Jamison had hardly moved since I got up this morning. He was sprawled on the ground with a thin blanket on top. Sweat clung to his brow and soaked through his shirt. His skin had a decidedly grey cast to it.

I nudged him with my foot. "Wake up. We're about to eat."

He didn't stir. There was only the shallow rise and fall of his chest.

"Jamison, come on," I said, digging my toe into his side.

This time, he groaned, shifting a fraction.

"If he doesn't want to eat, that's not our problem," Taylor called after me.

I ignored her, crouching down. I shook Jamison's shoulder. "Are you ok?"

"Go away," Jamison mumbled.

"What's going on?" Taylor asked.

Shivering, Jamison strained to pull the blanket above his shoulders. "I don't feel good."

"I can see that. Can you tell me why?" I asked. I felt like a parent trying to coax answers out of a toddler. "Was it something you ate? Are you hungover?"

"Yeah…but that's not the problem."

"Then what is?"

"I can't say."

"Why not?"

"You'll be mad."

"Jamison, we're trying to help you!"

"You can't."

"Oh my god…" I clenched my fists, wanting to slap him back to his senses. I settled down, cross-legged, taking a few moments to calm myself. Hitting him wouldn't help, however satisfying that might be. He wasn't well, and this wasn't his usual type of complaining. I touched his forehead. His skin radiated heat. "Guys, you might want to come over here."

Taylor, Olivia, and Mark bent over Jamison, their faces twisted with concern.

"He's burning up," I said.

Taylor pressed a hand to his forehead. "What's wrong?"

"I don't know, he won't tell me," I said.

Jamison's head lolled to the side. Taylor patted his cheek until he opened his eyes. He looked at us in confusion, voice croaking. "What's going on?"

"You're sick," I said.

"Oh…right…" Jamison said, my words taking him back to the present.

"Tell us what's happening," I pleaded quietly.

"Ok…" he said.

Jamison grimaced in pain, jaw clenched. His right hand shakily reached down his side. I grabbed it, thinking he wanted someone to hold. With considerable effort, he jerked out of my grip, pointing down his side again.

"No…it's my leg…" he said.

He watched the ceiling, unable to meet our eyes. The rest of us silently looked at the indicated area, unmoving. I frowned.

Nausea hit me like a fist, taking away my air. I shook my head against the thought of what it might be.

Images flashed in my mind.

Jamison running in the woods with a bloody shin. Saying it was a cut. Cleaning it by himself. Limping through the mall. Grey skin and bloodshot eyes. Everything he said last night; the resignation, the pain, trying to justify his actions.

And, always, getting worse instead of better.

I should have seen it sooner, but I couldn't even consider the possibility. I wouldn't let myself. My mind screamed as I threw off Jamison's blanket.

No, no, no, no, no…

I rolled up Jamison's right pant leg, doing my best to ignore his whimpers of pain.

No, no…this isn't happening…FUCK!

I unwrapped the stinking bandage and the truth slapped me hard across the face. There it was, right in the center of his shin.

A bite.

The teeth marks were unmistakable. Mottled grey skin surrounded the festering wound, and yellow puss bubbled from deep inside.

Taylor recoiled, hand over her mouth. Mark went still, eyes

bulging.

Olivia gasped. "Oh my God."

"Surprise…" Jamison said with a morbid laugh. "Is it bad?"

"You're going to be fine," Taylor said, voice shaking.

I didn't move. There was nothing we could do to help him. Not this late. Even if we caught it when it happened, who knew if we could have helped?

Mark dropped to his knees. "When did it happen?"

"In the woods…when I went to find the gun."

Jamison's face was like a sheet of paper. His brown eyes were dull. I couldn't think. Disbelief clouded my mind.

Mark whispered in my ear. "Do you think…we could take off the leg? Would that help?"

I bit my fist at the thought. "He's barely breathing," I whispered back. "It would probably kill him."

"So we leave it?" Mark asked.

I had no response. Instead, I turned back to Jamison. "Why didn't you tell us?"

"I was scared…I'm so scared," Jamison said.

"We're here," I said.

"It doesn't matter now," Jamison said. It sounded like he was breathing through waterlogged lungs. "I didn't want to tell you because if no one knew I could almost pretend it wasn't there…and I didn't want you to worry…" He broke into a fit of coughing. There was blood on his lips when he recovered. He wiped it away. "I wanted my last days to be normal."

I gripped Jamison's hand. No one knew what to say. There were no more false assurances. Not *it'll be ok* or *we'll get help*. There was nothing we could do, which was the worst feeling of all.

Just watching. Waiting.

He didn't deserve this. No one did.

I wanted to scream and pound the floor until my knuckles bled, but my body was paralyzed. The lump in my throat made it hard to swallow.

"I can feel it taking over," he said.

"We're here," I said. I couldn't imagine his pain.

His words came in whispers. With each one, I could see the life fading from his eyes. "Tell Mom and Dad I love them…"

"I will."

"…I love you…"

"I love you too," I returned, voice cracking. "We all do."

"…take care of each other…"

"Of course."

"…don't let me turn into one of them…" he trailed off. For a few seconds, he was silent. Then panic overtook his face. "…I can't… I can't breathe…" He squeezed my hand until it hurt. "…I can't breathe…"

He wheezed as the air left his lungs. His chest stilled but his throat worked, desperate for air. It wouldn't come. Fingers twitched. His eyes darted, pleading.

His agony tore my soul. Heavy tears blurred my vision.

A few terrible moments later, everything was still.

His grip slackened and I was left holding a lifeless hand.

"No…please…" I said, unable to let go. "No…"

It couldn't be over. It *couldn't*. Not like this.

I looked at his body. His face was hollow. Devoid. No sign of confusion or pain or laughter. Just a body. A husk.

Unable to take it anymore, I dropped his hand and stumbled away. Mark solemnly removed a knife from his belt and flipped it open. The blade flashed in the lantern glow. Grimacing, Mark aligned the point with Jamison's temple and shoved. Blood trickled from the wound.

Olivia buried her face in her hands. Taylor turned away, head down, figure shaking. I touched her arm. She faced me, tears running down her cheeks. We embraced, holding each other like we'd never get the chance again.

And for the second time in my life, my heart shattered.

Just like that, Jamison was gone.

NINETEEN

SHOCK ENVELOPED MY mind as I cycled through emotions. Suffocating disbelief and overwhelming pain. Blinding anger. Numbness. Manic at points, then perfectly still. One after another.

I felt like I was drowning. Each breath sent a stabbing pain through my chest. My head spun, and I thought I might throw up.

I paced the floor, ignoring the others. I sat. Stood. Laid down. Began pacing again. I squeezed my head in both hands, telling myself this couldn't be real. Sometimes I convinced myself that was true, but something would bring me crashing back. A glimpse of Jamison's body. The others comforting each other.

Things seemed to blur. Moments of clarity, then blackness, like my memory cut out. Flashes of time. At one point, I was looking at Jamison's uncovered body, then he was wrapped in a blanket. I glimpsed Elliot and Rose, unsure when they returned. Then they were gone.

Slowly, like a relieving of pressure, the world filtered back to me. The panic and anger and pain coalesced into a single, terrible grief. It was a stone on my back, in my chest, weighing down my limbs. I collapsed into a cross-legged position in the middle of the floor. Taylor settled next to me and laid her head on my shoulder. I hardly acknowledged her presence.

I couldn't stop looking at Jamison's body, barely holding its shape under the blanket.

I felt cheated. He should have told us. He should have let us know what was going on. But he kept it to himself, and for that, I cursed him. He didn't trust us and was probably scared of what we might do when we found out. For that, I felt guilty.

I ran through the last few days, going over every sign I had missed. Everything I could have done differently. Words I should have said. The time with Sullivan and getting to the mall. Shooting pucks with Jamison. Playing games and drinking last night.

Through it all, he kept it to himself, knowing he was going to die. Such a terrible burden. Maybe I would have done things differently. Maybe not.

In the end, no matter the reasons for secrecy or the way I felt or what I could have done better, it didn't change the simple fact that he was gone for good. All the years at each other's side, simply over.

I missed him already, and it hurt more than I could describe.

Part of me never thought this could happen. When the trip began, I never imagined that this would be the outcome. Of course, I knew we could die, and it might happen at any moment, but that seemed so far away when we decided to leave. It was like our group would be safe, simply because it was *us*. Things happened to other people, not you.

I knew now, in the deepest way possible, that wasn't the case. Next, it could be Taylor, Mark, or Olivia. Elliot or Rose. It could be me. My parents might already be gone, and I would have no way of knowing.

Those thoughts stormed through my head. Only Taylor touching my face brought me back to the present. Her hand was warm against my cheek.

"Cody," she said tentatively. "Do you want to bury him?"

It took me a moment to process the question. I nodded.

"Ok," she said, getting to her feet.

She helped me up and I realized everyone was standing around, even Elliot and Rose. I carried Jamison's body to the car. It was heavy and limp, with a smear of blood at his head. The walk through the mall was mournful. I dimly heard Mark say we needed to stop somewhere to find a shovel.

We halted at the food court entrance, the car just beyond. A handful of corpses circled the area. I realized I didn't have a weapon, but it didn't matter. The others had more than enough to cover me.

We pushed through the doors. Taylor opened the trunk and I gently laid Jamison on the floor, climbing in after him. She slammed it shut as Mark and Elliot fired on the dead. The gunshots were like distant thunder in my ears.

Once again, I slipped into a daze. The car lurched. My surroundings blurred. The buildings turned to trees and grassy plains. Jamison's body shook with the movement of the car. I didn't realize we'd stopped until Taylor was opening the trunk again.

I climbed out, Jamison in my arms.

We'd arrived at the edge of a quiet meadow. Trees sprouted throughout, leaves twisting in the wind. I squinted, unable to recognize the beauty.

I laid Jamison down, wiped my eyes, and picked up a shovel. I didn't remember stopping to get it. With an angry thrust, I dug it into the ground, turning up coffee-colored dirt and patches of grass.

Shove, dump.

I worked with quiet resolve. Every movement seemed to loosen the paralysis on my mind.

Shove, dump.

It was over.

Shove, dump.

We still had the mission of finding my parents. I could cling to that, but it didn't lessen the pain. It didn't take away the hollowness in my gut. I knew it would never truly go away.

This time, when the shovel stuck into the ground, I didn't pull it out.

I looked up, my senses rushing back. My hands throbbed, red. The rich scent of earth filled my nose. Birds chirped. A breeze whispered in my ears and hair.

For a singular moment, I felt nothing at all.

I shuffled away from the partially dug grave. I sat underneath a tree, wiping the sweat from my forehead. Mark took up the digging. I watched in silence. I sensed a shift within myself, like I was settling into the new reality. All I felt was a terrible ache in my chest. Everything else was gone. The fluctuating emotions had completely burned away.

Soon, the grave was complete. It beckoned, dark and gaping.

Mark and I lowered Jamison's body inside and began filling the hole. Dirt tumbled over his blanketed form. In minutes, only a few patches of cloth could be seen. Then it was just a mound of tightly packed earth.

Biting back tears, I said a few words, keeping it heartfelt and simple.

My hand in Taylor's, I turned away.

We piled into the car and left. I forced myself to not look back.

WHEN WE ARRIVED at the mall, I returned to the hockey net between the aisles. I donned a pair of gloves, retrieved a stick, and pushed a dozen pucks to the side. Hockey had always been a solace for me. Every time I stepped on the ice, everything else vanished. It was the only time—the only place—I could simply *be*. No worries. No cares. Just a singular focus on the next moment. A blissful escape.

Today, for a while, it worked.

I ripped pucks at the net. Gathered them up. Did it again. I broke two sticks during the hour. The second time it happened, I dropped the pieces, and then my gloves.

My thoughts slowly turned back to Jamison, so I searched for another distraction. I ended up gathering my rifle and two boxes of ammunition, wondering if I could find a way to the roof of the mall. I told the others what I was doing and left the base.

Ten minutes later, I emerged into open air. The roof was sectioned in tiers and I traversed across, climbing up a ladder to the side with the most corpses. My insides fluttered as I neared the edge. The ground swayed far below. If I didn't die from the fall, I'd certainly shatter my legs and be instantly overwhelmed by corpses.

I basked in the sun. For a while I stood, taking it in.

Straddling the lip of the roof, I removed the rifle from my back and loaded a bullet into the chamber. I easily melted into the gun as I sighted on a corpse. The tattered remains of a dress fluttered on the body. Grime and gore covered the fabric. Its hair was stringy. I tracked its head as it disappeared behind a car and emerged a few seconds later.

I squeezed the trigger.

The corpse crumbled. I ejected the shell, the little casing sparkling in the sun as it fell to the concrete below. Corpses cocked their heads at the gunshot, confused. I aimed and dropped another.

By the third shot, they'd located my position and began lumbering in my direction.

Would they ever realize I was out of their reach?

No. They were mindless creatures, driven by animal instinct. They pressed against the storefront below, necks and arms straining into the air. Collective growls rose to meet me. I took aim again, unloading shot after shot into the horde. Shells twinkled as they fell. Bullets whizzed, slamming into skulls.

The rhythm soothed me. The killing helped burn away my simmering anger.

I shot my way through the first box of ammunition and half of the second. I lowered the gun to take in the carnage. More than fifty bodies were sprawled on the concrete, but a hundred more corpses closed in from every direction in a never-ending stream of the dead. No matter how many we took out, there were always more.

I shifted in my perch, right leg still dangling over the edge. The corpses dispersed as other things caught their attention.

I reflected on how they were drawn to sound and movement. It was like those things triggered an instinct to attack. The louder the sound and quicker the movement, the more aggressive they became. They were basic predators, plain and simple.

I wondered what else I was missing, and the single news broadcast I had watched came to mind. I remembered the reporters talking about the scale of the Collapse, how countless cities were attacked virtually at once. The theory that somehow, this whole disaster was orchestrated. In a terrible way, it made sense, and it made me sick to think about.

How could someone purposefully cause this level of death? What kind of resources did they have? Was there a cure? If the corpses were man-made, there had to be, right?

I had too many questions and no way of finding out the truth. I shut down my spiraling thoughts before they could consume me.

I returned to the group. We had freeze-dried spaghetti for dinner. I didn't have an appetite, but Taylor made me eat anyway. Tension lined our conversations.

"We can leave tomorrow if you're ready," Mark said to the group.

"I think that's a good idea," Olivia said. "I don't want to stay here any longer."

I didn't have the energy to say I agreed with her. I finished off my food and retired to my sleeping bag. All I wanted was to put this day behind me. I closed my eyes. Unbidden, Jamison's voice came to me in words he'd said after my parents' deaths.

"*...you have to make it through. They're not here anymore, but you are, so live for them and don't forget. That's what they deserve...*"

I would live for him, even when it felt like I couldn't continue.

Burning pain consumed me, choking off my air.

I would live for him.

And silently, comforted by the dark, I wept.

TWENTY

THE NEXT MORNING, I numbly went through the motions of gathering supplies and filling a duffle bag with clothes and a new pair of boots. Next, we gathered to finalize our plans to leave.

Mark outlined our path to Tampa Bay. If things went smoothly—which seemed impossible—it would take us four days to get to my parents' hotel. That included regular stops to siphon gas, navigating around roadblocks, and hopefully avoiding other survivors.

I wondered what it would be like when we reached our goal. Would I feel relief? I considered how my dad talked about the hotel banding together. A whole community of survivors. What would that be like? They could be friendly, or they could be a group of murdering psychopaths. Survivors were cagy, protective, and desperate. The unfamiliar was a threat. They might not even let us in.

It was clear to me, in my limited experience, that this new world bred two types of people. The ones who gave, like Elliot and Rose. And the ones who took, like Sullivan—the looters, opportunists, and killers.

The Collapse only brought out what was already inside. You

became one or the other. And during the worst disaster of all, humanity was deteriorating at an alarming rate.

It made me wonder about Jamison's place in all this. He killed someone. A terrible fact, but it was done to protect the rest of us. No malice. Did that make him evil?

And who was *I* becoming?

I desperately wanted to be good, but sometimes that wasn't an option. Sometimes, you had to choose from an increasingly awful series of options. Good people could do bad things for the right reasons. Who could blame them?

It was a new world with new rules. And without a doubt, the line dividing right and wrong would only continue to blur.

I didn't like that conclusion, so I stopped thinking. It was almost blissful to mindlessly go about the store, only looking for the next thing to move. In the back of my mind, fear and grief tumbled around, but I kept them locked away.

With the help of Elliot and Rose, we transported the rest of our supplies through the mall, piling everything inside the doors leading to our car. There was a tent, sleeping bags, a stove and propane, bags of food, a half-full cooler of water, guns and ammo, chairs, blankets, and many other loose items. I evaluated the heap. It would get us where we needed to go. The only problem would be loading it into the car while corpses closed on our position. Speed was essential.

Mark cleared his throat. "We should go."

"Stay safe," Rose said, hugging us all in turn. There was sadness in her eyes; fear that we were heading to our deaths.

"I'll cover you," Elliot said, cocking his pistol.

I hoisted the tent in a two-handed grip as he pushed through the doors. Few corpses lingered in the area. Elliot posted up on one side of the car with Mark on the other, their weapons raised. The rest of us darted back and forth, dumping gear into the trunk.

On the third trip, a pan slipped from Taylor's overflowing arms. It resounded like a gong on the concrete. Everyone froze. Taylor hastily tossed her things into the car and snatched the pan. Seconds later, Mark and Elliot opened up with their pistols. Corpses fell with thuds. Many others stumbled over the bodies.

"Time's up!" Mark said.

I made a final dash for the remaining supplies and threw them in the car, slamming the trunk shut. Mark jumped into the driver's seat as I dove in the back. Elliot retreated to the safety of the mall.

"Good luck!" he shouted.

Mark put the car in gear. We bounced as a corpse disappeared underneath the tires. We steamrolled another as we squealed around a corner.

"The highway's still blocked," Olivia said.

Mark grunted in acknowledgment. He led the car down abandoned streets. Vacant storefronts lined each side. Corpses watched us pass. It took an hour to find a suitable on-ramp to merge onto the highway.

I was unexpectedly grateful to be outside again. The fresh air was cleansing. Even the burning afternoon sun was a welcome change from the cavernous shopping mall. I kept my window down as we drove, sticking out my hand for it to float on the wind.

When I wasn't driving, I let myself get lost in a book or fiddle with one of the many brainteasers I had. It was soothing to focus on something but not think, to work through problems that had clear answers. These were things that could be fixed and understood.

Taylor kept trying to get me to talk. Half the time, I didn't respond. The others, I gave a sharp answer to shut her up. It felt good for a split second. Then I'd see the hurt on her face, and guilt would fill my chest. I didn't apologize as I returned to my Rubik's Cube. She proceeded to ignore me for the rest of the afternoon, not even looking in my direction.

We stopped for lunch around 2 p.m. Olivia parked on a bridge, and we climbed down the embankment. A river sparkled below. Trees and boulders sprouted from the hillside. I dropped a bag of snacks on a flat boulder, letting my legs dangle off the edge. I closed my eyes to take in the whispering trees and trickling water.

Taylor sat as far away from me as possible, which meant Mark and Olivia were between us. I sighed, steeling myself as I got up to sit next to her. She picked through a bag of trail mix, only selecting the raisins, peanuts, and M&Ms.

I didn't know how to begin, so I asked, "What are you thinking about?"

Taylor spared me a tiny glance. "Nothing..." she said, studying the trail mix again. "Why are there so many *fucking* almonds?" She flicked one over the boulder's edge.

"I'll take them," I said.

She dumped some into my hand. I popped one into my mouth, chewing uncomfortably.

"I don't know why I did that. I hate almonds," I said.

Taylor almost smiled, but she caught herself in time to turn it into a grimace.

"Are you alright?" I asked.

"I don't know why you won't talk to me. I can't help if you cut me out," she said quietly.

I picked through the trail mix. "I'm not good at this sort of thing."

"Talking?"

I shrugged. "Letting people in."

"Yeah, you've mentioned that," Taylor said. "But you talked with me after we found my parents."

"That was to help you. I…" I trailed off. "I don't like to ask for help."

Taylor grabbed my hand. "Well, I'm here. We all are."

I nodded. I probably should have said more, but I let the conversation lapse. The river drew my attention. My skin itched with dirt and grime. "Did we pack shampoo?"

"What?" Olivia asked.

"Shampoo, body wash…"

"I think so?" Olivia said.

"I'm going to wash off," I said, getting to my feet.

"The water will be freezing," Mark said.

"I don't care. I just want to be clean," I said.

It took ten minutes of digging, but I finally located a bottle of shampoo in the trunk. There weren't any towels, so I took a blanket instead. Mark followed me to the water's edge. I ran my hand in the shallows. Cold leeched into my arm. I shook it dry.

Stripping out of my clothes, I piled them on a rock and waded into the stream. I gasped as it reached my knees. My feet went numb after a minute and I almost passed out when it reached my groin. Bracing myself, I dove under. I came up gasping as the water squeezed my chest. I hastily poured shampoo into my hands and lathered it through my hair. My teeth chattered as I dunked again, soapy bubbles floating away. I scrubbed my body with the shampoo and scrambled to shore a few minutes later.

It was only when I was drying off that I realized Taylor and Olivia had watched the whole thing from the boulder.

"Really?" I called, arms spread wide.

They laughed.

"Unbelievable," I said, pulling on my shirt.

"It's not a big deal," Mark said.

"That's because you have the body of a Greek God," I said.

Mark shrugged. I shook my head, tugging on the rest of my clothes. I pointedly sat in the car until the girls had cleaned themselves up and we were ready to set out again.

We drove until it was almost dark. Mark pulled over in a grove of trees and set to work building a fire. Taylor, Olivia, and I set up the tent. We'd barely gotten the poles in place when booming thunder shook the ground. The sunset disappeared as clouds overtook the sky like spilled ink over paper. A raindrop splashed on my cheek.

Mark ran over to help with the tent. Heavy drops pattered through the trees. We hooked the rainfly in place moments before the heavens opened. Taylor and Olivia dashed to the car for sleeping bags. Mark and I frantically secured a tarp to the trees above the sputtering fire. I fumbled with the knots, shaking in the icy downpour. Water dripped from my face. Tarp secure, we huddled underneath, but it was far too small for four people.

"I think we need another," I said, wiping my face.

"Yeah…" Mark said.

He retrieved our second tarp and we tied it to partially overhang the first. Tiny rivers of water soaked through my tennis shoes. I shivered. Lightning flashed. Thunder pounded my chest.

Mark tended the fire, coaxing it back to life. He stacked wet logs next to the flames and began organizing our supplies. Setting up the camp stove, he connected the small bottle of propane and twisted it on. Flames shot out and I caught the scent of gas.

I trudged through the rain to bring over chairs from the car. I was thoroughly soaked by the time I sat down. The pitiful fire gave little warmth. I shivered again, blowing on my hands. Taylor and

Olivia approached, wearing dry clothes.

"We set everything up and brought over your stuff," Olivia said. "You can change now if you want."

"Thanks," I said, jumping to my feet at the invitation.

Mark and I made our way to the tent, leaving our mud-caked shoes outside. A small lantern hung from the ceiling. Four sleeping bags lay cramped together, small pillows and bags of clothes sitting on top.

I stripped, shuddering as my freezing clothes clung to my skin. I rifled through my duffle bag, pulling out a flannel shirt, pants, socks, and underwear. A waterproof jacket and my new boots topped it off. Once dressed, I immediately felt better. I dumped my old pile of clothes in the car and plopped in front of the fire. Warmth slowly crept back into my stiff fingers.

Mark added another branch to the flames, sending up a shower of sparks. He doled out the food; stew this time. I took my bowl and comfortably leaned back in my chair.

"Does anyone know a good ghost story?" Mark asked after a while.

"I don't like them," Olivia said.

"I'm sure you could handle it," he returned.

"Don't try it."

Mark cleared his throat. "There once were four kids. They were alone in the woods as rain—"

Olivia smacked Mark and he shut up, smiling.

"What did you want to be when you grew up?" I asked.

The others adopted thoughtful looks.

"You first," Olivia said.

"I wanted to play in the NHL," I said.

"Do you think you would have made it? I saw some games and

you were really good," Taylor said.

I tried not to laugh outright and settled for an appreciative look. "Not good enough…"

"I wanted to be a model," Olivia said. "I immediately found out that wasn't going to happen."

"I think you're beautiful," Mark said.

"That's nice of you to say."

"It's true."

"Thank you," Olivia said. I thought I saw her blush. "But then I settled on music, which was *slightly* more realistic. Things were going pretty well too, but here we are."

"That song you played back home…all of them, really," Mark began. "I didn't want it to stop."

"Same," I said.

Olivia continued shrinking in her chair. "What about you?" she asked Mark.

"I thought about the military. Navy SEALs. I was going to join up after high school," Mark said. I raised an eyebrow but wasn't all that surprised. "I still get to kill things now…"

Taylor leaned forward. "Don't laugh, but I wanted to be an astronaut. I eventually decided to be a pilot. I even had a few lessons before all this."

"Are you saying you could have flown us to Florida?" I asked.

"If you wanted to risk crash landing, sure," Taylor said.

We lapsed into silence. It wasn't torrentially raining anymore, just a calming patter on the tarp above. The fire was mostly coals by now. I finished my soup. Mark and Olivia got up to find one of the board games we'd taken with us, leaving Taylor and me alone. After a minute of uncomfortable silence, I got up to leave.

"Do you have a minute?" Taylor asked.

I stopped. She stood to face me but didn't say anything. Her face weakened, then cracked.

"What's wrong?" I asked, tentatively touching her arm.

Taylor sniffed and wiped her eyes. "I don't know why I'm crying…"

I hugged her.

"I miss him," Taylor said.

"I miss him too."

"I didn't even know him that well, but you knew him for years."

"He was like a brother…" I whispered. "We did everything together, and…I can't believe he's gone."

Footsteps sounded from the car. Olivia waved the Monopoly box over her head. "You guys coming?"

"In a minute," I said.

I squeezed Taylor's hand and we followed Mark and Olivia into the tent.

TWENTY-ONE

I WHITTLED A stick in the morning as Mark and Olivia prepared breakfast. Taylor methodically tore apart pine needles next to me. She had a small pile at her feet by the time Mark handed out packages of freeze-dried scrambled eggs.

I looked at them apprehensively. They wiggled and slid around like they were coming alive. I hesitantly spooned some into my mouth, gagged, and spit it out on the ground. Taylor made a disgusted noise in the back of her throat.

"Incredible," I said, giving Mark a thumbs up. Glowering, he set aside his portion and rifled through our bag of food. He tossed each of us an energy bar. I tore mine open, the corner fluttering to the ground.

It took an hour to break camp. Mark and I folded up the tent while Taylor and Olivia packed the car. After breaking down the poles, we began scraping mud from the bottom of the tent. Mark wouldn't let us roll it up until it was nearly spotless and had dried in the sun.

Mark untied the tarps above the fire, and I was in the process of wrestling the tent into its bag when a twig snapped behind me. I twisted to face a corpse two steps away. My heart jumped into my throat as it lunged for my face. I fell backwards, the tent slipping out of my hands. I scrambled in the dirt. A hand closed around my ankle. I lashed out with my other foot. The corpse's head snapped back, loosening its grip enough for me to make a mad dash away.

I reached top speed in three strides, then my foot caught a root and I pitched hard into the ground. My right shoulder blossomed in pain as dirt and pine needles shoved under my shirt. A gunshot sounded and a body thumped to the ground next to me.

"Thanks," I said to Taylor as she helped me up with one hand, pistol in the other.

"Grab the tent, I'll cover you," Taylor said, then shouted, "Someone start the car!"

More than a dozen corpses streamed from the trees, but the tent was only ten feet away. I sprinted forward as Taylor emptied her clip into the dead. Bodies tumbled. Additional gunfire sounded behind us. I snatched the tent, careful to keep it all together. Taylor dumped the magazine and loaded another.

We turned tail for the car. The engine roared. We dove into the backseat as Mark pressed the gas. He obliterated a corpse and clipped a tree, snapping off the right mirror. I fell against the door, then Taylor, as Mark continued his erratic weaving. We launched onto the road a moment later.

I slumped in my seat, heart thudding in my chest and ears. My hands shook, and my entire body tingled with adrenaline. I touched my shoulder. It flared with pain. Blood streaked my fingers. I inspected the two-inch gash with odd detachment.

It's not a bite, you're fine.

"Cody…oh, God," Taylor said, eyes widening as she saw the

wound.

"It's fine," I said.

"That's *not* fine. Let me help."

"I can clean it out," I said, attempting to remove some of the needles and dirt. The car hit a bump and my fingers dug into the exposed flesh. "Fuck!"

"Cody!" Taylor grabbed my hand. "Let me help. Mark, pull over."

"One second," he said. The car ground to a halt next to an open field. He and Olivia twisted around to see what was going on. Olivia's mouth dropped open.

"Come on," Taylor said, hopping out of the car.

I reluctantly followed. She told me to sit down at the side of the road while she searched for a water bottle and first-aid kit.

"Take off your shirt," she said when she returned.

"No cuddling first? Just going straight for the good stuff, huh?" I asked.

Her eyes narrowed.

I took off the shirt, wincing at the movement. "I could take off my pants too. This might get messy—"

She responded by splashing my arm with icy water. I clenched my jaw against the burning pain.

"How'd you do this?" she asked.

"I tripped," I said. She inspected the gash with a critical eye. Guessing her thoughts, I added, "I wasn't bitten."

She poured more water on the cut and dried it with a cloth. I warily eyed the tiny bottle of antiseptic as she squeezed it directly into the wound.

She might as well have poured lava over my skin.

"*Jesus!*" I sprang to my feet, squeezing my hands together.

"Sorry…" Taylor said.

I paced the edge of the road.

"We'll need to sew it up."

I vigorously shook my head. "Absolutely not."

"We can't let it get infected," Taylor said.

"She's right," Mark added.

"Stay out of this," I said.

"Do you want to lose your arm?" Taylor asked.

"That's a bit dramatic," I said.

"It could happen," Taylor said, gravely.

"She's right," Mark said again, matching her tone.

"Don't you think *you're* being dramatic?" Olivia chimed in.

I halted, anger rising. "Does this look like I'm being dramatic to you?" I pointed at my shoulder. The pain had subsided to a dull ache by now, but blood continued to stream down my arm.

Taylor shrugged vaguely. "Sit down, we're doing this," she said, patting the ground next to her.

"I hate you all," I said, slumping to the concrete.

Taylor rummaged through the first-aid kid and pulled out a needle and surgical thread. She fumbled with threading the needle but managed to tie it off. For a moment, she shifted her hand from one end of the cut to the other, unsure where to start. I swallowed uncomfortably.

"Do you know what you're doing?" I asked.

"I think so."

"You *think so?*" I pulled away. "Mark, get over here. Can you sew this up?"

"I haven't done it before, but I could try," he said.

"*Great*, the one time I need you for something, you can't do it…"

"Hold still," Taylor said, pinching the torn flesh to insert the needle.

"*OW!* Be careful!"

"Stop squirming."

I clenched my teeth again. Each time the needle entered my skin, the wound was shocked with a bolt of pain. Taylor's brow furrowed in concentration, curly hair falling over her eyes. She tucked it behind an ear and returned to the work.

"Will you stop staring at me?" Taylor asked without looking up. "It's making it hard to focus."

I sighed, looking away. Olivia had taken up wandering the road, either no longer interested or too uncomfortable to watch. Mark rubbed his chin with interest, probably taking mental notes.

"Done," Taylor said ten minutes later.

I examined her work. The gash was now a haphazard line of shaky stitches. No finesse. I'd certainly have a thick scar once it healed. Taylor finished up by applying more ointment and wrapping it in gauze.

"Thanks," I grumbled.

Taylor flashed a pure smile and kissed me. "Anytime."

Hours later, Mark stopped on an overpass as we neared Atlanta. Cars flooded the highway leaving the city, but there weren't many on the one leading in. There were still enough cars to scavenge gas from. The city itself sprawled for miles. Skyscrapers pierced the air. They looked normal from our position, but we were too far away to see the real destruction.

I got out to stretch my legs, making sure I had my rifle and hunting knife in hand. There was no point in being surprised by a corpse again.

I walked to the edge of the overpass. The sunset bathed everything with an orange and purple glow, sparkling off the distant city. I leaned my elbows against the barrier to take it in. Corpses wandered the roads below, going from car to car without clear direction.

I swung my legs over the barrier and sat down, stomach fluttering with vertigo. A gust of wind pushed at my back. My knuckles turned white as I clutched the concrete to keep myself in place.

Taylor appeared at my side, hair blowing across her face. She attempted to brush it away, but the wind had other plans. "Hell of a drop," she said, leaning over the edge.

I took a moment to respond. "I can't believe we're almost there."

"One more day," Taylor said.

"I don't know if I'm nervous or excited," I said, squinting against the sunset. "I don't think I'm ready to find out they're gone…"

"I believe they're safe," Taylor said, squeezing my hand. "We'll find them, then we'll move into a house by the beach where we don't have to worry anymore. Soon enough, we'll find a way out of this."

I remained quiet and still as I observed the city. I desperately wanted to believe her, but that reality seemed impossible. Maybe my parents *were* alive, and maybe we could build a good life for ourselves, but I couldn't imagine the world would ever fully recover.

"Just picture it for a moment," Taylor said, reading my thoughts.

I closed my eyes to dream of a peaceful life. Taylor and me. My parents. Mark and Olivia. All of us living by the water somewhere. No corpses or angry survivors. No more quests. No more running.

"I've been thinking," Taylor said, tapping the barrier with a finger. "What if we went to the beach? Just for a few hours before we get to the hotel. We could use a break."

"I don't know if that's a good idea. Something could go wrong," I said.

"Look around. *Everything's* gone wrong. We might as well enjoy things while we can," Taylor said. "Besides, we won't have to deal with crowds."

"Or parking," I added.

"Exactly! It's perfect."

"I know a good one, too."

"So, we're going?"

"I think you're right. We should do it," I said.

Taylor beamed, her eyes twinkling with excitement. She hugged me from behind before running off to shout, "We can go!"

I couldn't help but laugh to myself as I returned my feet to solid ground. Because of the new plan, we drove another few hours that night. We would still make it to the hotel tomorrow, but it meant more time at the beach in the afternoon.

We made slow progress through Atlanta. Mark had to keep the car at a walking pace to get around certain obstacles. I caught occasional glimpses down ruined streets where rubble littered the ground. Corpses wandered like so many ants. Some wore military uniforms, and I caught sight of a tank, its cannon pointed toward the heart of the city.

Then we were past it all, and the buildings faded into tiny spires. I leaned back in my seat, watching clouds build outside my window. It rained for an hour and turned to mist by the time we stopped for the night.

As I lay in my sleeping bag, a tinge of excitement flared to life, mixing with the pain. I held onto it, hoping it wouldn't fade just yet. It seemed like forever ago that we left home, but now, for better or worse, our goal was just ahead. It made me wonder what would happen after we found my parents—for I no longer doubted we would. I just wondered how I would break the news about Jamison.

TWENTY-TWO

AFTER FINISHING MY reread of *The Hobbit* in the first hour of our morning drive, I returned to my Rubik's Cube. Now that I'd memorized all the algorithms, I could do it in less than three minutes each time.

"Can I see it?" Mark asked, looking up from a book I'd lent him. He and I sat in the middle seats. I handed it over. He examined it for a moment before rolling down the window to toss it outside.

"What the hell?" I threw my hands in the air.

"The clicking is driving me insane," he said.

I considered doing the same to the book I'd lent him, but I couldn't. I hadn't read it yet.

We stopped for gas one last time and I drove the last leg. More than once, I had to double back to find a new route because the roads were blocked. Palm trees began lining the highway. Weathered green road signs marked our progress.

Tampa Bay: 42 miles.

23 miles.

16 miles.

I had to stop watching the signs. Every time I looked at one, we'd hardly traveled any distance.

15 miles.

I sighed, rubbing my forehead.

"Cody, I just thought of something…" Mark said from the passenger's seat. "How will we find your parents' hotel?"

I looked over at him, realizing I never mentioned why I was so confident we could do this. "They're at the Grand Hyatt, right next to the airport. We've stayed there a few times, so I'll be able to find it."

"Huh…" Mark said. "What were they doing there?"

"It was their anniversary. Well, technically they missed it. They stayed for Jamison and my…" The words stuck in my throat. "They stayed for our last game and flew out that night."

8 miles.

The longer we drove, the more things began to filter back to me. The sights. The buildings. The streets. I remembered the last time we all went on vacation here, only a week after school ended. Watching the Lightning in the playoffs. Stamkos scored two goals that game…

My chest ached at the memories. I almost pushed them away, but it was a good kind of pain, so I let them linger.

I exited onto a new highway, and a few minutes later, signs for the airport popped into view. We slowed to a crawl as I navigated the clogged road. The airport opened on our right and the bay came into view on our other side. Sunlight glistened on the open water.

A clump of buildings sprouted at the water's edge. Adrenaline surged in my body at the sight. "That's the hotel," I said.

From this distance, I couldn't tell if anyone was there. What if they'd all been wiped out? I snuck glances at the hotel but mostly focused on the road. I didn't want to think about it. And I didn't have to. Not for a few more hours, at least. Until then, I could pretend everything was exactly how I wanted it to be.

"Where are we going?" Mark asked.

"Clearwater. It's on the ocean, so it's a bit nicer," I said.

We continued west for another thirty minutes before I parked in a mostly full lot. Several corpses roamed, linen shirts fluttering on their frames.

That might be a problem. We were far from alone out here, but the others didn't seem to care. They jumped out of the car. I gathered my rifle, bat, a handful of blankets, and headed for the steps leading to the beach.

Waves crashed and seagulls floated in the swampy sky. I sucked in air through my nose, smelling salt as the sun warmed my back. My shoes filled with sand as I neared the water. I spread everything out, laying my weapons on top.

Without hesitation, I ripped off my clothes. Standing in just my underwear, I let my feet sink into the burning sand until they reached the cooler layer below the surface. On instinct, I scanned the surrounding area for additional corpses. A handful lurched to our right, half a mile away. The ones from the parking lot slowly made their way forward.

I hoped we'd be fine. Small numbers of the dead no longer scared me. Besides, they wouldn't be able to swim and catch us. As far as I knew.

The others caught up and dropped their things. Taylor removed everything until she was just in her bra and underwear. She pursed her lips suggestively and I couldn't help but take her in.

The ocean drew my attention. I bounced impatiently on the balls of my feet. Unable to stand the wait any longer, I sprinted off, kicking up sand and letting out a triumphant whoop.

Brilliantly warm water splashed on my legs and chest, and then a wave pulled me under. The wound on my arm blazed at first but soon fell into a dull throb.

I came up for air and wiped my eyes. Another wave crashed over my head and filled my mouth with water. Diving under, I swam further out until my toes barely skimmed the bottom. Mark and Olivia paddled over, and Taylor broke the surface a few feet away.

"I thought I lost you," I said.

"I'm still here," she said, trying to float on her back.

A wave rocked her body in a spray of foam. She vanished for a second and came up sputtering. I snuck behind and dunked her again. She cursed and flailed her arms. I laughed as she bobbed to the surface. I dove away, but her hand caught my ankle. I was suddenly underwater as she dragged me down. She let go a few seconds later. I coughed, and it was her turn to laugh.

Her hands found my chest. I held her around the waist, our bodies brushing against each other. I kissed her as we rose and fell on the waves.

I never wanted to leave this moment. Even if it was temporary, it was like every burden had been lifted from my shoulders.

We splashed around for a long time. I contentedly moved with the waves, looking out over the ocean. Mark and Olivia hovered on our right, talking quietly.

Tired of treading water, I made my way back to the shore.

"Cody, you should sterilize your arm again before we leave," Mark said as I passed him.

"Thanks, Mom," I returned.

He was right, though. I couldn't let it get infected. I probably shouldn't have swam in the first place.

I scanned the shore. Four corpses languished in the shallows. I paddled around them and ran to retrieve my bat. With a little coaxing, I lured them back to solid ground and took them down one by one.

I sprawled out on one of the blankets, sand and water drying on my body. I focused on breathing. In and out, eyes closed. Lost in the perfect moment. Crashing waves lulled me into a trance, but I fought sleep. I couldn't let myself be surprised by corpses. I kept my ears open for the sound of crunching sand.

I perked up at movement, but it was only Taylor. She laid down next to me. I scanned the beach again before dropping my head. We didn't have to share a word. It was enough to be here, together.

For a little while, I forgot who I was. Where we were. What we were doing. I could almost pretend I was back on vacation with my family. The phantom shouts of a busy beach filled my ears. I was happy. And yet...

I abruptly sat up. This wasn't right. We shouldn't be acting like the world was back to normal when everything we knew was gone.

I took a long look at the beach—the shimmering water and turned-up sand, the gulls running along the edges of waves—before standing up. I wiped the sand off my feet and pulled on my pants, socks, then shoes and shirt. I waited in silence as the others took the hint and began packing up.

Once everything was stowed in the car, I hopped behind the wheel and we set off. Trepidation coursed through my body the entire drive. Tension filled the car like stifling fog. My hands shook. I gripped the steering wheel tighter.

No more detours or distractions. The journey was over. We'd made it.

Well...most of us.

Now, to see if it could justify the pain.

We rounded a bend and the hotel came into view. It towered above the trees, in good condition. Four stories of concrete, and about a dozen of curving glass above. It caught the sunlight, like a wave stuck in time.

I had less than a second to admire the architecture before figures poured onto the road. Men and women, each with hostile expressions and weapons in hand. They trained assault rifles, shotguns, and pistols on our vehicle. A quick glance in the rearview mirror showed another four circling behind. I didn't see my parents.

"Keep calm, we're not trying to start anything," I said.

"Don't worry, we wouldn't stand a chance," Mark said.

"Turn off the car and step outside, slowly!" a man shouted. He had a buzzcut and grey stubble. "Keep your hands up!"

I removed the keys and opened the door, stepping outside with my hands raised.

"Drop what's in your hand!" he yelled.

"It's just the keys—"

"Drop it!"

I let them slip from my fingers. They clinked on the concrete. The hostiles closed in, just feet away now. The man with the buzzcut trained his rifle at my forehead.

"Get on your knees," he said.

I spared a glance at the others. Olivia dropped first. Then Taylor and Mark. I followed suit.

"We're just here to find—" I began.

"Shut up," the man with the buzzcut barked.

"Just listen—" I began to rise to my feet.

Before I could finish, the man slammed the butt of his gun into my face. I had a vague sense of falling before I slipped into darkness.

PART THREE
WHATEVER IT TAKES

TWENTY-THREE

I CAME TO in a sparsely furnished room. Yellow lights seared into the back of my skull. My head throbbed. It was like my brain was stuffed with cotton and set ablaze. I couldn't breathe through my nose, and it sent needles of pain into my face. I tasted blood. I tried to wipe it away, but my arms wouldn't move. Rope dug into my wrists and ankles, keeping me affixed to a metal chair.

"Welcome back," a woman's voice said.

I opened my eyes again. The room spun and took a moment to right itself. A woman stepped in front of me. Her black hair was pulled back in a braid. A pistol rested at one hip, a Bowie knife on the other. Two men flanked a closed door, their weapons ready but pointed at the ground. One of them was the man with the buzzcut who knocked me out. The other had short blond hair and a pointed face. The woman pulled up a chair and sat down. She leaned forward, hands folded.

"Where are my friends?" I asked.

"I'll get to them," she said. "How did you find us?"

"I just…knew," I said, trying to form a clear thought. I squeezed my eyes together, but the fuzziness wouldn't leave.

"Who sent you?"

"We came on our own."

"How many of you are there?"

"I don't know what you're talking about. It's just me and my friends."

"Alright, I'm done playing nice," she said. There was a *swish*, and something sharp pressed against my chest. I looked down to find her knife poised to slice into my pec. *"How many of you are there?"*

"I swear to God I don't know what you're talking about! I came here to find my parents," I said.

She barked out a laugh. I gasped as searing pain blossomed across my chest. Her knife dripped blood.

"Bullshit. Did they send you to test our defenses?" she asked. The tip of the knife dug into my forearm. "Where's your base?"

"We came from Minneapolis to find my parents—"

She sliced my arm. I clenched my teeth as blood dripped onto the ground. I jerked against my bonds. The ropes were so tight my hands were a tingling purple.

"Stop!" I yelled. "My parents are Jean and Daniel Calloway! They came here for their anniversary right before everything happened."

The woman paused, leaning back. She exchanged a look with the men flanking her.

"You have to believe me," I pleaded. "My dad mentioned someone else…" I frantically searched my brain, hoping she wouldn't start cutting me open again. "…Evelyn Murphy…she was helping organize everyone."

"What's your name?" she asked, ignoring this piece of information. Her eyes were dark and calculating.

"Cody. They had another son, Jamison…but he didn't make it."

"Alright," she said slowly. "We'll see if you're telling the truth soon enough."

"I am! What else do you want me to say?"

The woman stood, wiped the knife on her pants, and sheathed it. She nodded to the man with the buzzcut. "Untie him and lock him up, alone." She turned to the other man. "Have Daniel find me when he gets back. I'm going to chat with his friends."

"He's alive?" Relief overtook me, but the woman didn't respond. "Hey! They'll say the same thing!" I shouted after her as she and the blond-haired man left the room.

The man with the buzzcut crouched next to me, tugging at the knots holding my right arm. "I'm sorry about Murphy. She can be… erratic."

"*That's* Murphy? Jesus Christ…" I said. Arms freed, I rubbed my wrists, but it was a disembodied feeling with my hands completely numb. "What's your name?"

"Aaron," the man said, untying my legs. He helped me stand. "I'm sorry, but you can never be too cautious. We needed to know who you are."

Aaron led me down the hall, to the stairwell, and up four flights. We passed several people on the way. Men and women. Old and young. Each one looked me over, contempt hiding in their expressions. Aaron stopped at door 513.

"I'll have someone bring you food," he said, glancing at my wounds, "and a first aid kit. Sit tight, it might be a while before you're let out."

"You need a better system," I growled. "This is insane. We're not guilty of whatever it is you think we did."

"Just get in the room and everything will be fine," Aaron said.

He flashed a key card and the door unlocked. I stepped inside. "I'm sorry about the nose," Aaron said, apologizing for the third time.

The door closed between us. The inside didn't have a handle. They must have taken it off to keep people locked away. That was far from comforting.

At least the room was furnished. It was just like the ones I remembered. Two queen beds were pushed against the wall, a nightstand between them. A desk and office chair, TV and dresser. Sliding glass doors led to a balcony that overlooked the bay. Warm sunlight flooded the room, spilling over the carpet.

The lights worked, too. And the door locks. I'd been too distracted to pay proper attention. They must have salvaged a generator. A big one. It was a small comfort.

I entered the bathroom and tried the faucet. It sputtered clear water at a low pressure.

I looked in the mirror and grimaced.

My nose was bent a fraction to the right. Broken. Touching it sent stabbing pains into my skull. Blood streamed down my lip, chin, and into my mouth, coating my teeth and gums. I removed my shirt, wincing as the fabric pulled away from the gash on my chest. My left forearm was coated red and still seeped. I gently ran my fingers over these cuts, further streaking them with blood.

I looked at my hands. They wouldn't stop shaking so I gripped the countertop and forced myself to take measured breaths.

I realized then that Murphy never mentioned where my mom was. If she was here. Alive or dead. Nothing. My friends were gone too. Maybe being tortured for information.

Deeply rooted anger rose in my throat, making it hard to swallow. Fear squeezed my lungs as I tried to take calming breaths. I pressed a hand to my chest, my heart pounding.

I turned on the faucet. Lukewarm water ran over my hands, clearing away the blood in coppery waves. Icy needles jabbed under my skin as my fingers shook off the numbness. I soaked a small towel and used it to scrub my chest and forearm, then tenderly go over my face. It was stained pink by the time I was done. I didn't try setting my nose because I didn't want to make it worse by doing it wrong.

I sat on the bed, eyes on nothing until a knock came from the door. I stood but remembered there was no way for me to open it. A woman peeked inside. She deposited a paper bag on the ground and left without a word.

I investigated the bag, pulling out a first aid kit, an apple, and a granola bar. I sighed. Stomach grumbling, I ate first. The apple was bruised in places but sweet. Finishing off the last crumbs of the granola bar, I returned to the bathroom with the first aid kit. I applied antiseptic and taped gauze over the wounds. Thankfully, they weren't deep enough to warrant stitches. Still hurt, though.

I considered putting my shirt back on, but it was a filthy, ragged mess. I tossed it on the floor.

With no way to know how long it would take my dad to show up, I collapsed on the bed. My mind raced with every terrible possibility.

My mom, dead...fear over dragging my friends into a worse fate than staying home...being trapped for the rest of my life...guilt that Jamison died for a futile quest...

Guilt that he died at all...

I WOKE WITH a start. Faint moonlight came from the balcony. My skin was clammy with sweat. I rubbed my face.

Someone was knocking.

It took a moment for me to realize it wasn't my imagination. I sprang from the bed and fumbled with a lamp, filling the room with warm light. The door squeaked open. I peered around the corner and found my dad standing just inside the doorway. He'd propped it open with a block.

I went still. He had a short brown beard and wavy hair that was greying at the temples. For a split second, he wasn't the man I knew. He had a pistol at his hip, and his deep blue eyes were tinged with heaviness. They flicked behind me. Just a glance, but telling.

"Cody," he said, barely a whisper. He looked me over, face clouded by pain and relief.

"Dad," I said.

He wrapped me in a crushing embrace. I returned it, paying no attention to the burning cut on my chest. His beard scratched my cheek.

"I can't believe you're here. I never thought I'd see you again…" His voice hitched. "I didn't believe Murphy when she told me."

"Jamison's gone," I said, the words spilling out.

"I know…" he said. There was more, but I didn't ask. He said it anyway. "Your mom is dead."

The confirmation slammed into my gut. I clutched his shirt. There were long, terrible minutes of nothing but holding each other, crying. He pulled away, searching my face. He wiped away my tears. I winced at the touch.

"What happened to your face?" he asked.

"Aaron thought I was being confrontational," I said.

"Let me help," he said, taking my nose between two fingers. "Your mom taught me a few things over the years."

"What are you doing?" I tried to pull away.

"Stop squirming. You don't want it to heal crooked, do you?" he asked. "On three. One…two…"

He didn't finish the count. With a practiced hand, he cracked my nose back into place. I doubled over as pain knifed through my head. I touched my nose. It was bleeding again. I snagged my shirt to wipe it away.

"What about the rest?" He gestured at my bandages, concern etched in his brow.

"This one was my fault," I said, pointing to my shoulder. "Murphy did the others. She *tortured* me. What the hell is that about?"

My dad's face soured and his lips became a thin line. "We should probably sit down." I held off on questions as we sat on the beds, facing each other. "Before I start, tell me about Jamison. What happened? How did you get here?"

I clasped my hands together, twisting my thumbs in a circle. "Did you get my text?"

He nodded. "I tried to call you later, but it didn't work."

"Me too," I said. "My friends lost everyone…" I bit my lip. My dad didn't cut in. He was silent. Stoic. "But as far as I knew, you were still alive. We had to try to find you, so we started driving. On the second day, we ran into another group. They forced us to camp with them and then they stole everything in the morning. Jamison went back for a gun he had hidden and was bitten. He didn't tell us until a few days later…and then he was gone. That was a week ago, maybe."

My dad pressed his eyes with his thumb and forefinger. He shook his head, jaw clenched as he looked around the room.

I'd lost a friend. A brother. But I couldn't imagine what it was like to lose a child.

"I never got to talk to him again," he said.

"I never got to talk to Mom," I said.

"I'm so sorry."

"How did it happen?"

"I thought it would be safe here," he said, meeting my eyes. "I was wrong. So many people died, but everyone else began forming groups and fighting over supplies. Your mom wanted to set up a clinic, so last week we took a group to a hospital for medicine. People were already looting the place. Someone started shooting and she was hit. I…I killed three people that day."

I was at a loss for words.

My dad held his head in his hands. "The worst part is, part of me enjoyed it. I wanted to *hurt* them, but some of them got away…"

"It's ok—"

"It's not, Cody!" he snapped. Anguish flickered behind his eyes. "I *killed* people, and this isn't over! They're still out there, growing stronger and ambushing us at every chance. Just today, we had to fight off one of their groups. It's only getting worse. *That's* why Murphy didn't take a chance with you. Honestly, I don't blame her."

"How can you say that?"

"I hate what she did to you, but it's to protect everyone here."

"Dad, what do you owe these people? We can *leave*."

"And go where? There's no place on earth we can go to escape this. I can't do it. I'm responsible for keeping these people alive. We have a place here, a community. I can't give that up. I can talk to Murphy. I know she'll let you and your friends join us."

"I don't want to join your group of murderers."

"That's not who we are. We're survivors, and sometimes that means we have to protect ourselves. Sometimes, people die."

"That's messed up."

"Everything is! It's not a black-and-white world, Cody! You can't ignore what's going on. Things are different now."

"You're different," I said, fighting the bitter disgust rising in my chest.

"I know," he said. "But you have to understand that I'm doing this to protect my people—"

"*Your* people?"

"—and now that you're here, I have an even greater reason to fight. I would do *anything* to keep you safe. *I love you.*"

I stood up and paced the room as my dad watched me from the bed. Despite everything, I believed him. I believed he thought this was the best place for him to be. It still made me sick. "I can't be a part of this."

"I'm sorry, but you don't have a choice. This is our life now."

"This isn't living. This is justifying your actions because you can't live with yourself otherwise."

"It's not easy, but it's us or them. It's as simple as that." He stood and gripped my arms. "Look at me. I'm so glad you're here. I thought I'd lost everything. Listen to me, I love you."

I had a hard time saying it back. The words seemed to stick in my throat. "I love you too," I managed to get out. "I don't know what to do. Everything's messed up…"

He hugged me again, and I tentatively returned the gesture. "We're going to get through this," he said.

"Where are my friends?" I asked.

He tried to smile, ignoring the question. "Come on. I'll show you to your room. I can get you clothes, too."

I numbly followed him, hardly listening as he talked about the hotel. It was too much for me to process. It felt like my brain was shutting down, trying to protect itself. My mom was dead, but doubt clouded my thinking. I didn't see it happen, but my dad had, so it must be true. I never got to say goodbye. I couldn't remember the last time we talked.

I couldn't stop thinking about the way she died. And my dad, killing people. Or his promise that things were only going to get worse. Fighting against other survivors. *Really* fighting. I believed that things were bad, but was there any way to get out? Why did we have to be here, right in the middle of a brewing war?

All I wanted was to escape to somewhere safe and quiet, but that wasn't going to happen. There was no place to go, and I wouldn't leave my dad. He was one of the last people I had left. I had trouble understanding what he had done, but in a terrible way, it made sense. Could I really blame him?

I needed to go to bed. It was the only way to make the world disappear.

"Take this," my dad said. I snapped back to myself, realizing we were in another room. Probably his. He held out a backpack. "It's clothes. There's more in room two-twenty-four. It's where we put all the extra things."

"From the dead, you mean," I said.

"Look, we need to rebuild our society," he said. "That means using what we have."

I pulled on a shirt as we made our way to the lobby. My dad stopped at the check-in counter. Even though it was night, people milled around. Four guards stood inside the entrance, assault rifles in hand. Many others talked in small groups in the foyer. Or lounged in chairs, reading and playing games. Aaron and Murphy exchanged whispers next to a pillar. They watched me like predators.

"Here's your key. I'll send your friends up in a bit," my dad said. I looked at the key card. The room number was written on the back. He squeezed my arm reassuringly. "We'll talk tomorrow. I need to check in with them." He nodded at Aaron and Murphy.

I walked away, silent.

The room was nice. Two king beds in separate rooms. A small kitchen with marble countertops. A common room with artwork on the walls, two couches, and a coffee table. Magazines littered the top. I turned on the TV but it returned a NO SIGNAL box.

I stepped onto the balcony. The air was warm. A faint breeze carried the scent of the ocean. I took it in, looking over the dark bay. The water glimmered, silvery in the moonlight.

It was probably twenty minutes before someone knocked on the door. I opened it to find Taylor, Mark, and Olivia outside. Taylor threw her arms around me. I held her tight.

"We met your dad," Taylor said. "He seems nice."

"He's changed," I said.

"Where's your mom?" Taylor asked.

"She's dead," I said.

The others stood rooted in place. I didn't know what to say, and I didn't feel like trying to talk. I let the silence reign. Mark shuffled from foot to foot. After a minute, they began looking around the room.

Taylor scrutinized my face. "How's the nose?"

"It's fine," I said.

"Why did they lock us up?" Mark asked.

I sat them down and explained what I could. Murphy cutting me to get information—Taylor's eyes tightened at that—and the conversation with my dad. They kept interjecting with questions, but there was so much I didn't know.

"What do we do?" Taylor asked when I finished.

"I don't know," I said. "Right now, I want to go to bed."

The others nodded.

"There's only two, so I don't know what you want to do about that."

"We can share," Taylor said to me.

"Mark and I can take the other," Olivia said. She looked at Mark, who nodded.

I wasted no time kicking off my shoes and climbing into one of the beds. Taylor ducked under the covers next to me. We looked into each other's eyes. She gave me a gentle kiss.

"What can I do?" she asked, one hand on my cheek.

"Just be here," I said. "Tell me everything will be ok…that we didn't make a mistake coming here."

"It's going to be ok. We did the right thing," she said. "Do you believe me?"

"I believe you," I said, even though I didn't.

TWENTY-FOUR

BREAKFAST IN HAND, I sat at a round table in the middle of the complementary dining area. I pursed my lips at my portion. A small bowl of oatmeal, two pieces of bread, and an orange. The people in charge of the food line gave the same to everyone.

I numbly took a bite of toast as the others settled around me. Questioning looks followed our every movement. Some people glared, threatened by our very presence. Others cast furtive glances at us every few minutes. Some of them must have seen us dragged into the hotel like hunted animals. And now, we sat in their midst like friends.

I busied myself with my food, just focusing on the next bite, trying not to think. Every time my mind drifted to my mom, I focused on the watery oatmeal and how I would still be hungry afterward. It wasn't working very well.

I looked up as someone took the remaining seat at our table. He was about our age and had long blond hair tucked behind his ears. He had brown eyes, but the right one drifted, unfocused.

"I heard you guys were here," he said, elbows on the table.

"Why'd they let you in?"

"Go away," I said.

"What happened to your face?" he asked.

I unconsciously touched my nose. I'd seen myself in the mirror this morning, and purple bruises outlined my eyes. It would be weeks before it went away.

"So, where'd you come from?" he asked.

"How about you leave us the hell alone," I said.

Taylor glowered at me. The kid closed his mouth and slowly gathered his food. "Just trying to be friendly…"

"Hold on, what can you tell us about this place?" Mark asked.

The kid looked at Mark, then me, weighing whose directions he should follow. He sat down again, breaking into a smile. I shouldn't have wanted to punch him, but my fuse was burning low. I kept myself planted in my seat, eyes narrowed at the kid.

"First off, I'm Leo. And I'm glad you asked," Leo said. He leaned forward conspiratorially. "I know everything about this place."

I tapped my finger on the table, unimpressed. Leo spared an uncomfortable glance at me. I found it hard to not watch his drifting eyeball.

"How many people are here?" Mark asked.

"Eighty…a hundred…" Leo said. "A lot of 'em left when things went south."

"What about the people with the guns? How many of them?" Mark asked.

"Not as many as you would think. Twenty-five. Thirty, maybe. They're the leaders. They took over and started ordering people around." Leo ticked off fingers. "There's Murphy. She's kind of crazy, but she's in charge. And then Aaron, Daniel, Porter, Jessie…they're her council. I do my best to stay out of their way."

"Daniel…" I said softly.

"Yeah, brown beard and hair. Tall, angry, ruthless. You'd know him when you see him." The rest of us exchanged a look as Leo continued. "Then you have the Rangers. They gather most of the supplies, guard the hotel, that sort of thing."

"Is it good…" Olivia began. "Living here?"

"It's not too bad," Leo said. "They don't let the rest of us go out, but it's a nice place. Have they assigned you jobs yet?"

"Jobs?" Taylor asked.

"Come on, you can't believe we have a free ride," Leo said. "Everyone does something. You can cook, clean rooms, train to be a doctor, join the Rangers…lots of options. I'm stuck in the laundry room. I tried to join the Rangers, but they wouldn't take me because I'm blind in my right eye. They need fighters. Not a lot of people want to do it."

"I don't know what we're going to do," Mark said, looking at me.

"How did you get in again?" Leo asked. "They don't let anyone join up."

"Does it matter?" I asked.

Leo shrugged. "Not really, but I'm surprised they didn't kill you right away. Everyone's on edge. We lost a bunch of people last week. It was a big firefight. I heard Daniel killed at least six people." I scraped my bowl clean, unable to look at the others. "It's happening more often. Some trouble with another group. Something big is going down, but I just hear rumors…" Leo trailed off as he looked behind me. His face went white and he shoved a chunk of bread into his mouth.

"I'm glad to see you guys," my dad said. I twisted in my seat. He put a hand on my shoulder. "Get enough food? I can get you more if you want."

Mark looked ready to accept, but I said, "I'm good, thanks."

"Who's this?" my dad asked.

Leo petrified at his inclusion in the conversation.

"Leo," I said. "Laundry *expert*."

Leo ducked his head.

"How are you all with guns?" my dad asked, forgoing additional pleasantries.

"We can shoot," I said.

"Good…good…" my dad said. "Come with me, Murphy wants proof."

I plucked my orange off the table and stood up, wondering what this meant for us. The rest followed, but Leo didn't move. He fearfully watched us leave. My dad led us to the stairs, and we went down one floor, soon emerging into the parking garage. Fluorescent lights dimly lit the area.

A row of paper targets adorned a concrete wall. Bullet holes pocked the surface. Lines of duct tape on the ground marked off various distances. Fifteen, thirty, and fifty feet. Spent casings littered the ground and a rack of weapons stood to the side. Murphy and Aaron waited, arms crossed. We halted in front of them, and Murphy wasted no time getting into it.

"Daniel assures me we can trust you," Murphy said. "I fought him on it, but that's because I don't know you."

"You can trust us," I said. "I found what I came here for."

"Good," Murphy said, evaluating my face. "We'll let you stay, but you have to do your part. Don't give me a reason to go back on that."

"What do you want?" I asked.

"First, I want to know how well you can shoot. We need people who can handle a weapon," Murphy said, nodding to Aaron.

He selected an assault rifle from the rack and slapped in a clip. He extended it to me. I hefted the weapon, running a hand over the cool metal. My dad handed out ear and eye protection.

"Start at thirty feet," Murphy said.

I glanced at my dad. He gave a slight nod, skin tight around his eyes. Flipping off the safety, I approached the line and sighted on the target. The stock pressed uncomfortably against the gash on my chest as the outlined head floated to meet the crosshairs. The gun was heavy, but it didn't waver. Despite the obvious differences to the hunting rifles I'd been using, there was a familiarity to the way it felt in my hands.

I squeezed the trigger and a single shot thundered in the garage. Chips of concrete arced through the air.

My first shot was too high, but my next two tore through the head and shoulder of the target. Murphy directed me to stand at the fifty-foot mark, and I emptied shots until she told me to stop. I flipped the safety and handed the gun back to Aaron. I massaged my chest. Murphy silently looked down the range. I stood next to my dad.

"I knew you'd be good," he said. "You can't make it as far as you did on luck alone."

I pursed my lips.

Mark went next. He checked the clip before taking his stance, and his shots were faster and more accurate than mine. Strips of paper fluttered to the ground as he finished. Aaron changed the clip while my dad hung up new targets. Taylor stepped to the line, blasting the targets with precision. Olivia had the most trouble, but her stance was good and she didn't flinch away.

I watched Murphy as she silently took in the show, arms crossed, finger absentmindedly tapping her arm. Her eyes focused like a hawk, sharp and calculating. I could see the wheels turning inside her head. I wondered what she was looking for, what she was planning.

How did she become the one in charge? Where did my dad fit into this? Where did *we?* There was so much I didn't understand, but I didn't know if the truth would calm the pit of trepidation in my gut.

Murphy had us cycle through a few more times, then we switched to pistols. I had to stand at the closest distance, and I barely hit the target with half my shots. I grimaced, handing off the gun to Mark. We spent another twenty minutes practicing before Murphy had seen enough.

"You're going to need more practice—you two especially," Murphy indicated Olivia and me, "but you'll do."

I was slightly affronted, but she was right. I was sporadic at best with the pistol, and that was against unmoving targets. I doubted I would ever reach the level of Mark and Taylor, no matter how much practice I had. Handguns were not my choice. Rifles on the other hand…

"You can go," Murphy said. "I need to talk with Aaron and Daniel."

I chewed my lip and nodded, turning on a heel for the stairs. My dad watched us leave, still and brooding.

TWENTY-FIVE

FOR THE NEXT three days, we aimlessly wandered the hotel. Murphy hadn't assigned us any responsibilities yet, so we were mostly free to roam. Even though it was a big hotel, there wasn't much to see. Each floor was virtually the same, with uniform hallways, locked doors, and beige walls adorned in stock photos of wildflowers and crashing waves.

People usually milled about on the first floor, playing games at coffee tables or lounging on the couches. I saw Leo a few times during meals, but he avoided being drawn into another conversation. Mark spent some time in the workout room, but the best part of the hotel was the pool, which they'd decided to keep open.

Still, guards made sure no one wandered to the beach. They posted themselves along the paths to the water but didn't stop us from walking around close to the hotel.

A few hours a day, I laid in the sun and strained to hear the ocean. When it got too hot, I jumped in the pool and stayed under the surface as long as I could.

I relished those fleeting, weightless seconds, but no matter how long I stayed under the water, it was never enough. Nothing could dispel the knot in my stomach, or the unrelenting vice squeezing the air from my body.

When he wasn't out scavenging supplies, my dad let me patrol the hotel with him. After all we'd survived, I could hardly believe we were together again. Sometimes we'd get lost in conversation and I'd forget my mom and Jamison weren't going to join us for dinner. Despite everything I wanted to talk about, I had trouble finding the right words. More often than not, I lapsed into silence, forcing my dad to change the subject.

"I can't believe you used the basement for target practice," he said one afternoon. We stood in the middle of the road leading to the hotel. "Do you know how much we spent remodeling it?"

"We broke most of the dishes too," I added with a guilty smile.

My dad rubbed his head. "You two were never boring, I'll give you that."

"Never," I said, rocking back and forth on my toes. "What's it like being in charge?"

My dad glanced at the rifle in his hands. "It's better than following someone else. We get to decide how to move forward, what's best for the group. People respect us."

"Probably because your guards are the only ones with weapons."

My dad looked at me out of the corner of his eye. He scratched his beard. "Yeah, maybe…but we're the ones who keep them alive."

Rather than argue about his methods for establishing order, we fell silent again. I said goodbye and searched for Olivia so we could practice shooting in the parking garage. Only Aaron coached us, and he wouldn't answer why my dad wasn't allowed to do it.

"Probably so we don't steal the guns and escape," Olivia said when we were alone.

By the end of our third day at the hotel, I could confidently use the pistol from twenty feet out. Nothing worthy of praise, but Aaron encouraged our progress anyway.

"Cody, I want to see how far you can shoot with the rifle," Aaron said.

I accepted the challenge and stopped at approximately seventy-five feet.

"Keep going," Aaron said, walking with Olivia and me.

We halted around one hundred feet. Olivia raised an eyebrow at the distance. I apprehensively looked at the target with my naked eye. Even shooting off the roof of the mall wasn't this far. I raised the gun anyway. I fell into my stance, breathing slowly, sighting down the scope. I popped off a series of shots. Concrete blew apart under the paper. A few went wide or high, but they were close. I nailed the chest on the next shot.

"Go all the way back," Aaron said.

I stopped in front of the far wall of the parking garage. I couldn't guess the distance, but I doubted my ability to make this shot. Aaron rubbed his chin, eyes focused on the target. It took me a handful of shots to hit the outline three times. I lowered the gun in quiet surprise. Aaron clapped me on the back, awe on his face.

"Forget the pistol," he said. "This is what you're good at."

At that, we packed up for the day. I couldn't help but feel a small dose of pride. Olivia went back to the room, but I helped Aaron gather up the guns. Over these three days, he had lost his initial hostility. Oftentimes, he would give an easy smile with a subtle kindness behind his eyes. It reminded me that he was just another person caught up in the destruction.

"Do you have a family?" I asked as we headed for the stairs.

"I do—" he said, growing somber. "I did...my wife is here. We came out for our son's wedding, but we lost them at the beginning. I have one daughter in Seattle and one in San Diego. I don't know if they're still alive."

"I'm sorry," I said.

"There's nothing we could have done," he said, and that's all he offered.

Aaron led us through the hotel foyer and down a hallway. He unlocked the door to a conference room and we ducked inside. A full arsenal decorated the room. There were tables solely dedicated to pistols, rifles, shotguns, knives, and boxes of ammunition. I whistled at the display. Aaron returned the weapons to their places as I walked the room.

The door opened. Aaron and I turned as Murphy stalked inside.

"Good, you're back," she said. She addressed Aaron. "How's his progress?"

"He's a natural," Aaron said.

"And Olivia?" Murphy asked.

"She can shoot well enough to do the job," Aaron said.

Murphy nodded, facing me. "I want you and your friends to join the Rangers."

I balked at the offer. "Are you serious?"

"We need fighters, and you're good," she said.

"I keep hearing that, but I don't want to fight," I said. "None of us do. We'll help you with something else."

"You don't have a choice," Murphy said. "This is how you earn your keep."

"You can't force us to do this," I said.

"We'll see," Murphy said, lips a thin line. "Go tell your friends. I'll give you a day to think about it."

"What if we say no?" I asked.

All Murphy did was stare at me like she'd already fallen into the void. I took that as a sign to leave, unease building as I left the armory.

I FOUND THEM in the room.

Olivia gestured excitedly, Taylor and Mark sitting on the couch in the living room.

"…and then Cody made the shot across the entire parking garage," she said.

"It was a lucky shot," I interjected.

"No, you've got a gift," Mark said.

"That's one way to put it," I said, shuffling over to the couch. Taylor squeezed my arm as I sat down.

"Anyway, I saw Leo as I was coming back to the room," Olivia said.

"And?" Mark prodded.

"This is going to sound insane," Olivia said, "but he said there's a cure."

"*A cure?*" Taylor sputtered.

Olivia nodded. "At the Denver airport. He said it's a haven."

"You believe him?" I asked, rubbing my forehead. "How would he know that?"

"I don't know, I just thought I should tell you," Olivia said. "He heard it from someone who came from there."

Mark smirked. "I guarantee he made that up just so he could talk to you."

"Stop! He's nice," Olivia said.

"A nice lazy eye you mean," Mark said, earning a smack from Olivia.

I cycled through the obvious reasons why Leo's information was false. "First off, that's an *airport*, not a laboratory. Second, that's a hell of a distance to travel—"

"At least as far as we went," Mark said.

"—which would take time. You're saying this mystery person left a 'haven', which had a cure, just at the beginning of the Collapse? That doesn't make sense," I said.

"I'm just repeating what he told me," Olivia said.

There was a minute of silence.

"Do you think there *is* a cure?" Taylor asked.

I almost said a definitive *no*, but this entire situation wasn't right. It wasn't natural. The fact that the entire world had been overrun in a matter of hours was proof enough for me. Something bigger was going on, that much I was sure of. Maybe, somewhere, there was a way to end this.

The problem was we had more immediate problems to deal with.

"I have to tell you something," I said. When I was sure I had their attention, I dove into it. "Murphy said she wants us to join the Rangers."

"That's good, right?" Mark asked. "We won't be sitting around. We'll have a say in what we do."

"No…I said we didn't want to fight, but she told me we didn't have a choice," I said.

"So what? I'd rather be out there than stuck in the laundry room with Leo," Mark said.

"He has a point," Taylor said.

"It's the way she said it," I insisted. "She made a point of making sure we can fight, not just shoot. Murphy's planning something, and I think it has to do with the other group out there."

"What did your dad say?" Taylor asked.

"He wasn't there, and I haven't talked to him yet," I said. "I don't know what to do. What if she kicks us out if we refuse to help?"

"Or kills us," Olivia said quietly.

"Exactly," I said. "I can't imagine she'd let us go with what we know about this place. We could run into the other group and tell them everything."

"You're jumping to conclusions," Mark said.

I rubbed my hands together. "I still don't like it."

"Then we do what she wants," Mark said. "What other option do we have? Run away again?"

"I won't leave my dad," I said.

"We'll take him with us," Mark said.

"He won't leave, I told you that," I said.

"Are you hearing yourself?" Mark asked. "You bring up a problem and shoot down every solution. What do you want to do?"

"I don't know! I'm scared to make the wrong decision again," I said.

"It wasn't wrong to come here. We all knew the risks," Taylor said.

I rubbed my temples. "And Jamison died for it."

"We all chose to come here, and now we have to deal with that reality," Taylor said. "We can't leave, and we can't refuse Murphy's orders. That means we do what she says until something else comes along. It's that simple."

Mark and Olivia nodded. I laid my head back on the couch. I felt trapped, with no way to escape whatever was coming. Taylor was right, but that didn't make it easy to accept. I knew I had to let it go. Jamison was gone. My mom was gone. It was over, and dwelling wasn't going to help. Second-guessing everything we did before we did it would only drive me crazy.

"Well," I said, reserved, "I guess we fight."

TWENTY-SIX

KNOCKING BROUGHT ME out of sleep. Faint morning light with just a hint of gold streamed in the window. I rubbed my eyes. Taylor slept soundly at my side, hair sprawled over the pillow. I rolled over and placed my feet on the ground.

I opened the door to find my dad in the outside hallway, a cardboard box in his arms. I spotted the spines of my books inside and some of our other loose items. Four duffle bags slumped at his feet.

"I brought your stuff," he said. "It took a while to track down, but I think most of it's there."

"Thanks," I said.

I shoved everything inside the door and faced my dad. He scratched his chin.

"Murphy wants to know your decision," he said.

"About joining the Rangers?" I asked.

"Yes."

"We'll do it. It's not like she gave us a choice."

"Good…I know. It's best not to get on her bad side," he said. He gripped my arm in a comforting gesture. "It's a good place. You'll fit in here."

I grimaced. "I want you to know I won't kill anyone. That's not who I am."

"Things are different now, and there's not much you can do about it," he said. His eyes flickered with regret. He checked his watch and glanced down the hallway. "I have to go. We're sending out some patrols to try to find the other group."

"Why?"

"In case we need to act."

I opened my mouth, then closed it. We stood for a moment, not knowing what to say.

My dad squeezed my shoulder. "I should go."

"Wait, I was wondering…" I trailed off, unsure how to put this. "Do you have any condoms?"

My dad started, eyebrows raised. He rubbed his face, frozen between nervous laughter and uncertainty. "Wow, uh…yeah, I have some," he said, looking me over. "I'll find them when I get back."

I nodded. My dad chuckled and turned away again. I watched him stride down the hallway before closing the door to survey our stuff on the floor. I picked up the box and brought it over to the living room coffee table. After a few minutes of rearranging, the books went on a small shelf by the TV, and the brainteasers found a spot on the table.

I picked up *The Name of the Wind* and flipped through the pages.

"Who was that?" Taylor asked, yawning in the hallway.

"My dad. He dropped off our stuff," I said, setting the book down.

Taylor leaned against the wall. "Do we have an assignment yet?"

"No, but he knows we'll help," I said.

"Want some coffee?" Taylor asked.

I nodded, even though it always made me jittery. It was all we had in the room. Taylor busied herself with pouring the water and adding the grounds. I came up behind her and wrapped my arms around her waist. I rested my chin on her shoulder.

"I asked my dad for condoms. I think he took it well," I said.

"So…" Taylor said, facing me. The coffee pot gurgled. "Tonight?"

"Tonight," I said, kissing her. She returned it.

Taylor broke away, touched my cheek with a smile, and retrieved two mugs from the cabinet. We had to wait a few minutes before the coffee was ready, but we soon settled on the couch together, steam wafting under our noses.

I nestled my face close to hers. "This is nice."

"It would be more romantic if it weren't for corpses and the homicidal survivors," she said. "But yes, this is nice."

"At least we have a view," I said, gazing through the windows overlooking the bay.

"At least we have a view," she agreed.

I wanted to stay like this, but my mug was soon empty, and so was Taylor's. I filled them up again as Mark shuffled out of his room. I told him about the new developments, and he immediately started rummaging through the duffle bags. He lugged his and Olivia's back to their room.

I spent a few minutes unpacking my things. It wasn't much— just a handful of shirts and pants, and a small heap of extra socks and underwear.

We all headed to the lobby for breakfast and spent the afternoon at the pool, eventually ending up in the lounge near the hotel entrance. Olivia dumped a puzzle on the coffee table and we crowded around, flipping over the pieces. We'd been at it for the better part of an hour when a shout came from the hotel entrance.

I looked up, hand poised over the puzzle. Someone burst through the sliding doors, waving people out of the way. Murphy came running from the stairs, a radio in one hand. Two men stumbled through the entrance. Aaron hefted someone with one hand. His other arm was slack and covered with blood.

"Get the doctor!" he shouted.

The other man slipped from his grasp. I saw his face and my stomach flipped.

No...

My dad cried out as Aaron lifted him again. I sprinted over, skidding to a halt at his open side. At least three bullet holes marred his chest and gut, but it was hard to tell with so much blood. It trailed down the front of his pants, leaving red footprints in our wake.

Disbelief gripped my lungs and *squeezed*. I wrapped his arm around my shoulders, his feet dragging on the ground. Murphy walked at our side.

"What happened?" Murphy asked.

"Ambush," Aaron said. *"Someone get the doctor!"*

A man ran off.

"Dad, we're here. It'll be ok," I said.

He mumbled incoherently. I patted his cheek to try and wake him up. When he didn't respond, I pressed my left hand against his stomach to try and staunch the bleeding. It flowed over my fingers.

No, no, no...

"Where are the others?" Murphy asked.

"They're dead...or captured. I don't know. Jessie's group is still out there somewhere," Aaron said. "They told me to get Daniel out."

Murphy seethed. "This has to end."

I caught a glimpse of my friends' horror-struck faces, then we were heading down the first-floor hallway. A woman emerged from a room ahead, scrubs on, latex gloves painting her hands white. Her gaze zeroed in on my dad, assessing his wounds.

"Get him in here," she commanded.

Aaron and I heaved my dad through the door and onto a crude operating table. Just a table with a sheet over it. Murphy hovered in the background, arms crossed, jaw clenched.

"Keep pressure on the wounds," the doctor said, putting a finger to my dad's neck. "Pulse is weak…"

I pressed both hands against his stomach. Aaron did the same to his chest. My dad groaned. I didn't know if I was doing it wrong because blood kept pooling up between my fingers. His face was flushed grey. The doctor flashed a pair of surgical scissors.

"I need to remove his shirt," she said.

I fell back, hands dripping, forearms red. The doctor cut off my dad's shirt from neck to waist and swabbed his skin with gauze. Two jagged bullet holes marked his abdomen with another through his right pec. My dad wheezed.

"…collapsed lung…" the doctor said to herself.

I hardly heard her. I couldn't move. The doctor kept talking as she bent over my dad, trading out clamps, scalpels, and pincers. Her hands and scrubs were covered with blood. The room spun around me, but I was rooted to the floor. I didn't register a word being said. Everything was muffled and distant.

Someone else joined the doctor at the table. He pressed a finger to my dad's neck. He said something with light lips and began doing compressions. He paused, blew air into my dad's lungs with a pump, and did more compressions. He kept doing this. Over and over. The woman continued patching the bullet holes. Then there was an AED hooked up to my dad's chest. His body jerked. Another hand at his neck. He jolted again.

A minute later, the female doctor stopped her work. She stood up straight, both hands on the table. The man looked down at my dad. He wiped his nose with an arm, looked around the room, and flipped open a knife. It sank into my dad's temple.

The room was silent. Suffocating.

I felt their eyes on me. The woman's mouth moved. A hand touched my shoulder. Aaron looked at me with compassion and whispered an apology.

My feet moved an inch, then another. I found myself at the table, staring down at my dad. I couldn't process what this meant. I let my fingers brush his arm, maybe to see if he was really gone. He was warm. Blood still seeped from the hole in his chest. I couldn't help but look at the knife wound in his temple. His face had lost all color. A wax figure, now. A stranger.

I turned away.

Not again. Not him…

I couldn't do this again. I couldn't watch any more of my people die.

Numbness flooded my body. Air came in tiny gasps. It was all I could do to keep myself from slumping to the ground, catatonic.

I don't know how long I stood there. It could have been seconds or minutes, but the door burst open. Everyone but me jumped at the intrusion. I hardly tilted my head in the newcomer's direction. He looked thirty, with brown eyes and black hair. A pink scar ran down his chin.

"We got them," he panted. "Jessie's group is back. They found the ones who did this."

The man glanced at my dad, then at me. Murphy stepped forward. "That was quick. Where are they?"

"Interrogation room," the man said.

He led Murphy out of the room. Aaron followed, leaving me with the doctors and the body of my dad. I didn't know what to do. My bloody fingers trembled. My mind swirled, overcome with a pain that gnawed at me like acid. I shoved it down to keep myself from slipping into the darkness. I couldn't face it. Not now. A sick part of me burned for revenge. I held onto that. They were here—the ones who killed my dad.

I swayed, teetering on the brink of collapse and rage until the female doctor gently took my arm and directed me to the door.

TWENTY-SEVEN

My friends waited outside the room, mouths open and poised with a thousand questions. They took in the blood on my arms. On my chest. My expressionless face.

"What happened? Is he ok?" Taylor asked.

I couldn't find the words. I couldn't even shake my head. All I did was stare at the wall behind them. A fly landed on the surface. It crawled in a half circle and flew off again.

"Cody…" Taylor said quietly.

I had trouble focusing on her face. I blinked a few times and looked down at myself. "I need to wash my hands…"

"Come on," Taylor said. "We'll get you cleaned up."

She took my arm and we slowly walked to the stairs. I dumbly watched the people in the lobby. Most of them were back to talking. A few laughed, unfazed. I mentally cursed them with the energy I had left. One girl watched us pass. She looked away when I caught her gaze. I cursed her too.

I methodically plodded up the stairs, taking comfort in Taylor's grip. No one said a word, and I was thankful for that. They couldn't have said the right thing, anyway. Those words didn't exist.

I locked myself in the bathroom when we reached our room and spent long minutes running my hands under the warm water of the sink. Scrubbing away the blood with soap. Cleansing it from under my fingernails.

I couldn't bring myself to scream, but anger boiled inside. I couldn't stop the tears, but it wasn't a torrent like I expected. I kept my thoughts locked away, yet they pounded in the back of my mind, straining to break through.

I dried my hands, found a new shirt in my room, and returned to the living room. Mark and Olivia eyed me warily like one wrong move might shatter me like a vase. Maybe it would.

Taylor ushered me to the couch and placed a mug in my hand. I almost dropped it, but I squeezed my hands just in time. Scalding coffee washed over my skin. I winced and took a sip. Taylor made me eat a dinner roll she'd taken from downstairs the night before. I chewed mechanically.

I curled up on the couch, laying my head in Taylor's lap. She stroked my hair.

I must have fallen asleep because I jerked upright when someone pounded on the door. I rubbed my eyes.

"I don't have to get it," Mark said.

The pounding continued. "I know you're there," Aaron's muffled voice said. "Open the door."

Mark sighed and let Aaron in. "What do you want?" Mark asked.

"Murphy needs to see you," Aaron said, eyes settling on me. "All of you. I wouldn't ask if it wasn't important."

"What is it?" Mark persisted.

"You'll find out," Aaron said.

"It's the people you picked up…" I said, getting to my feet. "Isn't it?"

Aaron gave a grim nod. We followed him down the hall, and my heart rate picked up. I didn't know why Murphy wanted us there, but I was glad—focused. My head suddenly cleared, the fog replaced by a singular, burning rage. My teeth ground together. I clenched my hands, taking purposeful strides up the stairs. Taylor glanced at me and touched my arm. I hardly noticed.

Guards waited outside one of the master suites on the top floor. They let us pass without a word. My feet sank into thick carpet. Lounge chairs sat at the left of the room, and a minibar jutted from the wall. A rounded oak table took up the center of the room. Murphy and her council crowded around, maps and papers adorning the surface.

To the right, two women and three men knelt on their knees in a line. Guards pointed their weapons at the backs of their heads. Ropes bound the prisoners' hands behind their backs, and gags split their mouths. Blood, cuts, and bruises covered each of their faces. The man in the middle was the worst off. His eyes were purple and nearly swollen shut from his beating. Jagged knife wounds crisscrossed his forearms and chest.

The prisoners watched, eyes filled with terror.

I paused at the sight. It should have made me sick, but I didn't feel for them. Whatever was coming to them, they deserved it.

I caught myself.

Did I really mean that?

I didn't have a chance to ruminate. Murphy approached us, hands on her hips. Her shirt was speckled with blood.

"Do you know why you're here?" Murphy asked.

I didn't respond, eyes playing over the prisoners.

"It's because I believe in justice. An eye for an eye. A life for a life. It took some *convincing*, but they talked eventually. We have everything we need," Murphy said, absentmindedly running a finger over the handle of her knife. She stepped forward and pointed to the man in the center of the line. She met my eyes. "This man killed your father. He confessed."

I stiffened. The man looked up at Murphy, hardly able to see through his bruised face. He tried to speak, but the gag muffled his words. I flashed back to my dad stumbling into the hotel. Dying on the operating table. His blood seeping between my fingers as I tried in vain to hold him together.

I looked away.

"Kill him," Murphy said. "Get your revenge. Prove that you're one of us."

I faced her, taken aback, and then looked at the prisoner again. He vehemently shook his head at me, and I thought I saw tears in the corners of his eyes. No matter how much it hurt, this wasn't right. I didn't even know if Murphy was telling the truth.

"No…I can't…" I said.

"I'll give you three seconds to do it," Murphy said, "and if you don't, I'll kill you and your friends."

"*What?*" Taylor spat, stepping forward.

My heart lurched as Aaron leveled his weapon between her eyes. Taylor froze, hands up. Mark and Olivia looked ready to bolt; Mark for Aaron, and Olivia for the door.

"You can't make him do this," Taylor said. "It's not loyalty if you have a *goddamn* gun to your head!"

"I don't care about your loyalty. We need to act, and if threats keep you in line, so be it. Kill her if she says another word," Murphy said to Aaron. He spared a conflicted glance at me, but the barrel of his rifle didn't waver from its aim at Taylor. Murphy took the pistol from her belt, cocked it, and handed it to me, grip first. "Three seconds."

I trembled as I took the gun. My mind screamed for me to do something, to use the weapon on Murphy, but that would only kill me and my friends. I shut down my thoughts. I shut out the thudding in my ears and the dozens of people watching.

"Two."

The man on the ground choked on the gag. His eyes pleaded for mercy. I focused on the cool metal in my hands and leveled the pistol at his forehead. I focused on the anger and pain and grief, letting it come to the surface until I only felt the storm.

"One."

I pulled the trigger.

TWENTY-EIGHT

THE GUNSHOT WENT from a crack of thunder to a ringing in my ears, to nothing. The man's body slumped to the ground the same moment the gun slipped from my fingers. I couldn't tear my gaze away from the leaking hole in his forehead and the ever-expanding pool of blood soaking into the carpet. His eyes fixed straight ahead in silent judgment.

Something broke inside me. A painful *snap* in my chest, borne from guilt and horror as I realized who I was.

Murderer.

My body shook under the weight of what that meant. A cold and bitter numbness sank into my bones. My head swam as I looked around the room. The row of prisoners were statues, but their lips and eyes quivered.

Impassive, Murphy snapped her fingers and pointed at the dead man. Two of her guards hauled him away. Four other guards herded the remaining prisoners from the room. Aaron had lowered his gun by now. He rubbed his right arm. It was still bloody and untreated from his encounter with the group that killed my dad.

I avoided looking at my friends. I didn't want to see the revulsion on their faces. I didn't want them to see the shame on mine.

The image of the dead man kept replaying in my mind. Every time I closed my eyes, the bullet tore through his forehead. I had to remind myself I did it to save my friends, but that didn't make it right. He was unarmed. Tortured. Begging for his life. And I still pulled the trigger. It didn't matter how I tried to justify my actions, because this would haunt me for the rest of my life.

Murphy picked up her pistol and whispered in my ear, "You made the right choice."

"Fuck you—"

"Don't say that again." Murphy cut me off, drawing close. "I don't want to hurt anyone you care about," she said, squeezing my arm.

I fought the urge to launch myself at Murphy. My emotions faded as I let the numbness completely overtake me. I made no effort to fight it. I welcomed the way it burrowed into the depths of my being, bringing a sort of peace.

I watched, detached, as someone scrubbed the bloodstain with a rag. Nothing would clean it, not fully. He had to have known that, and he still worked at the ground.

Taylor tried to hug me, but I flinched away. She took my chin in hand and forced me to look at her, her soft face brimming with worry. "There's nothing you could have done," she said, eyes pleading for me to believe her.

I turned away. I didn't want to talk. I didn't want to think about it. Mark and Olivia's hands found my shoulders, but I remained motionless. They dropped their efforts to comfort me as guards filed back into the room.

Murphy looked over the small crowd. Her iron gaze quieted any hushed conversation in the corners of the room. She waited until all eyes were on her. Taylor shifted at my side. Murphy licked her lips and rocked on her heels like a bomb ready to explode.

"I need to make something clear to *everyone* in the room. *THIS HAS TO END!*" Murphy roared, eyes blazing. "We can't survive with these wolves snapping at our heels. I've tried for peace, and they still won't listen. We're done talking, and we're going to end this, *right now*. It's time we send a message to anyone who might stand in our way."

She paced in front of the bloodstain. "Anyone who refuses to fight will be shot. Anyone who refuses to do as I say will be shot. But follow me, and we *will* survive. I guarantee it."

No one cheered. No one so much as whispered to the person next to them. At that moment, everyone became a taught string, ready to snap at the slightest touch.

I shrank back, her words leaving me nauseous and hollow.

I couldn't do this. I couldn't be a part of what she was planning. The only thing I wanted was to get out of this room. To get away from this place.

I started inching towards the exit, but I felt a hand on my shoulder. Aaron steered me away, leaning close. "Don't try it. If she sees you trying to leave…" He shrugged. "There's not much I could do for you."

"I—"

"Keep your head down, follow orders, and you'll get out of this alive," Aaron said. He nervously looked around the room to make sure no one else was listening. "I don't like it either, but we do what we do to survive."

"She shouldn't be in charge," I said.

Aaron didn't respond. He gave me a final pat on the back and made his way to the war table. Murphy and her council discussed strategy while the rest of us—maybe twenty-five in all—hovered around them, watching in anxious silence. They pointed at the maps. Drew routes to the enemy. Plotted the best way to catch them by surprise.

Taylor cast glances at me every few minutes, and she kept touching my arm as if to let me know she was still there.

The battle plans continued to take shape over the next hour. It made me sick to think about what we were going to do. Lots of people would die, some at my own hand. That knowledge only added to my guilt—a massive stone weighing against my chest.

There was nothing we could do to avoid the battle. No way to escape without being shot by Murphy. It was fight and hope to survive, or die right now. No middle ground. No room for error. And by the end of the day, one side would be in ruins.

Possibly both.

I should have felt more than numb guilt. I should have been terrified for my life and what I was about to do. But I knew I didn't deserve to survive this. Maybe none of us did.

Then I looked at Taylor, and an electric jolt went through my body. She bounced on her toes, chewing her lip. She scanned the room. The guards. Their weapons. She observed Murphy through a crumbling mask. Mark was still, but the muscles in his arms tightened as he clenched his fists over and over. Olivia seemed on the verge of panic. She kept glancing at the door.

It hit me then: I would do anything to protect them. I would kill or die, because they were the last people I had left in the world. And so, the terror that began to rise inside my chest was for them. But no matter what I did, I couldn't guarantee their survival.

That was the worst feeling of all.

"…the first wave will take two cars," Murphy said, bringing me back to the present. Murphy rattled off six names, including Mark and myself. "You will take the prisoners and demand a meeting with their leader. Convince them we want peace and we're willing to trade their people for it. When they let their guard down, that's when you strike."

Murphy looked around the table. I shifted my feet, trepidation growing. I wasn't the only one who didn't like it. Uncomfortable nods accompanied her orders.

"And wave two?" Aaron asked.

"The rest of us will follow thirty minutes behind. That should give you enough time to complete the mission. If not, we'll attack, and the chaos will catch them off guard."

"How many people do they have?" Aaron asked.

"Around forty fighters. We're outnumbered, but we have the element of surprise," Murphy said. She placed both hands on the table. "I know you have questions about why we're doing this, but this is about securing our survival. No one is safe until we act. They already took everything from me, and I'm trying to make sure that doesn't happen to the rest of you. I didn't ask for this war, but they're the ones who started it. It's up to us to end it before we lose any more of our people."

"It's us or them," Aaron said, turning in a circle. "Think about the people we will save. Think about your families and their futures. *That's* who we're fighting for."

Grunts of agreement went up around the room. The guards exchanged meaningful looks from behind determined masks. A few of them took this moment to check the ammunition of their guns.

I backed away, overwhelmed by the muddiness in my head. Errant thoughts skittered around my brain. Just noise. Static. I rubbed my temples. I wanted to lie down but I wouldn't have been able to stay still if I got the chance. I tugged at my shirt. I was starting to sweat through it.

For a second, I was back in the school cafeteria, taking in the first minutes of the end of the world. Trapped and in shock. Only this time, dozens of armed men and women surrounded every exit, ready to kill us if we gave them a reason. And now, those people were forcing us to fight in their war.

I paced a strip of the carpet, the walls and people blurring into the background. I gasped for air, clutching my chest. Everything spun.

Taylor caught my arm. "What's wrong?"

I shook my hands at my side. I couldn't focus on a single point in the room. "I can't...I can't do this...they're going to get us all killed. I just..." I trailed off as I began pacing again. "It's too much...my parents...and Jamison...him..." I gestured to the blood-stain. "...I can't do this...I can't do this..."

"Cody, look at me," Taylor said. She cupped my cheeks with her hands. "We'll get through this. Take a deep breath, good. We'll make it."

I paused long enough to take in her half-hearted smile and the heavy flicker in her eyes. She didn't believe it. We all knew this was the end. I shook my head as the noise came back. My eyes kept drifting to the bloodstained carpet.

I bounced on my toes, shook my hands, and tried squeezing my eyes shut, but the panic had burrowed into my being. The void tugged, drawing me nearer to the inescapable darkness.

I couldn't stop it. I couldn't shut it out this time. It was like a storm cloud building on the edges of my mind, creeping ever closer.

"Let's go," Aaron said.

I looked up. Half the guards had already left the room and were stoically marching down the hall. Aaron didn't offer a word as he passed, but our eyes met for a moment. They were hollow, with dark circles around them. Sad and tired and afraid.

I wanted to pull him aside and say we didn't have to go through with this. I wanted to plead with him and say we could find a different solution. But I couldn't form the words and he was gone before I could stop him.

Taylor pulled me into line to follow Mark and Olivia. My feet moved, but I wasn't sure how. It was like I'd lost control of my body. My thoughts weren't my own. And somehow, in that moment, I retreated to a place where I didn't have to think. A place where everything was quiet and still.

As we walked, I couldn't help but think of animals being led to slaughter. Only, we were the ones doing the killing. I don't know if I would have preferred to feel like a soldier on his way to battle. Because soldiers had a cause. Soldiers felt pride. Honor. There was nothing honorable about this fight.

Few people spoke, and if they did, it was in hushed tones. We plodded down the hallway, footsteps echoing in the stairwell. Taylor squeezed my hand. I couldn't focus on any one thing, so I drifted with the crowd until I found someone handing me an AR.

Battle preparations echoed through the armory—the click of magazines being loaded and slides pulled back to check the chamber. The jingling of bullets. Someone made a joke, but the tension simmered like a pot ready to boil over.

I loaded my rifle, slung the strap over my shoulder, and tucked three more clips into my ammo belt. I took one of the remaining pistols and two extra magazines. I patted myself down once more. Just like that, I was ready. My hands rested on the stock of my gun as

I took in the room.

Aaron was one of a handful who wore bulletproof vests. Two grenades hung from his chest and his wounded arm was tightly wrapped with a strip of cloth. I didn't see Murphy, which made me wonder if she was planning on joining the fight.

I faced my friends. Mark pursed his lips, eyes drifting from person to person. Olivia eyed the rifle in her grip, and Taylor shifted from foot to foot.

"We'll be ok," Mark said.

"Nothing to worry about…" Olivia whispered.

I couldn't bring myself to agree with them. I couldn't bring myself to hope. Taylor's arm rested on mine as we stood around. I lost track of time. We left the armory and made our way in small groups to the parking garage. For all the urgency, we weren't moving fast. It was like getting a shot of adrenaline and being forced to sit still.

Guards ran from car to car, gathering supplies, shouting at each other, or occasionally standing idly by as everyone else made preparations. Loaded down with weapons, Murphy directed operations from the center of the garage. Her gaze halted when she saw me. I half expected her to revel in our inability to escape, but all she did was hold my gaze for a second before she continued shouting orders. Aaron posted up at her flank, scouring the garage.

For what seemed like twenty minutes without discernible progress, small groups formed to discuss strategy. Three guards under a flickering light. A driver, leaning out the open window of a Suburban.

I couldn't imagine what else had to be prepared. I was in a daze. Ready, yet embracing the extra time. It almost made me feel like we would never follow through with the raid. As long as we never piled into the cars, it was still theoretical, an idea we'd never realize. At some point, Aaron disappeared to retrieve the remaining prisoners. Still bound and gagged, they were split into two SUVs.

I observed the stairwell at the edge of the garage. Could I slip out the back without them noticing?

Mark snapped his fingers to gain my attention. "Time to go."

I nodded. Taylor gave me a long kiss, but I felt only a flicker of warmth. I searched her eyes for something that might break me out of this trance.

"Stay safe," she said.

"You too," I returned.

It was like an eternity passed before my fingertips. I saw a whole life ahead of us. Every possibility for joy and fulfillment and family. And then it was gone as Taylor drifted away.

Mark's gaze followed Olivia, his lips pursed. He gave me a silent look and I saw all his fear and pain and guilt over words unsaid and things unrealized.

We moved toward Aaron's position together. My steps were heavy, slow. My body was unwilling to recognize the importance of what was about to happen. The bustling of the garage faded into the background as I focused on Aaron and the others surrounding him. There were two women, maybe sisters. They looked to be in their late twenties, both with sharp chins. Aaron introduced them as Ali and Cameron. Ali had red hair pulled back in a braid and Cameron's was short and blonde.

The last person was a man, Patrick, and I recognized him because of the scar on his chin. Without warning, I was spiraling back to the room where my dad bled out on the table; to Patrick bursting in to report they'd captured the enemy.

I gripped the stock of my rifle with white knuckles.

As Aaron split us into two groups, the others sized me up the same way I did them. Calculating, wondering if we could trust each other.

"…do *not* escalate until we're face to face with their leaders. The whole plan hinges on our ability to follow through. Everyone here is counting on you. Your families, your kids…this is for them," Aaron said. "Any questions?"

I didn't feel the need to respond, but the others shook their heads. Mark patted my shoulder before following Patrick and Cameron to their car. I watched him leave, then did a quick survey of the parking garage. Taylor caught my eye. I wondered if this was the last time we would see each other.

A moment later, I was strapped into the passenger seat of one of the Suburbans, my AR and Aaron's nestled between my legs. The extra magazines dug into my back. I tried shifting in my seat, but nothing could have made me comfortable. Nothing could have dissolved the knot in my chest as Aaron put the car in gear.

I looked behind me and caught a glimpse of the two gagged and blindfolded prisoners, their arms awkwardly tied behind their backs. Ali sat in the last row, her gun at the ready. She didn't frown or grimace. All I got was a look of resignation, her lips forming a pale, thin line. I turned around as we emerged into blazing sunlight.

Toward the coming storm.

TWENTY-NINE

THE HOTEL RECEDED behind us. Shadows flickered over the windshield as palm trees blurred at the side of the road. We were on the main road in minutes. Abandoned storefronts beckoned with broken windows and dirty walls. Corpses watched us pass, their tattered clothing flapping in the breeze.

Aaron took it slow, careful to avoid abandoned cars and the occasional body sprawled on the concrete. I leaned back to study the roof. I had to fold my hands together to keep them from shaking. The rifles clinked against each other between my knees.

No one spoke. Hardly anyone made a sound. The silence pressed against me like an invisible hand. My vision blurred. I rubbed my eyes, feeling the first signs of a headache.

Aaron made a left and the momentum pressed me against the door. Every second seemed to drag. Every minute flew by too quickly. This ride was somehow the longest and shortest of my life.

I tried to imagine what awaited us.

Scared and desperate people, certainly. Enemy soldiers. A vengeful leader?

I wondered if they would open fire the minute we pulled up. If they would listen to our offer or refuse to meet. If they had more people than anticipated.

In minutes, it could all be over.

I wasn't ready for that, despite all that had happened and all I'd done. I wasn't ready for it to end like this. I had to try and see this through. Pain couldn't overcome my instinct to stay alive. Guilt wouldn't stop me from killing to protect my friends.

Maybe, in the end, this would all be worth it.

But maybe I wouldn't get that far.

Aaron turned right down a street lined with arching palm trees and untrimmed grass. Stone monuments jutted from each corner of the road, with cursive metal letters reading *Sherwin Country Club*. My heart pounded, and my body tingled with anticipation.

Weeds filled the gardens in front of the signs, choking out the remaining flowers. Single-story houses spread out in all directions. The clubhouse rose to meet us as we rounded another bend. It was two stories tall with glittering windows in front. A massive round-about appeared thirty feet ahead with a defunct fountain in the center. A few trucks were parked in front of the building.

We'd barely made it another twenty feet before a half dozen enemy soldiers poured from the clubhouse entrance. Two more ran up from the right. A few hung back behind trees. Our car inched forward as the first soldiers shouted at us to halt, guns raised to their shoulders.

Aaron parked. He blew out a breath, scanning the enemy's defenses. The guards continued to shout at us, voices muffled by the car windows. The other Suburban pulled to a halt on our left.

"Show time," Aaron said, almost too quiet to hear. The hesitancy in his demeanor evaporated as he opened his door, boots thudding on the concrete.

"Don't move!" one of the enemy commanded. His black T-shirt showed tattoos crisscrossing his arms. "Keep your hands up."

Aaron ignored the man. I handed him his rifle and he took three bold strides in front of our position. He didn't raise his gun but scoured the enemy with condescension, completely unfazed by their display of force. The grenades on his vest swayed. He stood casually, legs spread wide.

"Don't take another—"

"We're here to make a deal," Aaron bellowed, making sure even the furthest guards could hear. A woman spoke into her radio. Someone else disappeared into the building. "Believe me, you're going to want to listen."

The rest of us poured out of the cars at that. Ali directed the prisoners to stand behind Aaron. She'd removed their blindfolds but left their other bonds intact. Mark formed up on my side.

"This isn't going to work," he whispered.

I didn't answer him. I hefted my gun, choking down the fear in my throat. My palms were slick against the metal of the gun. I regretted my long-sleeved shirt. Sweat coated my back. I squinted against the sunlight as I scanned the line of the enemy. The back of my neck itched under the aim of more than a dozen weapons. They'd quietly bolstered their forces in the few moments we'd been here.

A glint caught my eye, like a mirror in the muggy, shimmering heat. It came from the roof. I barely made out a figure at the crest.

Sniper.

A few of the enemy exchanged hushed words. They looked us over warily, hostility creasing their faces. Taut bodies waiting for the signal to rip us to shreds.

"You have our people," the man with tattoos said, indicating the prisoners.

"We're here to discuss a truce," Aaron said. "We brought them along as a gesture of good faith."

"Let them go and we'll talk."

"Not with you, Judah," Aaron said. "You are Judah, right? They told me about all of you, and I'm only talking to Dalton. In person."

"That's not going to happen. I speak for him."

"He'll want to hear what we have to say."

"Take off their gags."

"We're just wasting time," Aaron said with a sigh. He nodded to Ali anyway, who began removing the gags from the prisoners. She left their hands tied behind their backs.

"Bitch," one of the men said.

"Quiet," Ali growled, poking the man in the stomach with the barrel of her weapon.

"We're not letting them go until we get a meeting with Dalton," Aaron said.

"You don't have the power to negotiate right now," Judah returned.

"I beg to differ."

"You shouldn't have come here."

"Maybe, but we're not the threat you should be worrying about," Aaron said. Judah's brow drew together. "Sure, we could throw everyone we have at destroying your group. We have the information to do it. The rest of our people are out there waiting, but we wanted to give you the chance to negotiate before that happens. We don't need a war, nor do we want one. We've all lost enough as it is."

Aaron checked his watch. "But if you don't listen to our demands, your entire community will be razed to the ground in less than twenty-seven minutes. It's your choice."

"You don't have enough people for that," Judah said.

"Are you sure? Of course, you could try to kill us, but if I don't check in with my people," Aaron raised his arms uncertainly, "that's it for your group. Are you willing to take that risk?"

"Maybe we should listen to him," the woman next to Judah said.

"Either way, you don't have much time," Aaron said.

Judah clenched his jaw. His eyes flickered across our line. He checked his watch. "Tell Dalton," he said.

The woman nodded and stepped away, taking the radio from her belt. "Let our people go and you'll get your meeting."

"Do it," Aaron said.

I gripped my gun. No one spoke as Ali and Patrick pushed the prisoners forward. They retreated quickly behind their comrades. Other guards stepped forward to untie their hands. Tension thickened the air. Now, nothing was stopping them from gunning us down except for their fear of what *might* happen if they did. Mark subtly drew closer to the Suburban.

"This is a mistake," one of the former prisoners said to Judah. He had dried blood on his forehead from an open gash. He pointed directly at me, and my stomach dropped when he said, "That one killed Greyson."

Judah's expression darkened. I tensed, ready to spring away if he raised his gun at me.

"He's ready," the woman said, returning to Judah's side.

"Twenty-four minutes," Aaron announced. "Better get moving."

Judah cursed. He looked down his line of guards, then at us. He pursed his lips.

"We don't have time to deal with that right now. Let's go," Judah said. The others behind him looked ready to protest. The man with the gash on his forehead opened his mouth, but Judah cut him off.

"Save it."

"Patrick, Cameron, stay with the cars. Don't do anything stupid," Aaron said.

Patrick's expression turned grim, and Cameron nodded stoically. In their eyes, I could read their silent wish of good luck and the acceptance of their own situation. They were on the enemy's doorstep, outnumbered and waiting for the signal to attack.

I didn't envy their position.

"Leave your guns," Judah said.

Aaron laughed, "Not a chance."

"You're not getting in otherwise."

"Then the offer's off the table."

"You'll be safe."

"I don't think so. We need to be able to protect ourselves, and assurances don't do that." Aaron pointed at the former prisoners. "We brought your people back. Isn't that enough to convince you we're serious?"

"Not all of them," Judah said.

"Bygones!" Aaron said. "You've killed some of ours, and we've killed in return, but if we keep this up no one will be left."

"I still can't do it," Judah said, shaking his head. "You'll get your guns back when we make a deal."

"No," Aaron said.

"Then you're not getting the meeting," Judah said.

My gaze flicked between Aaron and Judah. They stared each other down. Aaron's hands clenched his rifle, his shoulders tense. Judah shifted his weight from foot to foot and checked his watch. Mark glanced at me out of the corner of his eye.

The ten second silence felt like an eternity.

"Fine," Aaron said.

I felt the air hitch in my lungs. Aaron turned around, eyes brimming with uncertainty. He gave us a look that told us to stay calm, but trepidation only grew in my chest. Visions of our plan falling apart bounced around my head. It wasn't going to work. Murphy was going to attack, and we were going to be in the heart of their compound, defenseless and easy targets.

"Dump it in the cars," Aaron said. "We don't have time to waste if we want to make this deal happen."

I frowned. Was he suggesting we actually try to form a peace treaty? The possibility gave a glimmer of hope to the situation. He was right. We didn't have much time.

I set to work removing my weapons. I laid the rifle in the front seat. Placed the pistol in the glovebox. Removed the ammo belt. Without it all, I felt completely exposed. The only thing that remained was my knife. My skin crawled at the thought of Judah's guards cutting us down the moment we got rid of our guns.

Aaron stepped forward again. He still wore the bulletproof vest, the grenades, and the knife on his belt. Judah let it go, and he began the march toward the clubhouse. Patrick and Cameron watched us leave in silence, covered by six of Judah's people.

Eighteen minutes.

We marched past the fountain. Guards patrolled the outskirts of the facility, making a clear effort to protect the main building. Hedges lined the perimeter, and a parking lot sprawled on the right.

I glanced again at the sniper above before we passed under the edge of the roof.

Cool air washed over me the moment we passed through the double doors. I peeled my shirt away from my body as I examined the interior. Waist-high windows lined the walls. Easy chairs and coffee tables adorned the corners of rooms. An elderly couple looked up from their game of checkers, worry creasing their weathered faces.

The longer we walked, the more residents we passed. All were older and shrank back from our presence. No one stopped to question us or ask what we were doing. Clearly, Judah's people were in charge, but I knew it was more than that. They were protection. They were the force that would stop enemies from attacking.

The pit in my stomach grew as I thought over what we were about to do to their group. Judah gave reassuring nods to the people we passed, and his guards told the residents to lock themselves in their rooms until further notice.

Judah led us to a room at the base of a wide set of stairs. Patterned carpet covered the steps, and ornate gold decorations filled the corners of the walls and ceiling. We took a right at the top of the stairs and passed hallways on each side. Directly ahead, two guards stood in front of a set of double doors.

We halted.

"They're here to talk to Dalton about a truce," Judah said.

The guards nodded, opened the doors, and stepped aside. We emerged into what might have once been a conference room. It had raised ceilings and cream walls. Oil paintings and leather furniture. A rectangular wooden table took up the left portion of the room. Chairs sprouted around the table. Beyond it all was a sliding glass door leading to a large balcony. I thought I made out the beginnings of a driving range behind. Sunlight poured through the windows to pool on the ground.

The doors clicked shut.

Inside the room were the four of my group, Judah, and his five additional guards. I squeezed my hands together and focused on the final man at the conference table. He looked to be in his fifties but had short, jet-black hair. He wore a sky-blue dress shirt with the sleeves rolled halfway up his forearms. He clasped his hands together.

"My name is Peter Dalton," he said. "I've been informed you're here to discuss a peace treaty."

"Yes—" Aaron began.

"Please, sit," Dalton said.

We did as directed. I sank into the leather chair. Mark sat on my right, Aaron and Ali on my left. Dalton settled on the opposite side of the table. Judah and two guards flanked him, and the other two stood behind us. All were prepared to raise their weapons at a moment's notice.

I checked my watch again. Less than fifteen minutes.

"We've all lost too many people," Aaron said, jumping into it. "We want to end this before it turns into a full-blown war."

"Is that why you kidnapped our people and tortured them?" Dalton asked. He said it casually, but there was a knife edge to his voice. His eyes glittered sharply. He looked at Aaron with a stony expression that seemed to say, *I could do the same to you, right now. I could kill you with a single nod.*

"We were responding to your people ambushing us," Aaron said calmly.

"Which was because you massacred a group weeks ago," Dalton spat. "It's a cycle, always because of something else."

"We'll be here all day if we're going to list everything we did wrong," Aaron said, real pain in his voice. "All we want is to move forward without additional conflict."

"Why did you bring so many people to discuss peace when you're the only one talking?" Dalton asked, looking us over. "Does he speak for all of you? Where's Murphy? Why isn't she here?" Dalton raised his hands in question. "If you really want a ceasefire, shouldn't your leader be here? Why is she holding back?"

Aaron continued to tap the table. His eyes went from Dalton and the guards to the rest of our group. He shifted in his seat and leaned forward on his elbows. "She sent us to kill you. If we wiped out the leaders, it would be easier to eliminate the rest of your group in the ensuing chaos."

I froze at the confession, my heart rate skyrocketing. Dalton's vague amusement slipped from his face, and Mark and Ali looked at Aaron in horror. Judah pointed his gun at Aaron, who kept perfectly still, hands visible on the table.

"What Murphy doesn't know," Aaron said slowly, "is that we have no intention of following her orders. We want this to end. And if we can reach a deal, we can convince Murphy to call off the attack."

Dalton's chair squeaked as he leaned back. "How much time do we have?"

"Twelve minutes," Aaron said.

"How do you know she'll listen to you?"

"I'll convince her."

Dalton stood up and began pacing the length of the table. He rubbed his forehead, paused, and placed both hands on the back of his chair.

"We don't have enough time to determine the details of a treaty," Dalton said.

"I know," Aaron said.

Dalton put his hands in his pockets and faced the windows overlooking the driving range. "I don't want to see anyone else get hurt."

"No one does," Aaron said.

"You could join us," Dalton said.

Aaron hesitated before responding. "We want to be on our

own."

Dalton pursed his lips. He rubbed his forehead and leaned close to one of the guards. I couldn't hear what he said, but the woman nodded and left the room.

"What do you want?" Dalton asked.

"Stay out of our territory, and we'll stay out of yours," Aaron said.

"It would be easier if we banded together. We could share supplies. Expand our reach," Dalton said.

"I don't think Murphy will agree to that," Aaron said.

"Why not? Ask her and see," Dalton said.

Aaron opened and closed his mouth. He looked down our line, apprehension etched on his face. Lips pursed, he removed the radio from his belt and took a few strides away from the table.

The guards adjusted the grips on their weapons. Aaron cast a last glance at us before raising the radio to his mouth and pressing the button to open the line. I closed my eyes and gripped the arms of my chair, praying that Murphy would listen.

"Murphy, this is Aaron," he said.

A crackle of static filled the room, eleven lives hanging on her reply. I held my breath. A handful of seconds later, Murphy's disembodied voice came over the radio. *"Is it done?"*

"We're working on a deal," Aaron said. "Pull back your forces."

Four seconds passed. Five.

"Is it done?" Murphy prodded.

"They want to discuss a truce," Aaron said, voice strained. "We have a chance at peace. Hold back while we figure out the terms."

There was a terrible moment of silence. No static from the radio. Aaron looked at the device in his hand. I glanced at the guards. At Dalton. Everyone had their eyes pinned on Aaron. He scanned the room before trying again.

"Don't attack. You don't have to do this," he said.

"I want you to think about Jamie."

"I am! This is for all of us!"

"Who's Jamie?" Mark whispered to me.

"His wife," I said.

More silence, and then Murphy's sinister voice filtered through the radio. *"No deal. Do what you came for, or you won't see her again."*

THRITY

"Murphy! Listen to me!" Aaron shouted into the radio. He got no response.

I found myself reaching for my knife but stopped before I touched it. What was I going to do against their guns?

Mark clenched his hands, and I knew he was thinking about Olivia and Taylor. If we couldn't stop the attack, they would be caught in the battle. We couldn't let that happen. We had to do something, or else we'd never make it out of this room.

I got up from the table, Mark and Ali following suit. The guards shifted their weapons to cover us but looked to Dalton for direction. No matter how much Aaron yelled into the radio, Murphy didn't pick up. Dalton stopped in front of Aaron.

"Looks like you've run out of time," Dalton said.

"We all have," Aaron returned quietly.

There was a long moment of silence. Dalton's guards inched closer, a woman flanking Mark and me. The guard's radios sprang to life, drawing their attention.

"We have enemy forces approaching!"

"They're here—"

"—coming from behind—"

The unmistakable pop of gunfire filled the space between shouts. Dalton twisted to face the nearest guard. "Tie them up—"

Aaron lunged forward and wrapped an arm around Dalton's throat. He gasped as Aaron cut off his air. Guards raised their weapons. Mark reacted instantly, throwing an elbow into the face of the woman behind him. She fell back. Mark yanked the shotgun from her grasp and slammed the stock into her temple. He blasted a hole in her chest and wheeled on the nearest guard before the first body hit the ground.

Blood puffed in the air as the second guard dropped. I threw myself to the ground as Judah opened up with his rifle above my head. The right side of my face flared in white-hot pain. My ears rang. Ali took two steps away from the table before Judah filled her back with bullets.

Mark pumped his shotgun as I scrambled in a daze for the rifle of the other dead guard. I came up and sprayed fire with no direct target. The windows to the balcony shattered into a million pieces of crystal. I sprinted to the other side of the room and dove behind a couch, bullets whizzing by my head and into the wall behind me. Tufts of padding flew into the air.

Mark backpedaled in my direction, blasting the air repeatedly with his shotgun. I had enough time to watch Aaron yank a grenade from his vest and toss it in the direction of the remaining three guards by the conference table. He didn't wait for it to hit the ground before he removed his knife and sank it into Dalton's back. Dalton screamed. Aaron stabbed him again. The grenade bounced under the table and the guards dove away.

The room exploded.

Shrapnel sliced the air. Smoke and fire filled the room. I peeked around the corner of the couch and saw Mark sprawled on the ground. He sluggishly picked himself up, blood streaming from a dozen cuts on his face and arms. A guard appeared in the smoke. I sighted on him before I could think, finger squeezing the trigger. The man fell.

There were still two guards out of sight. Mark limped to my position and slumped to the ground next to me. Aaron dropped Dalton in a heap just as the doors to the conference room burst open. I wheeled on the intruders as they entered. Bullets thudded into the wood, splintering the door. One of them fell backward out of sight and the other pitched forward through the doorway, a hole through the right side of his head. Blood streamed from the wound and soaked into the carpet.

Exposed and weaponless, Aaron yanked the second and final grenade from his vest as Judah stood and opened up on him. Aaron sank to the ground, a bullet through his neck. The grenade bounced at his feet. I ducked behind the couch again as it went off with a thunderous explosion. A painting crashed to the ground.

Mark's shotgun roared two more times from his position behind the couch. He fell back behind cover. "I'm out."

I sighted over the couch. Judah came into view. I squeezed the trigger, filling him and the wall with bullets. The last guard attempted to upend the remains of the conference table. Too easy. I cut him down just as my gun clicked.

I shakily got to my feet, chest heaving. My ears rang. Bright spots danced in my vision. My lungs burned from the gunpowder and smoke hanging heavy in the air. I touched my temple, fingers coming away slick with blood. My head throbbed.

"You're hit," Mark said.

"Just a graze," I said.

The adrenaline faded, leaving me weak and sick. My hands shook. I didn't have the strength to keep holding the rifle. It slipped from my fingers. I swayed on my feet. Mark placed a steadying hand on my shoulder. Blood trickled down his arm, leaving a print on my shirt.

"Maybe you should sit down," he said.

I shook my head, which sent the room tumbling around. "We have to get out of here, help the others."

Mark nodded, but for a minute all we did was stand amid the carnage. My gaze went from body to body. Ali, sprawled out with bullets in her back. The guards with shotgun blasts in their chests. Gore covered the carpet. My stomach turned at the scent.

I glanced at Aaron and Dalton's bodies and immediately regretted it. Aaron's legs were blown to pieces, and the rest of his body was a ragged mess. Charred in some places. Mushy in others. I only recognized Dalton because I knew where he fell. Not much of his upper half remained.

I turned away from the sight and threw up on the ground. Tears formed in my eyes as the full weight of what we'd done crashed into my chest. For this, I knew I could never be forgiven.

That was when I heard the first sounds of bodies transforming into corpses. A gurgling in the throat. Low growls. A clicking of teeth.

Mark and I exchanged a look. He hefted the shotgun and took slow strides to Aaron's corpse. He brought the butt of the gun down against its head with a sickening *thunk*. Mark looked at Dalton's body long enough to realize it wasn't coming back.

Ali's corpse came to its feet. Its grey eyes flickered in my direction. Mark gripped his shotgun by the barrel and swung. The corpse's neck snapped backward as the metal *cracked* against its skull, leaving a sizable dent in the forehead.

The other three corpses rose to their feet. I retrieved an abandoned AR and dropped them all before they'd taken more than a few strides in our direction. I silently skirted the bodies, gathering ammunition. I stuffed two extra magazines for the rifle in my back pockets and tucked a pistol into the front of my belt. Another pistol clip went in my front pocket. Mark did the same.

Glass crunched under my feet as I made my way to the balcony. The sun neared the horizon, a hazy ball of flame in the muggy air. Golden light spilled over the countryside. I guessed we had an hour before sunset.

Movement at the fringes of the driving range drew my attention. Scattered corpses closed on our position, drawn by the gunfire echoing from the front of the clubhouse. I turned around and saw a ladder propped against the lip of the roof.

"Cody, let's go," Mark said from inside.

"Hold up," I said. "We'll get a better view from up here."

"We want to get out, not go up," Mark said, coming over.

"It's a better vantage point. Better to protect Taylor and Olivia… if they're still out there," I said.

Mark looked at me for a long moment. He wiped a cut on his cheek with his forearm. He considered the ladder and followed the line of the roof. "Alright."

I slung the rifle over my shoulder. The ladder shook as I climbed. Mark steadied it and I reached the top, crawling on the burning shingles. Mark followed me up. I carefully picked my way across the slant. I nearly lost my balance twice as shingles disintegrated under my weight.

The sounds of battle grew louder as I neared the crest. I slowly approached the lookout position where I'd seen the sniper. He had a chair bolted to a small platform. His figure was slumped to one side, bolt action rifle in his lap. I skirted him with my gun raised and found a bullet hole through his forehead. Blood still seeped from the wound and coated his face and the front of his shirt.

I turned my attention to the battle below. Our forces hadn't made much progress in their assault. Four SUVs had charged the compound and were being used as cover for our forces. Bullets thudded into the metal. One of the cars was on fire. A dozen bodies from both sides were sprawled on the grass and concrete.

I laid my arms over the edge of the roof and sighted down my rifle, leaving the rest of my body to hang on the other side. The boiling shingles made it feel like I was being cooked alive. Sweat rolled down my forehead as I scanned the ranks.

Every second I didn't see them drove a wedge of fear deeper into my chest, but I finally spotted Taylor hunkering behind the fountain. Chips of stone blew into the air under enemy fire. Taylor sighted over the lip and loosed a storm of bullets. I glimpsed Olivia in her shadow.

"By the fountain," I said.

"I see them," Mark said to my right, sprawled on the roof like me.

I focused on the enemy again, searching out the ones closest to Taylor and Olivia. The back of a man's head slid between my crosshairs. He ducked away, red hair blurring at the edge of the scope. I found him again and breathed out. Squeeze. One shot. The rifle kicked and the man crumbled to the pavement.

I dropped my head, teeth clenched.

I was doing this for them.

Shoot. Don't think.

A woman made a mad dash across the lawn toward the cars. I followed her path, popping off a dozen shots before catching her in the leg. She pitched into the grass, rifle flying from her hands. I easily finished her off with a single shot. Her body rested only twenty feet from Taylor. She didn't notice.

I lined up the next shot, but my gun clicked. Empty. I ripped out the spent magazine and inserted another. The old one slid down the roof and clattered to the ground in front of an enemy soldier. Confused, he looked up and found my position. I pulled back the release and filled his chest with lead before he could bring his own weapon to bear.

Every distraction faded as I continued my hunt. The doubts left. The condemnation numbed with every shot. My rifle and I became one. It felt unlike anything I had ever experienced. It was thrilling. I was dangerous, invincible.

Death manifested.

Every shot connected. One here. Another behind a monument. Two women crouching out of sight behind a row of bushes. They all fell. Too many to keep track of, and I didn't want to count. I didn't want to know.

My sights unexpectedly floated over Murphy. She advanced with purpose, peppering unseen enemies. My crosshairs remained over her head and my finger itched to pull the trigger.

Do it, the darkness whispered. *Take the shot.*

I knew I could, and no one would be able to pin it on me. I hovered, trigger already half suppressed, as if daring me to finish the job. A split second later, the choice was gone. Murphy's head snapped back as she took a bullet.

I swallowed the lump in my throat.

The enemy's forces fell back under the onslaught. I shifted my sights to a new target. My rifle clicked after three rounds. I cursed as bullets slammed into the roof a few feet away. Probably from my own side. They had no way of knowing Mark and I were up here.

I ducked under the lip of the roof, the skin on my fingers ripping as I kept myself from sliding all the way down.

The fog in my head broke as I snapped back to myself. I rested on my back, face to the sky. I didn't fully understand what I'd done, but I knew what it meant.

I had become evil.

I had to remind myself it was for Taylor. All of the killing at my hand was for her. And maybe the act wasn't so bad as the way I'd done it, cowering behind cover and shooting people in the back of the head. Assassinating their leaders under the guise of peace talks.

It would have been stupid to rush the enemy at ground level, but that did nothing to erase my steadily growing shame. I busied myself with loading my remaining magazine before peering over the edge of the roof. Taylor and Olivia still crouched behind the fountain. Olivia pointed away from the main building. I followed her line of sight, heart lurching.

At least a hundred corpses poured from the retirement community. One of the bodies rose in the middle of the battlefield. I faced the driving range again. In our short time on the roof, their ranks had swelled until they were a sea of death, marching steadily forward.

I spun on the roof to take it in. They emerged from nothing until they were all I saw. I clutched my gun, realizing the real battle hadn't even begun.

"Time to go," I said.

Mark inched back from his position and surveyed our surroundings.

"Shit," he said, scrambling for the ladder. Mark didn't bother climbing down. He gripped the gutter and let himself swing over the balcony. He dropped with a thud. I followed suit, the gutter bending beneath my weight as I dangled in the air. My boots smacked the ground.

I scanned the shredded room again, noticing more blood on the walls and some on the ceiling. The walls and floors were blackened and peppered with shrapnel where the grenades went off. Adorning the carpet were red shells and sparkling gold casings.

We carefully approached the double doors. I clenched my teeth against the gore of Aaron and Dalton's bodies. The guards who had been stationed outside were charred, and only one of them moved. I was about to step through the doorway when three enemy guards came barreling our way. I ducked behind the wall to keep out of sight.

Mark readied his gun from the other side and whispered, "I'll take the two on the left."

I nodded. He counted down from three and we stepped into the doorframe. My target came into view. He was bald and heavyset, which was all I would ever know about him. Caught unprepared, they dropped like stones as we fired. I ignored the corpse at our feet as we entered the hallway. Mark emptied one round into each head as we reached the guards. I pulled away from the sight, feeling like another part of my soul had died.

"So they don't come back," Mark said.

"We should save our ammo," I said.

He gave a slight nod and we continued down the hallway. Mark peeked around the corner to the stairs and dashed forward. I followed him down. A few guards ran past but paid us no mind.

We sped through each room toward the entrance of the clubhouse. The closer we got, the louder the battle became. It was a medley of gunfire, explosions, and terrified screams. I jogged to a window at the far wall of the foyer. Plants obscured my view of what was beyond, but I could see the occasional figure run by. Smoke rose from some place I couldn't see. Things chased people.

Mayhem reigned.

Pounding feet twisted me around. Guards sprinted through the rooms. No one raised a weapon against us as they disappeared further into the building. A corpse wandered into the room, head cocked, fresh blood trickling down its chin. Mark blew its head off just as another two guards ran behind us.

The window at my back shattered. Glass showered my body as a corpse fell through, bullets flying in after. I took it out before it could get to its feet. Another figure jumped into the room from the garden. I trained my gun on him, but he made no move to stop me. He ran off to another section of the building.

I looked out the window again, all of hell beyond.

THIRTY-ONE

I REMAINED SUSPENDED by the chaos.

People screamed and ran in every direction, corpses at their heels. Bloody men and women shoved each other out of the way in their attempts to find safety.

Something *crashed* with a splintering of wood and glass. The noise broke me from my reverie. Mark motioned me forward. We jogged through another doorway and were nearly knocked off our feet by three people charging past. A corpse thrashed on my left. I kicked it in the chest, creating enough space for me to blast it in the head.

More people poured through the room, a corpse or two in their midst. I stopped when I saw the car. The SUV had come through the front door, taking out the frame and creating a jagged opening to the outside world. Its front bumper was shredded. I could hardly fight the stream of people coming through. The building swarmed with soldiers from both sides looking for shelter.

"We need to find the others," I said. "Mark!"

Where'd he go? I dashed to a wall and hopped on a chair to

survey the room. There! He was pushing forward through the mass of people to approach the car. I ran after him, shouldering through the crowd. I caught his arm. "Come on!"

"I don't see them," he said, searching the windows.

I turned my back to him and held up my rifle against the incoming flood. A man fell, a corpse at his neck. It ripped at the flesh, sending up a gush of blood. I pasted the corpse as the figure on the ground moaned. I shot him too, a mercy killing, then yanked Mark away from the window.

"This isn't helping! We'll find them," I said.

A wall of corpses fought their way into the building. I knew the chances of Taylor and Olivia making it out were slim, but we had to look. I wouldn't stop until we found them. We let the stream of people guide us further into the building.

I frantically tried to put myself in Taylor's shoes, wondering where they would have escaped. I continued through doorways and expansive rooms, weaving between panic-stricken people. We arrived in a pastel room with panoramic windows. Everything glowed with a sickening brightness. Corpses threw themselves against the windows, smearing gore on the glass.

There were two doorways. One behind us and one to the right. I headed for the second door as more of the dead poured into the room. I fired again and again into the flailing bodies, dropping them like meaty boulders. It wasn't enough. They kept coming, only a few tripping over the fallen. I continued to give ground.

My rifle clicked.

I gripped it by the barrel so I could swing it like a bat. The nearest corpse crumpled with a seeping hole in its forehead. Dropping the gun, I retrieved the pistol from my belt in time to fire a round into the eyes of a charging corpse. Shots *cracked* at my side where two strangers held off a second pack of the dead. Mark wrestled with one on the ground. His hands barely kept its teeth from snapping chunks out of his nose. I aimed a savage kick at the thing's head, stunning it long enough for Mark to get back to his feet and stomp it into oblivion.

The four of us fell back under the attack, returning the way we came to the front of the clubhouse. I replaced my mag as we escaped down a side corridor. Someone wrenched open a door and jumped through.

I emptied shots until the floor was covered in bodies and my pistol clicked. I launched through the pitch-black doorway and fell down a flight of stairs. Mark slammed the door shut behind us. I tumbled to the bottom, vision blurring when my head hit the floor.

Pain blossomed over every inch of my body. Stars danced before my eyes. I groaned, letting the pistol clatter to the ground. My side hurt when I breathed, but for once we weren't being chased. The door occasionally shook as corpses bumped into it on their search for easier prey.

I just laid on the ground in the darkness, hands on my chest. I could hardly believe we'd made it this far, and we still hadn't found any trace of Taylor or Olivia. I didn't want to dwell on the possibilities, but I couldn't get the images of them as corpses out of my head.

I knew we couldn't stay here forever. At some point, we were going to have to make a break for it. The longer we waited, the more corpses were going to show up and the worse our odds became.

I rolled over and propped myself against a wall. A light turned on, searing into my eyes. Two figures approached.

"Cody?"

I immediately recognized her voice. Taylor's weapon fell to her side, and I jumped to my feet so I could wrap her in a tight embrace.

Olivia threw herself into Mark's arms. Taylor pulled back and I scanned her face. Relief and elation filled my body.

"How did you get here?" I asked.

"We were fighting, then corpses started to show up. The closest cover Olivia and I could find was a car. The keys were still in the ignition. We weren't going to leave you, so I drove it through the building…" Taylor said, trailing off.

"That was you!" I laughed.

"She wouldn't leave you," Olivia said.

"What about me?" Mark asked Olivia.

Olivia kissed him. "I'm not going anywhere."

"How much ammo do you have?" Mark asked.

I patted myself down and inserted my last magazine. "Twelve shots."

The girls still had their rifles but hardly any ammo. Mark grimaced as he reloaded his rifle. It was a dismal display of force.

"We need to get out of here before it's too late," Mark said. "Is the car still working?"

"The one I crashed? I have the keys if it still runs," Taylor said.

"We'll make for that," Mark said.

"What about us?" a man asked. He and the other stranger stepped forward from deeper in the room.

I'd completely forgotten anyone else had followed us into the basement. Mark cocked his gun and looked them over. "We're leaving now. Join us if you want."

They nodded as we moved to the stairs. Mark stepped quietly and I followed his example. We listened at the top step for a minute. Occasional shadows slid under the doorframe, and sporadic gunfire sounded from distant portions of the building. Mark carefully turned the handle and peered through a crack in the doorway. He opened it all the way and disappeared. I went next, followed by the girls, then the strangers.

We went right and four corpses appeared in the hallway. They snarled, blood and flesh dangling from their mouths. I leveled my gun at the first one and blew its brains out. Mark cut the others down, clearing our way as corpses streamed behind us.

We ran for an open room, firing as we went. Bodies thudded. One of the men yelled as he was tackled from behind. Agonized screams filled my ears as a pack of corpses fell on the man.

Mark led us through a side room, and we sprinted across the dining area. We emerged into a room at the far left of the building, windows showing the front of the club. Corpses filtered through every doorway, forcing us into the corner of the room. Mark upended a table, giving us minimal cover. Gun clicking, he tossed it away and flashed his knife, dodging back and forth as he sunk it into the skulls of corpses.

I carefully picked each of my shots, but there were too many for it to make a difference. My gun clicked for the last time. Dread seized my chest as I hurled the gun and dazed a corpse. It didn't matter. We were trapped. There were no more side rooms to escape to. This was our last stand.

I took my knife and came close to the others behind the table. The dead thronged like swarming ants, but we kept them at bay with our tight formation. One came around the side and I kicked it in the chest. It fell and was crushed underneath the feet of a dozen others. I used this short second to glance around the room one more time. Windows at our back…

That was it.

"Shoot the windows!" I shouted.

Olivia twisted to spray the glass, but only one shot punched through. Spiderwebs spread from the hole. Mark threw his elbow into the center. It shattered, but jagged pieces stuck from the frame. He helped Olivia outside and jumped through himself. I fell back under the sudden push from the corpses. My hands and face were slick with their blood as we continued our dance.

Kick one. Dodge another. Stab through the eye or at the base of the skull. One after another.

Bodies heaped on the ground like an ever-expanding moat, slowing their advance. Everything blurred together. My arms burned with the effort, but I couldn't allow myself to give up.

I spared a glance at Taylor in time to see her take a step back and trip over a leg. Corpses crawled over the barrier and were on her the moment she hit the floor. She blew off the heads of the first two, but she was too slow to hold off the third.

It bit her shoulder. She screamed.

My veins turned to ice. I thought I heard my name, but everything went quiet. All I could see was the corpse pulling away from her arm, face red, blood bubbling from a patch of missing flesh.

I dashed to her side and stabbed the corpse, then hurled the body into a wall of the dead. I shoved Taylor toward the window and fought at her back as the others helped her climb outside. Another yell came from the second stranger. He vanished under a swarm of bodies, giving me just enough time to dive through the waist-high window.

My right leg caught a piece of glass. Hands grasped my ankles. Mark yanked me forward, deepening the gash. I weakly got to my feet, the pain not yet registering. Corpses strained through the window. I stepped out of reach and looked down, shocked at how much blood was pouring from my leg. It began to soak into my shoe, squishing in my sock.

Olivia ran in front of Taylor, who was clutching her wounded arm. Mark and I followed, dodging around corpses and strewn bodies. Rubble from explosions speckled the parking lot and grass. Smoke rose from an SUV. Another blazed in the distance. We rounded the front of the country club, seeing that the rest of the cars had been taken.

The clubhouse entrance came into view.

There it was! Our only escape was still wedged in the doorway.

I shouldered a corpse out of my way. Countless others swarmed our position. I plowed through the masses. Hands scrambled for purchase on my arms and chest.

Ahead, Olivia and Taylor reached the car. Mark jumped into the driver's seat. I broke through the last stretch of corpses and dove into the backseat.

The dead surrounded the vehicle in moments, throwing themselves against the doors and windows. The engine turned. Mark tried again, shouting at the car to start. I almost fainted with relief when it roared to life.

I fell forward as Mark reversed out of the building. Wood splintered and dozens of thuds came from the swarming corpses. Mark slammed on the gas and plowed through the sea of attackers. He swerved back and forth, jumping a curb and demolishing a row of bushes. The tires squealed when they returned to the road.

The country club faded and we left the ravenous corpses behind, black smoke rising into the perfectly blue sky.

THIRTY-TWO

I SANK INTO my seat, head swimming and the outside light seeming much too bright. I ignored my condition so I could check on Taylor. Her arm continued to bleed, and her face was pale from shock. I reached over the aisle and grabbed her hands.

Hollowness overtook me as I watched her grapple with the knowledge that her fight was over. Her shirt was ripped at the bite. Blood streamed down to her hands. I tore off my shirt and furiously ripped it into smaller pieces. Using one to plug the wound, I tied another around her arm to keep it in place. Taylor whimpered, her green eyes flickering as they pleaded for something I couldn't understand.

I clasped her cheeks, smearing blood over the pale skin. "Look at me. It's ok, you're going to be ok."

She nodded weakly.

"We'll figure this out. I'll make sure nothing happens to you," I said.

She didn't say a word but continued to look into my eyes. It was almost too much for me to bear. I held her against my chest. It was all I could think to do.

It suddenly felt like I was floating high above the car. I wondered if this was what it was like to die. I must have made a sound because Olivia shouted in surprise.

"Cody!"

Her voice was distant. I looked down at my leg, but I couldn't figure out why one was red and the other wasn't. I wanted to laugh, but I only felt myself sinking deeper into the abyss. Lights blended. I barely registered Olivia yelling something at Mark.

Someone patted my cheek. I wanted to keep sleeping. I was so tired.

"…stay with me."

I brushed away the hand, confused. Mark intently searched my face.

"What's going on?" I asked.

"You're an idiot, that's what," Mark said.

"Who's driving?" I rubbed my forehead. It felt like I was rocking in a boat.

"We pulled over. You've lost a lot of blood."

"We should get back on the road. They're going to come for us." I tried to sit up, but Mark's hand kept me pinned to the ground.

"We're safe," Mark said.

I realized now we weren't even in the car. When did that happen? Trees towered above us, and fresh air touched my skin. I looked at the others who were crowding around, and it all came flooding back. Taylor's weathered face furrowed as she watched me. This wasn't right. We should be trying to help *her*.

"Cody, I need you to look at me," Mark said. "You're hurt pretty bad, but I've slowed most of the bleeding. I want to stitch you up, but we don't have a first aid kit, so you're going to have to stick it out for a little. Think you can do that for me?"

I nodded.

"Good. Let's get you back in the car." He grunted as he lifted me like a child and helped guide me into the back seat. "Olivia, keep pressure on the wound. Say something if it starts bleeding again. Sit with him and make sure he doesn't move."

I kept my leg extended, silently taking in what had become of it. My jeans were ripped wide open from my upper thigh to my knee. Dark blood had completely soaked the fabric and covered my skin. My hands were coated in it as well, along with spotty portions of the back row of the car. Makeshift bandages sprouted from the cut, and strips of cloth were tied around to keep them in place. My leg pulsed with every heartbeat.

Olivia never took her eyes off me as she relaxed on her side of the row. Her gaze played over my body in grim amusement. "You know, you look *real* bad."

"Well, girls like scars, right?" I asked, mentally taking stock of my injuries. Broken nose. Stitches on the shoulder. The cuts on my pec and forearm from Murphy. The bullet graze at my temple. Now the leg. I chewed my lip, not sure if the cut on my thumb counted. "If you ask me, I think that makes me a badass."

"I think it means you're bad at avoiding injury," Olivia said.

"I'd do it again to keep—" *you safe* was the unfinished sentence. But I'd failed that too. Taylor wasn't going to get better. "Do you have any scars?" I asked to change the direction of the conversation.

"Besides emotional trauma?" Olivia asked.

I didn't know if I was allowed to laugh at that or not. Mark glanced at us in the mirror. The glimmer of humor was soon swallowed by the seething pool of darkness I felt inside. I was slipping into it, and I didn't know if I had the strength to fight it anymore.

I tried not to think about the blood on my hands; the blood of the people I killed. It had to have been a dozen. Fifteen. Maybe twenty. I didn't want to count, but I kept seeing images of bodies falling under my aim. They flashed in my mind like a reel. I squeezed my head, temple burning where the bullet had grazed me.

I watched Taylor in the front seat. Her head lolled to the side. "Is she ok?"

Mark reached across and felt her wrist. "She's good. She's strong."

Taylor mumbled something but didn't wake up.

"What do we do now?" I asked quietly.

Mark ran a hand through his hair. "What *can* we do?"

"What if we went to DIA? Olivia, you said there's a cure there," I said.

"I said there *might* be. It was just a rumor, from *Leo*."

"But we have to try, right? If there's a chance, we have to take it," I said.

Mark switched lanes to avoid an abandoned car. The sun was nearly gone by now. Mark turned on the headlights.

"There's no cure," Mark said after a long minute of silence. "Not yet. Maybe never."

"I don't care—"

"Cody," Mark said. "*Think.* Jamison hid his bite from us for what, two days? All I'm saying is we have no idea how much time we have. Jamison was still running around with his. Maybe that helped fight the infection, maybe it made it worse. Maybe the location of the bite has an effect, or the person. We *don't* know."

"I'm just—"

"*I'm* saying to look at the reality of the situation. We have no food. No supplies. We'll need gas, and believe it or not, this car isn't going to last all the way to Colorado. Next time it's turned off, it might never start again. *That's* what I want you to think about."

"So, we're giving up?" I clenched my teeth.

The thrum of the engine held the silence at bay.

"No, but we need to take it one step at a time. Car first. Maybe we can find a dealership. Then we can head that way and hope for the best."

I hated the truth of his words. Taylor had a very limited, but unknown, amount of time. With periodic breaks and *hopefully* no encounters with other survivors, we might be able to make it in four or five days. There was no way we could go any faster. And Mark was right, I knew it in my gut. There wasn't a cure. Not yet.

"No pressure," Taylor said. I didn't know how long she had been awake. "But this is literally life and death."

I pinched my eyes, screaming on the inside. How could she not be taking this seriously?

"I shouldn't have said that," Taylor said.

I couldn't look at her. I couldn't do this again. It wasn't fair. But what was fair? Nothing was right in this world anymore. All you could do was survive as long as possible.

And when things became too much to handle…what then?

We were driving for twenty minutes before Mark abruptly stopped in the middle of the highway. He turned around to head toward the previous exit. I was about to ask what he was doing when I saw the dealership. Rows of Cadillacs went by my window. Mark came to a halt in front of the main building. He took a deep breath before turning off the engine, then flipped around in his seat.

"Here's the plan. Olivia and I are going to go in there and find the keys to a new car. You two are going to stay put and not even think about helping." Mark nodded to himself and opened the glove box. "Thank God..." He pulled out a pistol and checked to see if it still had ammo.

I watched them jog to the front of the store where show cars gleamed through the panoramic windows. Mark tried the handle, but it didn't open. He looked around before leveling the pistol at the lock and blowing it to pieces. The shot reverberated in the twilight, and they lost no time entering the store. Taylor waited until they were out of sight before she climbed out of the front seat and into the row with me.

My smile was faint.

"What?" Taylor prodded.

"They're like our parents, making us stay here."

"Like you'd be able to help with your leg like that."

"I hate not being able to help. It's like I'm letting them down."

"By being hurt? You can't control that."

"I know, but I feel like I should be doing more than sitting around..."

"It's fine with me if they want to do all the work," Taylor said. She was silent for a few minutes, and it was like the air had been sucked from the car. "I know I'm going to die."

I looked everywhere but at her face, bouncing my good leg and fiddling with my hands. I couldn't comprehend that possibility.

"I'm sorry," she said. "It still feels like it's a bad dream, but every time I look at the bite, I'm reminded I won't make it...the same thing happened to Jamison. I don't know how he kept it a secret... I..."

Her whispering voice broke like a fraying string. I covered my face with a hand so she couldn't see the tears streaming down my cheeks. I gathered myself enough to look at her and see the tears forming in her eyes. I reached across the seat to take her hand. I squeezed it with what strength I had.

"You're going to be ok," I said.

"We both know that isn't true. Even if there was a way to make me better, there's not enough time."

"Why is this happening?" I asked, desperate for any answer I could hold onto.

"I don't know," she said. "I think, sometimes, things just happen."

We watched the entrance of the dealership. No corpses had appeared from the gunshot, and it was another ten minutes before Mark and Olivia pushed through the doors again. Mark jogged by, flashing a single key. Then they were off to find our new car. They returned soon enough, pulling up in a pure white Escalade.

Taylor helped me into the back row so I could keep my leg extended. The new car smell still hadn't left in the months of sitting around. I rubbed the perfect leather seats and tried not to smear too much blood on them.

"They used this one for test drives, so it has barely enough gas," Mark said.

I went back to putting pressure on my sliced leg as Mark pulled out of the dealership. We returned to the highway and settled into a quiet drive. I watched the world pass by, glancing over abandoned houses and storefronts.

I fell asleep at some point and woke to Mark and Olivia getting out of the car. Discarded vehicles clogged the road. It was completely dark by now.

"What's going on?" I asked, rubbing my eyes.

Taylor glanced back. "They're looking for supplies. You were out for a while. Are you feeling alright?"

I lifted a hand. It trembled. My entire body was weak from

excessive blood loss and no food. My stomach growled. "I'll be fine."

"Mark found a siphoning pump. It might help pick up our pace," Taylor said.

"That's good," I said.

I watched Mark and Olivia move from car to car. I could see them in the middle of a heated discussion. Olivia gestured wildly at something, and Mark just shook his head. They moved on to the next car.

"They're good together. I wouldn't have guessed," I said.

"Love is surprising," Taylor said quietly. "I'm glad they're happy."

We watched them, the silence between us expanding like a gulf.

Taylor's soft expression drew taut. "Do you think we would have worked?"

I looked at her for a long while. I took in her messy hair. Her small chin and soft eyes. The way they twinkled, even amid such terrible circumstances.

"I think we would have done great things together," I said, barely a whisper.

"I think so too," Taylor said. I swallowed the lump in my throat. She looked out the window. "They're coming back."

Through the windshield, I saw Mark hauling a cooler with a cardboard box stacked on top. Olivia carried a shopping bag and a heap of blankets in her arms. They opened the trunk and began piling in our new stock of supplies.

"Got clothes for you," Mark said, tossing me a pair of jeans and a shirt. "We found a first aid kit and a bit of food, too. We'll stop for the night soon."

Mark drove until we passed over a bridge, a stream below. He set to work gathering stones for a fire pit. I struggled to get out of the car, my head swimming. I nearly face-planted, but Olivia caught me with strong arms. She helped me limp down the embankment. We made slow progress in the dark as we avoided rocks and shrubs. Taylor followed close behind. Only once I sat next to the water did Olivia release her grip on me. She ran back to the car to retrieve the first aid kit, towels, and my clothes.

My left hand grazed the icy water. I dug into the sand and pulled out a handful of mud. It plopped in the water with small ripples. I washed off the dirt and splashed water on my face, enjoying its soothing chill. I gently scrubbed my temple. The blood on my hands came off easily, but some remained under my fingernails no matter how hard I tried to get it out.

My left leg was stiff as a board, which made removing my pants awkward and terribly painful. With trembling fingers, I began peeling away the bandages. Some of them had dried to my flesh, bringing tears to my eyes as I was forced to rip them free.

I took a minute to calm myself. I leaned my head back to observe the stars between tree branches. The half-moon provided barely enough light to see by.

Clenching my teeth, I soaked a towel and ran it over the gash with the gentlest of touches. Searing pain shot to my foot and up my side. The water itself sent shivers across my skin.

"Fuck me…" I gasped.

"Not looking like that, I won't," Taylor said.

I glared at her. She looked up with a smile. A genuine one, where I could make out the dimples in her cheeks. I wondered how she could be so lighthearted with everything going on. I shoved away the thought and let myself smile back. I would do it for her if no one else.

I went back to cleaning my leg. I gritted my teeth through the shooting pain as I washed the gash. At first, I could only brush the towel against my skin, inches from the cut. In a few minutes, I could run it over the exposed flesh. Soon, the blood was washed away, except for the stretch that continued to bubble up from the center of the cut. It burned all the while but was mostly a throbbing pain.

I wrung out the towel again and observed my leg. The gash was jagged and inflamed. It ran from the top of my thigh to four inches above my knee. It might have been a quarter of an inch deep. I was lucky it hadn't nicked an artery. It was going to make one hell of a scar.

Steeling myself one more time, I spread a generous amount of antiseptic over the entire cut. It burned like I'd laid hot coals over my leg but subsided to a dull ache after a few minutes. Now came the important task of sewing it back up. I wondered if there would be enough surgical thread in the first aid kit to do the job. If there was any at all.

I washed my hands in the stream again, nearly falling over this time. My body shuddered as my hand sank into the mud. Sudden vertigo twisted my head. I fell backward on the sand, right arm still in the water. Someone came to my side, pulling my head into their lap. It was Taylor. She looked down at me, face clouded with concern.

"Are you alright?" she asked.

"So good," I said, closing my eyes. I didn't know if I felt sick or hungry or completely exhausted. A mix of the three, I concluded.

"Mark! Get over here," Taylor said.

"No, I'm fine," I said, uncomfortable from all their attention. It wasn't me who deserved to be fussed over. "I'm just tired, and I'm a bit lightheaded."

"The fire is ready. What's up?" Mark asked, crunching under-brush as he made his way over.

"Fix him," Taylor said. "I'm going to get him something to eat."

"I'll get food," Olivia said. "Stay with him."

Mark pursed his lips and bent down next to me. I tried to shoo him away, but Taylor grabbed my arm and wrapped hers over my chest. I didn't have the energy to fight her.

"I'm going to sew this up, ok?" Mark asked in a voice you'd use for a toddler.

I shrugged. Things were *really* spinning now. Mark donned a headlamp and I watched with halfhearted attention as he threaded a needle. Olivia returned with an energy bar. I peeled it open and tried to take a bite, but the bar was more stone than food. I set my efforts to gnaw a corner when a needle of pain came from my knee.

"Watch it," I said.

"This will hurt," Mark said, not looking up.

For what seemed like hours, Mark worked on my leg, sending needles of pain into the muscles. He finally stood to stretch his back.

"Alright, you're good," Mark said.

Energy bar half gone, I looked down at my leg. It was a jagged line of uneven stitches.

"Thanks," I said.

"Sure," Mark returned.

He made his way to the dancing fire. I bent over my leg and gently covered it with a strip of gauze, then secured the ends and sides with medical tape. It took a bit of effort, but I managed to pull on the new pants. I tied my shoes and shuffled over to the others. Taylor draped a blanket over us. I extended my injured leg on the ground, unable to bend it more than a few inches.

We ate cans of tuna, and Mark excitedly presented us with a bag of dried fruit for dessert. We didn't talk much. There wasn't a lot to say.

After the coals died out, we piled into the car because it was safer than sleeping in the open. I took the back row, blanket wrapped around my shoulders. I spread out as much as possible and fell asleep within minutes of closing my eyes.

THIRTY-THREE

I CHECKED ON Taylor the first thing the next morning. She was curled up in the middle seat with a blanket wrapped tightly around her body. I touched her cheek. Her skin was warm, and I let out a sigh of relief. Her eyes fluttered open.

"Stop, your hands are cold," she said.

I sighed, looking her over with pursed lips. She shifted around and popped a hand out from under the blanket. I squeezed it. She seemed to fall asleep again, but she could have been pretending, not ready to talk or answer questions about how she was feeling.

Mark and Olivia were still asleep in the front seats, so I tried to wiggle out of the car as quietly as possible. The chill morning air cut through my shirt as I closed the door. The first hints of sunrise streamed over the horizon, coating everything with a purple glow. I massaged my aching neck, taking it in by twisting in a slow circle.

I shuffled to the side of the road like an injured turtle. My leg protested with every movement. It was stiff and aching. A streak of blood had soaked through my jeans and bandage, making the fabric stick to the cut. I'd worry about peeling it off later.

I went to the bathroom at the edge of the road before continuing to walk the length of the car. I was careful to not force my leg to bend. The last thing I wanted was to rip the stitches. Last night's surgery was likely the peak of Mark's medical abilities, and it would only mess up my leg further to do it again. Still, I refused to be a burden, so I forced myself to get used to walking on my own.

The first ten minutes were terribly painful. I felt it in my hip and lower back, in my calf and foot. I focused on the ground, making sure my steps were steady. I went the length of the car over and over. Back and forth. Fourteen small steps, turn, fourteen back. I didn't venture further than that because I wouldn't be able to outrun a corpse if one happened to surprise me.

After twenty minutes, the soreness began to fade. I reached the front of the car and leaned heavily against the hood, lightheaded. My hands began to shake. After losing so much blood, I'd be weak for a long while.

I didn't feel like climbing back inside, so I let myself sink to the asphalt against the front tire, soaking in the first rays of sunlight. Here, in the quiet, I could close my eyes and pick out the occasional chirping bird. I could almost forget about the last few days.

Almost.

It wasn't long before the others began to stir. Mark broke out more cans of tuna, and we hit the road soon after eating. Mark took the first stint behind the wheel. Olivia propped her feet on the dashboard in the passenger's seat. Taylor and I took the middle seats.

I spent most of my time watching her, and she spent most of hers sleeping. I didn't know if that was due to exhaustion or hopelessness. Probably both. And even then, that couldn't begin to describe how she was feeling. It tore at my heart to see her this way and not be able to do anything to make her better.

I wondered if she slept because she didn't want to think about what was happening to her. It happened to Jamison, and he'd barely lasted two days. Three, maybe. I wasn't sure anymore. Everything was blurring together in my mind.

If we were lucky, we still had a few days before the infection completely took over. A part of me wondered if that was lucky, not cruel, to know you only had a few days left. Just waiting for the end. Was it worth it to prolong your suffering so you could say goodbye?

I rubbed my eyes. My headache was coming back. I was sure now I'd gotten a concussion falling down the stairs at the country club. My ears still occasionally rang as well. There wasn't much I could do about either of these problems, so I tried my best to ignore them.

THE REST OF the day passed slowly.

Olivia drove after Mark, and they did their best to keep the conversation going, to distract us from the situation at hand. Mark continued to ask me questions about hockey. I knew what he was doing, but I took the bait anyway. For an hour or so, it felt good to share stories of my years playing, to talk about my favorite players, or to explain the rules in as much detail as he allowed.

All the while, we made frequent stops for gas and to scour abandoned cars and supermarkets for anything useful. I made sure to stretch my leg every chance I got, and Mark made it his job to yell that I was only going to make things worse. I waved him off with a middle finger.

On one of the breaks, I took a loop up and down the road, then stopped Mark outside our car. Taylor wandered aimlessly around rusting cars. Olivia worked the siphoning pump a short distance away.

"Where are we going?" I asked, shielding my eyes against the sunlight.

"I thought we'd decided on Colorado," Mark said.

"Sure…but why? There's nothing for us there," I said.

Taylor looked in our direction but she was too far away to hear what we were saying.

I rubbed my hands together. "The airport doesn't have a cure. We both know that. *Taylor* knows that."

"Sometimes it's better to have a goal than a reason," Mark said. "Something to look forward to, to keep you going."

I studied my feet. "What if there's no one there, or if it's overrun?"

"Then we'll figure something else out," Mark said. Even though I wasn't looking, I could feel him staring intently at me. "Cody, are you alright?"

"Nobody's alright anymore," I said. I meant it as a quip, but it came off sharply.

"I'm serious," Mark said.

I forced myself to meet his gaze. His face showed concern through the creases at his eyes and the way his eyebrows drew together. I looked away after a moment. I shook my head. "No…I don't know how to deal with this…"

There were a few seconds of silence between us. I looked around the highway. I focused on the sparse trees, the swaying grass, and the way the sun felt like it was burning the back of my neck. Mark's hand touched my shoulder, then he wrapped me in a hug. It took a moment for me to return the gesture.

Mark pulled away. "I'm here for you. Olivia's here for you. You're not alone."

All I could do was nod. Mark squeezed my arm and went to

check on Olivia. I returned to shuffling around the road, peering through dirty windows.

We'd hardly made it two hundred miles before the light started to fade. We gathered around a fire and ate a dinner of canned stew. I didn't have utensils, so I had to drink the broth before I could stab pieces of potato with my knife. I kept close to Taylor, both of us sharing a blanket. The flames made shadows dance across everyone's faces.

"Do you remember what it was like before?" I asked.

"Feels like it's been forever," Taylor said.

"A couple months, at least," Olivia said.

Mark shook his head. "Not even close."

"I honestly have no idea," I said.

Mark and Olivia proceeded to argue over how long it had been since the Collapse. I held Taylor's hand under the blanket.

"I was worried about what college I would go to," I said softly. "And now everything I knew is gone."

"We'll always be with you," Taylor said.

"Sure," I said, rubbing my chin uncertainly.

"What were your parents like?" Taylor asked.

I wrapped my arms around my left knee. The right remained extended close to the fire. My back hurt from sitting without anything to lean against.

"They used to get mad at me for rollerblading in the house, then for shooting pucks at the garage door. Still, I think a part of them liked it because they knew I'd found something I loved." I paused to think. It had been too long since I'd thought about my real parents. A deep ache made it hard to swallow. "My dad would come home from work early so he could surprise us before dinner. My mom always invited everyone over, even strangers, just to be friendly…"

Taylor rested her chin on her knees. "When was the last time you saw them?"

I took a while to respond. Long enough for Taylor to open her mouth, close it, and look back at the fire. "It was after a tournament in St. Paul. Our team went back on the bus and everyone else went home on their own. It was snowing, and…the police told me they went over a guard rail into a river—" I choked on the last words. My chest blossomed with pain.

Without warning, I was back on a bench in the police station, still wearing my game-day suit. Dazed and unbelieving. Jamison sat next to me and his parents hovered nearby, watching anxiously. Officers meandered past, occasionally glancing in our direction.

Taylor gripped my arm and I came back to the present. She wiped my cheek. She didn't have to say anything. I knew what she meant through the firm hold on my arm, from her head resting on my shoulder. It was only when I looked up that I saw Mark and Olivia watching me as well. I turned my attention back to the fire.

The flames burned down to coals. Mark added the occasional log, and the others shared stories over the next few hours. The more everyone talked, the more I realized how little I actually knew about them. I was content to let the others talk, which let me soak up the conversation. I didn't know how long we stayed up, but I didn't care. Nothing else mattered.

These were the moments that made life worth living.

I only wished Taylor had more of them.

THIRTY-FOUR

TAYLOR SHOOK ME awake.

"What's wrong?" I asked.

"Nothing, look outside," she said earnestly.

I squinted through the window. Fog undulated over the road and swirled between trees. I barely made out the circle of the sun in the grey. Simple awe washed over me.

"I thought you'd like it," Taylor said. Her eyes glimmered with excitement. The corner of her lips played upwards thoughtfully. "We should get going. We don't want to waste time."

"Sure…" I said, rubbing my eyes. "How are you feeling?"

"Good. Really good," she said. Her face was flushed, but it was a good change from the colorless cheeks I expected to see. "I jogged for a while."

I raised my eyebrows. "How long have you been up?"

"An hour, two. I don't know," Taylor said.

She proceeded to shake Mark and Olivia awake. Mark stretched, irritated. Olivia immediately began to bombard Taylor with questions about how she was feeling.

"Forget about that!" Taylor threw her hands in the air. "It's a beautiful day. I don't want you to miss it."

At that, Taylor jumped out of the car and ran along the road. Her jacket fluttered behind in slow ripples. She twirled in the middle of the street, spinning on the double yellow lines. Her hair shifted with the breeze. She faced the car again, joy across her face.

My heart broke in that moment. I did my best to smile back, but I doubt she saw. I found it impossible to move. I should have joined her, but I stayed in the car, watching through a dirty windshield. She danced on the concrete, feet barely skimming the ground, arms splayed wide.

I covered my mouth with a hand.

I should have moved. I should have joined her, but it was all I could do to keep myself from collapsing under the weight of what lay ahead of us.

Tears rolled down my cheeks.

And Taylor, impossibly light and free, spun endlessly in the fog.

THIRTY-FIVE

THE END CAME faster than anticipated.

Despite her morning strength, Taylor's condition only worsened throughout the day. It was almost unnoticeable at first. For a while, she kept up with our conversations, but her attention continued to wander. She stared out the window for long periods at a time.

By late afternoon, sweat glistened on her brow and dark circles appeared under her bloodshot eyes. The skin around her neck had turned a permanent, ashy grey. Her once vibrant cheeks lost all color. Even the sparkle in her eyes flickered here and there. A few times, I wasn't sure she recognized me as I watched her face. Her brow creased before an imperceptible smile appeared on her pale, thin lips.

Every bump in the road caused her to let out a quiet groan. I bit my lip against the pain of watching her deteriorate before my eyes. I tried to assure her that everything was going to be alright, but I don't think she believed me. My voice cracked when I tried to speak. The hope I tried to convey through my words echoed hollowly as soon as I said them. Taylor didn't mention it, and she didn't always reply.

Taylor doubled over in a fit of coughing. She wiped blood from her mouth with a blanket, wheezing as she pulled it tighter around her body. Olivia glanced back, concern etched deep into her brow.

We stopped in the midst of a swath of abandoned cars.

"We need gas," Mark said.

He looked back at us for a moment before stepping out of the car. Olivia joined him. I watched them go from car to car, peering into windows and trying the doors. We sat in the back row, and I had both arms wrapped around Taylor's waist. I grimaced as she pressed against my stretched-out leg.

"Cody," Taylor said.

"What?"

"You're a good person. Don't let this change you. You'll see the world get better, I know you will."

"You will too."

"Don't think I won't miss you." She touched my face. Her hand was like ice against my skin, but I didn't move it away. I gripped it instead, the back of her hand pressed against my lips.

"I didn't mean for any of this to happen. I—"

"It's ok."

I shook my head. "None of this should have happened—"

"It's ok, we did what we thought was best. It's done," she said, fingers playing over the collar of her shirt. "You're so kind. Don't let that change."

"No…" My voice hitched. I didn't even see that in myself. How could she?

Taylor pressed her head against my chest. I rested my chin on top of her head. I understood what she wanted without her saying it. Hold her tight. Show that I would be there as she slipped away. It was a while before Mark and Olivia returned. They took one look at Taylor and settled into their seats, watching from the corners of their eyes. Taylor's eyes remained closed, her breathing unsteady.

"Tell me about a happy place," Taylor said, voice a whisper.

Mark squeezed his hands together. Olivia wrapped her arms around her knees.

I only hesitated for a moment. "There were woods behind our house growing up. I used to go down and explore every few days. There was a tree that grew over a stream. I used to sit over the water and close my eyes. I listened to the birds…and the trickling water… it was so peaceful, and only I knew about it…"

I looked down. Taylor didn't make a sound. She didn't move. I felt her wrist, heart sinking.

She was gone.

Anguish flooded me like a ruptured dam. I clutched her body, tears streaming down my cheeks. I rocked back and forth. It couldn't be over. Not yet.

Mark and Olivia kept their eyes on their hands. It was minutes before anyone moved. Mark removed the knife from his belt and offered it to me.

"I can't…" I said.

Mark gave a slight nod. He bent forward and aligned the blade with Taylor's temple. It was in and out before I could avert my gaze. Olivia looked out the window, hand over her mouth. Her shoulders shook.

I didn't know what to do, so I just held Taylor's limp form and tried not to look at the blood coming from her temple. Mark regarded me for a long minute before gently pulling a blanket over Taylor's face. I helped wrap the rest of her body, my mind falling into a haze.

I hardly registered the actions around me. Mark started the car at some point. Rolling hills blurred in the windows. I continued to hold Taylor's stiffening body. At some point, we were traversing the streets of a town. I didn't remember us exiting the highway. Mark halted in front of a hardware store.

"We thought it would be good to give Taylor a proper burial," Mark said as he parked the car.

Twisting in his seat, he looked apprehensively at Taylor's blanketed form still in my arms. I glanced down, suddenly understanding what it must have looked like for them to see us this way. I slowly positioned Taylor's body along the back row of the car and settled into a middle seat.

"We'll be back soon," Mark said.

They disappeared into the store and I closed my eyes. I came to again as Mark and Olivia approached the car. Mark carried a shovel in his hands. I rubbed my forehead. It was becoming more difficult to keep track of events.

In time, Mark parked next to a small grove of trees at the edge of an expansive meadow. We all took turns digging the grave. Part of me thought the physical action would break me out of this paralysis. It didn't happen this time.

The numbness didn't release as we lowered Taylor's body into the hole in the ground. It didn't go away when we covered her form with upturned earth. It didn't fade as Mark fashioned a makeshift headstone, or when we shared a few words over her grave.

The shovel thumped to the ground, having slipped from my limp fingers. Never again would I hear her laugh. Or see her constant smile. Or feel giddy at the way she looked at me.

It was over.

I turned away and hobbled to the car, ignoring Mark and Olivia's concerned looks. I didn't register the pain in their own eyes. I leaned my head against the window.

We drove in silence. But sometimes, silence was good.

THIRTY-SIX

I DREAMT OF our first day on the road.

Everyone was there: Jamison, Taylor, Mark and Olivia. It wasn't dark yet, but we sat around a fire, laughing and sharing stories. Everything seemed to glow with a golden haze. It took me a while to realize what was different, and it dawned on me that my chest didn't ache. It wasn't weighed down with terrible pain. For the first time I could remember, I was at ease.

I turned to my left and saw my parents approaching from the woods. My mom kissed my cheek and my dad wrapped me in a crushing embrace. Even Jamison's parents were there, setting up a tent a short distance away. Jean looked up and waved while Daniel wrestled a pole into place.

And in that simple moment, everything was perfect and nothing could go wrong.

I smiled to myself as I took it in.

Muffled voices came from somewhere I couldn't pinpoint. I twisted in the woods. They spoke again. It sounded like Mark, but he was stirring a pot on our camp stove...

I woke up in my seat in the middle row. Head foggy, I took a moment to orient myself. Mark and Olivia talked outside the car. Judging by the position of the sun, it was already late morning.

I didn't make an effort to move, and instead closed my eyes so I could better cling to the remnants of my dream. I tried to visualize myself back in the forest, but it was already slipping away like water in a cupped hand. The elusive joy and comfort I'd felt dissolved into a hollow ache, which soon turned into a hopeless pit. Guilt and buried grief threatened to swallow me whole.

I shoved it down until I didn't feel much of anything. I wrapped my arms around myself and leaned my head against the window.

Mark and Olivia managed to coax me out of the car and forced me to eat from a bag of trail mix. They walked with me up and down the road to strengthen my leg, trying all the while to get me to talk. When I didn't respond, they settled for talking over me, seeming to hope I would join in.

The next handful of days went by in a blur. I lost track of our stops and how many days it had really been. For all the time I spent looking out the window, I hardly noticed the changes in scenery. I helped gather supplies and fill the car with gas, though Mark didn't trust me to drive.

I knew deep inside there were things I had to deal with. All the pain and darkness boiled just beneath the surface, waiting. The thought of letting it out—of *talking* about it—sent panic coursing through my body. I clutched the blanket to my face as I hyperventilated and fought the urge to jump out of the moving car.

The episode passed without Mark and Olivia noticing, but I was still on edge. Still restless. Sinking ever lower.

THE FIRST MARKING caught us by surprise. Black spray paint covered the weathered green road sign. An arrow pointed directly ahead with, DIA - 25 miles, scrawled below.

Did this mean people were there? And they wanted others to join them?

We got out of the car to marvel at the sight.

"I told you it would work!" Mark said, grinning widely. He shook me with enthusiasm. Olivia placed her hands on her hips, controlled excitement on her face.

I didn't know how to deal with the faint exhilaration swirling in my gut. It felt wrong to be happy about something like this.

I wondered what this group would be like. They advertised their presence, which seemed to bode well for us. I couldn't imagine why a hostile group would do that. Either way, we were close, and it didn't scare me so much anymore about what we would find.

It could be a trap. But maybe it was a haven. And maybe we would find a way to move forward.

I wondered if that was still possible for me.

The airport broke the horizon within the hour. Its canopy glowed in the afternoon sun like a white circus tent. The "W" shaped hotel glinted brightly, and thousands of abandoned cars sat in the expansive parking lots. Signs for non-existent airlines passed over-head. The roads leading up to the terminals became more clogged the closer we got, and our progress halted long before we reached the fork between the east and west terminals. Cars were pressed bumper to bumper with barely enough room to walk between them.

Mark shut off the car and dropped his hands into his lap. "I guess we should get out," he said.

It took a few minutes to gather our supplies. I shouldered a backpack of clothing and carried one of our new pistols in my right hand. I grimaced at every step. Mark slowly led the way through the maze of vehicles. I followed Olivia and glanced into the cars we passed. Some had broken windows. Many had corpses in the seats, but each body had a bullet in its forehead. Another spray-painted sign directed us to the west terminal. Mountains sprawled across the distant horizon.

The blockade of cars ended on the top floor reserved for arrivals and departures. Here, the cars were arranged in such a way that we had to climb over them to reach the other side.

"Hold it!" someone barked.

I halted on the trunk of a sedan. Looking up, I saw three figures positioned around a white, twelve-passenger van about twenty feet away. I'd been so focused on my next step that I hadn't seen the group.

A woman sat in a chair on the roof, and two men stood at both ends of the car. The woman kept her red hair in a ponytail. The man on the left watched us from under a thick beard and sunglasses. The other wore a mustache and stubble. All three were muscled, and from the way they carried themselves, they might have been ex-military.

"Hand over your weapons," the woman said. Her eyes were hidden by reflective sunglasses.

I laid my pistol on top of the car and removed the knife from my belt. Mark and Olivia did the same with their weapons, though it wasn't much to unload.

"Climb over," she commanded.

I inched to the edge of the car and carefully lowered myself to the ground. I massaged my leg. Mark and Olivia stood next to me. The men were content in their silence, guns no longer raised.

"Are any of you infected?" the woman asked.

"No," Mark said.

"Why are you here?"

"Safety."

"Where did you come from?"

"Florida."

"Long way to travel."

"It was."

The woman lowered her rifle. She hardly moved otherwise, but I could tell she was evaluating us carefully. "Have you killed anyone?"

My face twitched. I dropped my eyes to the ground.

"Yes. I don't know how many," Mark said.

"Why?" the woman asked.

Mark looked at me. "Wrong place, wrong time. We were taken in and they forced us to fight another group while holding her hostage." Mark indicated Olivia, sharing a version of the truth. "And one other, but she didn't make it. We escaped and headed here…" Mark broke off, face cracking as he surveyed the surrounding area. "I don't know why we're here…"

The woman mulled this over. "Check them."

The man with the beard slung his rifle over his shoulder and stepped forward. The other leaned casually against the van. None of them seemed worried. We clearly didn't pose much of a threat, especially in our condition. He patted us down.

"They're clear," he said, retrieving our weapons and dumping them in the van.

The woman raised her radio to her mouth. "We have three survivors. Sending them your way."

"*Copy,*" the voice on the other end said.

"They'll meet you at door six-twelve," the woman said, motioning for us to get moving.

The indicated doors were permanently wedged open. A woman

greeted us inside, two more guards standing watch. The woman wore a charcoal blazer and navy skirt, a spotless white blouse underneath. She kept her brown hair in a tight bun.

"Welcome," she said, smiling as she clasped her hands together. "My name is Katrina. Allow me to show you around."

Katrina walked slowly to keep pace with my uneven gait. Check-in counters went by on our left and right, and we emerged onto the walkway overlooking the west security checkpoint. The screening machines were still intact, but the long, snaking lines had been taken down, leaving a cavernous, open floor. High above, the tented ceiling glowed in the afternoon light, making the area feel even bigger.

Katrina started down the defunct escalator as she continued to explain life at the airport. "We have nearly two hundred survivors. More come in every few days, and we're slowly retaking the rest of the airport."

"How much is cleared?" Mark asked.

"Here and the hotel. They're working on Terminal A now. It's a slow process, and dangerous work. It all depends on volunteers, finding ammunition…" She trailed off and looked us over once we reached the floor. "We can always use more fighters and scavengers. Everyone helps out in some way, but we especially need people in those jobs. You're compensated well—"

"We'll think about it," Mark said. He glanced at me. "We're not ready for any of that right now."

Katrina gave a knowing nod, eyes softening. I looked at the ground. My chest tightened and I tried to shove away the lurking darkness. Katrina led us to the back of the security checkpoint and pushed through one of the many doors that opened to the hotel. It loomed above our heads, at least ten stories tall. The windows and glass canopy glimmered in the sunlight.

We crossed the courtyard of benches and artificial grass, other residents watching us pass. I kept my head down as we went through the lobby and down a side hallway. We entered a small meeting room, and a man and woman talked at their desks on the opposite wall. They wore light blue scrubs. Doctors, likely. Four chairs and a coffee table filled the corner on the left.

"You need a quick evaluation before we can continue," Katrina said.

I took a seat in the corner while the doctors led Mark and Olivia into separate rooms. Katrina hovered for a minute before taking a seat herself. I stared at my hands.

"...kid..."

I snapped back to myself, realizing Katrina was talking.

"What's your name?" She asked.

"Cody."

I didn't know what else to say, so I went back to fiddling with my hands. How long had Mark and Olivia had been gone?

"It's good here," Katrina said after a while. "You don't have to worry about that."

"Sure," I said.

Another pause, then, "Are you alright?"

I was saved from answering by the click of an opening door. Mark reentered the meeting room and the male doctor waved me forward. Mark patted me on the shoulder as we passed each other. He had a small bandage on his upper arm.

"You can take a seat," the doctor said, closing the door behind us.

The exam station was a fold-up table with a thin pad on top, covered by a white sheet. The room was sparse and had a modest selection of medical equipment. There was a scale in one corner, a wooden chair next to it. A small desk with another chair on the opposite wall. Jars of cotton balls, swabs, and ointment lined the desk.

The man faced me and extended his hand. "I'm Doctor Ward."

I shook his hand. "Cody."

"How old are you?" he asked.

"Eighteen."

"Well, Cody, the first thing I want to tell you is you're safe here," Dr. Ward said, giving me one of those pure smiles that reached the eyes. His were brown, and his hair was mostly grey.

"I don't think anywhere is safe anymore," I said.

"Safe as it can be," he clarified. "Can I have you take off your clothes?"

"Why?"

"To make sure you're not bitten—"

"I'm not."

"—and to check your other injuries," he said, indicating the streak of blood showing through my pant leg.

I reluctantly pulled off my shirt and set it next to me on the table. It took a moment to wiggle out of my pants, and Dr. Ward's eyes widened at the bloody bandage on my thigh. I laid down, and he carefully removed the strip of gauze. The cut was inflamed and raised. A bit of puss leaked from some areas. The surrounding skin was a tapestry of green and purple bruises.

"There's a minor infection, but we'll be able to take care of that," Dr. Ward said, gently probing the cut with gloved fingers. I clenched my teeth against the pain. "I'm sorry about the discomfort. What happened?"

"I climbed through a window. There was still glass on the bottom."

"You must have lost a lot of blood. How do you feel?"

"Weak. Tired."

"You should take it easy for the next week or so. Eat as much food as they'll let you, and you'll recover in time. Try to avoid walking as much as possible until it fully heals," Dr. Ward said, standing up. "Who stitched you up?"

"Mark."

"He did a good job. I'll have to clean it a bit, but he did well."

Dr. Ward had me drop my underwear long enough to make sure it wasn't covering a bite. He then inspected the slowly healing gash on my shoulder, and I had to explain that I'd gotten it by falling on a stick. He proceeded to clean my arm with stinging disinfectant, applied ointment, and finished up by wrapping it in gauze.

I laid on the table as he worked on my leg. I clenched my teeth through the pain. He offered me two Ibuprofen and apologized for not having anything stronger. The last thing he checked was my thumb. It had been a few weeks since I'd gotten the cut, but healing was slow since the injury kept breaking open when I strained it.

"Were you ever exposed to their blood? The dead, I mean," Dr. Ward asked.

"Plenty," I said.

"Did it ever come in contact with an open wound?"

I looked down at my hands, running a finger over my newly bandaged thumb. "Right here. I cut it by accident. A few days later, we were moving bodies, and my hands were covered."

"Interesting…" Dr. Ward said, taking down the note. "And you've never felt sick? Fever, cough, chills…"

"Nothing," I said.

Dr. Ward wrote for another minute, then set down the pen and clipboard. "Almost done." He donned the stethoscope and pressed the chest piece above my heart. I breathed in and out as instructed while he moved it over my stomach and back.

"You can put your clothes back on," Dr. Ward said, returning the stethoscope around his neck. "Do you tend to have high blood pressure?" he asked.

I shook my head, pulling on my shirt.

"Compared to others your age, your heart rate is much faster than normal. That can be attributed to blood loss, but…are you anxious, Cody?"

"I don't know," I said.

I focused on putting my pants back on. Focused on the next movement, on telling myself that I wasn't, in fact, drowning. I sat back down on the evaluation table, fingers tapping the edge. Dr. Ward watched me carefully. His gaze dropped to my hands. I squeezed the table to keep them from moving.

Dr. Ward pulled up his chair and leaned forward, elbows on his knees. "Are you depressed?"

I fought the increasingly desperate urge to spring into action, to pace around the room. Forcing myself to stay still made it feel like I was going to explode.

"I…" Words failed me. I looked around the room. At the jars of medical equipment. At the walls. Anywhere but Dr. Ward's soft expression.

"It's alright, Cody. You don't have to be scared or ashamed. I'm here to help, and there are plenty of other people who are ready to listen. We have groups for people who have gone through the same things," Dr. Ward said.

"Not quite the same things," I whispered. The next part slipped out before I could stop myself. "…they haven't killed like me…lost who I have…"

"We've all done things we regret, and we've lost so much, but there's always a way forward," Dr. Ward said. He remained silent for a long moment, still watching me. "Do you think about hurting yourself?"

I shook my head, even though a part of me was desperate for a way out. It was the part clawing for quiet, for an escape from the heaviness.

"Can you say it for me?" Dr. Ward asked.

"I'm not going to hurt myself," I managed to get out.

"If you feel that way, please, talk to someone. There's no shame in it. I'm here. Groups are here. Your friends are here," Dr. Ward said. He squeezed my good shoulder, concern and warmth overtaking his expression. "It's not all on you, and you're not alone, Cody."

I nodded, internally trying to make sense of his words when it felt quite the opposite. The only people I had left were Mark and Olivia, and I'd hardly talked to them before the Collapse. No one here knew me. I was, without a doubt, completely and utterly alone.

"I should get going. They've been waiting a while," I said, getting up.

Dr. Ward stepped aside. He seemed ready to let me go but spoke up again as I reached for the door handle. "Would you mind coming back tomorrow?"

I paused. "What for?"

"I'd like to keep talking. I think I can help, if you're willing," Dr. Ward said. "I think you should talk to somebody, and maybe your friends aren't the right ones."

I chewed my lip. Almost every part of me wanted to deny his offer. I longed to put on a smile, say *I'm alright*, and never see this man again. But a smaller part of me knew that wasn't true, and I knew I couldn't keep this up on my own. Somehow, he could see that. And still, I deliberated for a long moment. Dr. Ward waited patiently for my answer.

I brought myself to give a slight nod, and it was the hardest thing I could have done. "Sure."

"Good…good…" Dr. Ward said. "Tomorrow at two."

"Thanks," I said, turning the handle to leave.

UNCERTAINTY SEIZED MY body the moment I left the room. I shouldn't have said yes. I was fine. There was no need to talk. I turned back to tell Dr. Ward I'd changed my mind, but the door clicked shut with him still inside. My heart raced.

Mark and Olivia jumped to their feet. I looked at them like a deer in headlights. I didn't know what to do. Everyone regarded me warily. Katrina fiddled with the button of her blazer. I checked my watch, realizing I'd been gone nearly thirty minutes.

Far too long.

I knew it, and they did too.

"You didn't have to wait for me," I said, shifting from foot to foot. I did my best to casually look around the room.

"It's no problem," Mark said.

"We're not leaving you," Olivia added.

Katrina led us back to the hotel lobby, and we paused in front of the check-in desk. "I'll leave you to get settled," she said. "Don't hesitate to ask for help if you need it."

"Thank you," Mark said. He turned to the middle-aged woman behind the desk. "So…what do we do?"

"Fill out these, and I'll assign your rooms," the woman said.

She handed us three sheets of paper and pens. I read mine over. It was a list of questions in neat handwriting, probably made with a copier. The longer questions left extra space to answer.

Full name.

Age.

Partner.

Where are you from?

How can you help/what skills do you have? (E.g. Cooking, bookkeeping, weapons training, scavenging, etc.)

Questions continued on the back of the page. I made my way to a table to fill it out. I didn't know what to say for how I could help the community. I knew I could fight if they needed me, but the thought of doing that again filled my insides with knots. I wrote that I could help scavenge for supplies. After thinking about it for a few minutes, I added that I could help clear out the remaining corpses from the other terminals.

I reviewed my shaky handwriting and crossed out the second part. I wrote it again, then crossed it out. For the next few minutes, I stared at the paper, squeezing my head between my hands.

Confusion muddied my ability to think. I tried reading the next questions, but I couldn't understand what they meant. It was like my mind had shut down. A flood of thoughts but nothing I could grasp onto.

I gave up when Mark turned his paper in. The clerk looked me over with concern after surveying my sheet. Anger rose in my chest at that look, the one I got anywhere I turned. I tried to ignore her as I bounced on the balls of my feet, scouring the ceiling.

Mark handed me the key to my room and directed us through the lobby. I studied the number written on its back in Sharpie.

528.

I watched each step as we climbed, repeating the number in my head.

528.

528.

5—

Shit.

I studied the keycard again.

528.

We stopped in front of our rooms.

"Do you want to be with us?" Olivia asked. "Cody?"

I looked up. "Oh, no…I just need some time…later, maybe."

"Sure," Olivia said. "Knock if you need us."

I flashed my keycard and shoved the door open. It slammed behind me. I took small steps into the center of the room. It had a queen bed. A nightstand with a lamp on top. A desk and swivel chair. Lastly, a TV. Weak lighting came from the window.

Almost exactly like the room in Florida.

I dropped my keycard.

I couldn't stop it this time.

In seconds, everything I'd been pushing down crashed over me like a tsunami of unquenchable pain. Frantic gasps of air filled the room as I paced. I tugged at my shirt collar and focused on my steps.

Left. Right. Left. Right.

The thought of returning to Dr. Ward tomorrow sent panic surging through my veins, making everything tremble. I held my neck as my throat seemed to close. I would have to talk. Part of me was desperate for that, but I was terrified of facing everything I'd done. It didn't seem real. It wasn't. It couldn't be. I hadn't killed those people, because that would mean I'd done something unforgivable.

A gunshot cracked in my mind. The prisoner fell again, a bullet in his forehead.

No…I didn't do it…

People tumbled at the country club. One after another.

No…stop…

Visions flashed, and I was there as each one happened.

Training in the parking garage…Aaron and Dalton's mangled bodies…shooting pucks with Jamison in the mall…finding his bite, and his desperate clawing for air…diving into the ocean…Murphy, dropping like a stone in my scope…

I picked up my pace, knives shooting through my leg. The memories continued, strangling me from the inside out.

Jamison and I on the bench in the police station…learning how to shoot in the basement, glass and drywall everywhere…my dad's body on the operating table…late night drinking and board games at the house…people flying past the cafeteria windows, filled with terror at the end of the world…

It wouldn't stop. My heart pounded against my ribs.

My first kiss with Taylor at the party…her last moments in my arms…smirking at Jamison as he skinned a rabbit…digging his grave…digging Taylor's…lowering them into the ground…

It all came back to me. The times when we laughed and fought, killed and sat together. When we drank and ate and watched the world burn.

I shook my hands. Squeezed my head. Screamed into a pillow. I circled the room, doing it all over again. And again. My lungs fought for air. It felt like my whole body was collapsing in on itself.

Hot tears streamed down my face, and I began sobbing uncontrollably. I covered my face with a pillow so no one could overhear me weeping over the times I wouldn't get back. For both sets of parents. For Jamison and Taylor. My hockey team, and everyone else I would never see again. The injustice of it all consumed me. It wasn't right, being forced to kill and make decisions that only led to death.

Suddenly, the tears slowed and I could breathe again. Then another body fell, accompanied by chilling screams and the sounds of battle. And I was back in pieces.

This happened twice more before I had nothing left. I sank against the wall, arms wrapped around my good leg. Exhaustion reigned. I wiped my face on my shirt. My head throbbed and I took deep, shuddering breaths.

It was hard to notice at first, but the fog gripping my mind had lessened a fraction. It wasn't gone, but it felt like I could think again. The storm had pulled back as well, but it continued to swirl, angry and relentless, waiting for me to slip again. And next time, it might swallow me whole.

But in this moment, I'd surfaced. Somehow.

It didn't take me as I stood up, or as I washed my face in the bathroom. It didn't come as I scrubbed myself down with a wash-cloth and soap. Even when I thought about meeting Dr. Ward—anxiety squeezing me like a vice—the darkness held back.

It might not last. But for now, it did. And for that, I was truly grateful.

THIRTY-SEVEN

I AWOKE TO faint orange light pooling on the floor of my room. I remained still, and for those first moments of consciousness, I was completely at peace.

Thoughts slowly filtered back.

The memories. The hurt. Anxiety over meeting with Dr. Ward. Facing Mark and Olivia. Having to get through another day without Taylor.

I rubbed my eyes and told myself it would get better, somehow, because there was no other option.

Inspiration hit me. I could get dressed. Take a walk, maybe. Bask in the fresh air outside the hotel. I hesitated for a split second, and the idea slipped into nothingness. So, I continued lying in bed, staring at the ceiling until a knock came on the door.

"Cody, you in there?" Olivia's voice filtered through the door. I closed my eyes. "Cody?"

"Yeah, one second," I said.

With considerable effort, I sat up in bed, then slipped out from under the covers. I shuffled to the door in my boxers. Olivia, ready for the day, looked me over.

"We wanted to find food and see if we can get new clothes," Olivia said. "We'll wait for you to get ready."

"Alright," I said.

I shut the door, Olivia still standing outside. Alone again, I did my best to prepare for what lay ahead.

THE BREAKFAST LINE was long, but it moved efficiently as it snaked through the lobby. I took in the other survivors. There were people of every age, even a few babies in carriers. I wondered how many of them had been here since the beginning.

It must have been awful.

Thousands of people stuck inside with no easy way to seal the exits. All it would have taken was a few of the dead to overrun the entire airport, and by the time anyone realized what was happening, it would have been too late to fight back.

The lucky ones probably hid in the right spot. Set up a base. Worked their way out…

I put aside my theories as the three of us settled at a small table and ate in relative silence. The buzz of other conversations filled my ears. My hands shook with nerves.

"I'm meeting with Doctor Ward later. To talk," I said.

"That's good, Cody," Mark said, squeezing my shoulder. "Olivia and I might check out one of the groups."

"Really?" I asked, stirring my soup.

Olivia chewed a piece of bread. "Maybe it'll help, maybe not, but it's probably best to try. Do you want to come?"

I thought it over, giving a small shrug. "I guess it can't hurt."

"Great, I think there's one tomorrow," Mark said, returning to his food.

Once again, the claustrophobic knowledge that I couldn't back out made it hard to eat. I took tiny bites until half my soup was gone. I pushed it forward, bread untouched. "I don't think I can finish this."

Mark and Olivia looked up, scraping their bowls. They exchanged a telling glance. I shrank in my seat.

"No problem," Mark said, dividing up the food. Olivia got the soup and Mark the bread.

They kept talking and I did my best to seem relaxed. Agitation gnawed inside, making it difficult to keep still. My legs bounced and my eyes flicked from person to person.

Meal finally over, we wandered the airport to look for clothes and get a feel for our new home. We passed storefronts and abandoned restaurants. It was impossible to go anywhere without passing other survivors. Most were friendly. Some had distant expressions, hardly acknowledging their surroundings.

I tried to keep my mind from wandering. It took little nudges here and there; counting my steps instead of thinking about the meeting; studying faces instead of dwelling on the weight of Taylor's death, or Jamison's, or my parents'…

I clenched my jaw and focused intently on the floor, counting the white marble tiles. I was able to relax again after a few minutes. It was like I was balancing on a knife edge, miles above the ground. Any single thought or word or situation could send me tumbling through the air.

Two o'clock arrived.

I left Mark and Olivia and reluctantly made my way back to the hotel. Every step sent a spike of uncertainty through my body. Every stride was more difficult than the last, but I kept moving. And before I knew it, I was standing in front of Dr. Ward. He shook my hand in greeting, his smile returning. He directed me to the screening room where I sat in the chair next to the scale. Dr. Ward sat in the chair across from me, a small notepad in hand. I stuck my hands under my legs, left foot tapping the floor.

"How are you feeling today?" Dr. Ward asked.

"Fine, I guess. The same," I said.

"And what's that like?"

I wasn't sure what to say, so I began with what I thought he wanted to know. "It's as if I'm…trapped, or something. There's a weight, right here…and it doesn't go away." I put a hand over my chest, feeling my rapid heartbeat through the bones. I took shallow breaths. The room shrank. Half-buried emotion nearly overtook me. "I don't know how to do this, or what to say…"

"It's alright. I understand if you're anxious, but I'm here to listen. There's no pressure to share before you're ready," Dr. Ward said, closing his notebook. He leaned forward an inch, compassion in his eyes. "Let's start over, get to know each other a bit. Just a conversation."

I nodded, relieved. He was just another person, doing his best to help. Still, the millstone holding me down argued otherwise. I thought I could ignore it if we kept things light, so that's what I intended to do.

"What do you do for fun?" Dr. Ward asked.

"I played hockey growing up, and I read when I get the time," I said.

Dr. Ward nodded along. "I've always loved reading. What's your favorite book?"

And we were off, talking about the little things; what we still had, and what we used to take for granted. He carefully nudged the conversation along, never prying or forcing me to answer. Always patient. Listening.

I slowly relaxed, but I still skirted the big topics and fought the unrelenting urge to cry. Every time that reaction came up, I shoved it away, holding out for just a bit longer. Only a few minutes until I could leave…

After avoiding yet another question, Dr. Ward rubbed the palm of one hand. Forehead creased, he seemed to be choosing his next words carefully. He sought my wandering eyes, somehow picking out the things I found impossible to say. "I know this is hard for you, but it's normal to feel your emotions, to let them out. It's also normal to want to hide them. The problem is, ignoring what's wrong doesn't solve it. The longer something goes without being said, the harder it is to voice, and the worse things get."

My shell cracked, threatening to break apart at any moment. Unconsciously, I knew he was right. I'd felt it. Every day, I was less and less alive.

He continued. "Oftentimes, healing can be just as painful as the initial trauma. That's why it's so difficult." Dr. Ward said the next part slowly, with nothing but warmth in his voice and expression. "If you truly want to get better, I'll do everything I can to help when you're ready, but the choice is up to you. I can't force it to happen, and I certainly wouldn't try."

I didn't know what it was. It might have been what he said, or the *way* he said it, or even the fact I *did* believe he cared, but something about his words made the walls of my carefully built world crumble around me. And maybe, also, I was tired of holding it in.

Vision blurring, I finally let go.

The grief of death and guilt of surviving coiled together, but it was the shame of my actions that broke through the doors holding these emotions in check. And unlike the previous night, there were no desperate attempts at keeping myself together. I simply let it happen, no longer thinking about who heard or what it looked like. Because this was the only thing left to do.

Dr. Ward produced a box of tissues. I had a small pile at my feet before I could speak again.

"Alright," I said, wiping my nose. "Where do we start?"

Dr. Ward spread his hands. "What's on your mind?"

I began with Jamison.

It felt strange to talk about him with a man I'd just met, but I *did* know Dr. Ward—who he was, at least, the kind of person I could trust.

And he was right. It *was* difficult, but opening up wasn't as terrible as I imagined. I left the session imperceptibly lighter. Not free. Not unburdened. But lighter. A glimmer of hope sparked to life. Like a candle in a storm. Flickering, maybe. But there nonetheless.

That's all I needed.

THIRTY-EIGHT

I STRUGGLED THROUGH the first month at the airport.

There were days I felt mostly myself; when I could laugh at a joke or think about Taylor and Jamison—or my parents—without it crushing me. Other days, I hardly dragged myself out of bed in the morning. And some, I didn't even try. I laid on my back with covers up to my chin despite the heat. It might be noon before I had to go to the bathroom badly enough to get up, then I'd crawl back into bed and fall asleep.

Sometimes, I would be on a walk and suddenly start crying or be overcome with panic. Sleep was fitful and occasionally filled with the recurring nightmare of seeing my friends as corpses. It left me groggy the next day, with dark circles under my eyes.

I continued to meet with Dr. Ward, and he assured me those things would pass in time. All the while, I attended group meetings with other survivors. Mark and Olivia went with me to those. For the first week, all I did was listen. I tried sharing a few times the second week but only succeeded in choking up after a couple of minutes.

Progress was slow at first, but it was around the third week I noticed small changes. I began to sleep through the night. My appetite returned. The panic attacks became less frequent.

My physical injuries also continued to get better. I could walk fairly well by now, though the gash in my leg wasn't quite healed. The cut on my shoulder had almost completely scarred over. You could tell my nose was slightly crooked too, but only if you looked closely. Most people didn't do that, thankfully.

One day, Dr. Ward brought up the issue I'd been avoiding.

"What job will you take?" he asked.

I'd been trying not to think about it, because the only option I felt I was good at, I didn't want to do: Fight, scavenge, kill corpses. Mark had already accepted his position with the guards and was actively working to clear the airport of corpses. Surprisingly, Olivia took the same job. Something about Mark needing someone to watch his back, as if he couldn't handle himself.

They'd taken the positions two weeks ago, and when pressed by the community leaders, Dr. Ward provided a note saying I wasn't ready to work. That extra time seemed to be up, but it was more generous than I deserved.

"I don't know what I'll do," I said.

I had already made it clear I didn't want to return to an action-based role, at least not for the time being. The problem was everything else seemed menial after what I'd experienced. I wasn't sure if I was ready for that either.

Dr. Ward clicked his pen, deep in thought. "What if you worked with me? Trained to be a doctor?"

I almost dismissed his suggestion with a laugh, but the longing for something *more* made me pause. Could that really be an option?

"I don't have any training. I would just get in the way," I said.

"Hey, most people here had no idea what they were doing until they started. We've built so much in so little time, and that's because people stepped up. Why are you any different?"

"I'm too young, and I'm not very good with blood…or injuries."

"Too young?" Dr. Ward raised his eyebrows. "You've already experienced more than most people do their entire lives. And sure, I have to deal with messy injuries, but there's more to the job than stitching people up. You have the heart for it, that's what matters," he said, leaning forward on his elbows to meet my eyes. "I know how badly you want to help, and this is the kind of work that *saves* lives, not takes them. I think you'd like it."

I mulled this over, absentmindedly tracing the scar on my thigh. Dr. Ward had one eyebrow raised, waiting for my answer. I nodded, knowing the truth deep inside. "Yes, I would."

THE FIRST HINT of purpose filled me as I left the session.

I found myself on the outside veranda between the hotel and the security checkpoint. I paused in the middle of the open area, hands in my pockets, looking toward the mountains. Evening sunlight warmed my face. Crisp air cut through my shirt. Eyes closed, I took a deep, cleansing breath.

For a minute, I was back on the road with my friends. I heard their laughter. Took in their voices. Remembered what it was like to be in their presence.

Taylor's steadiness. Her confidence. The dimples in her cheeks, and the way she looked at you with kindness and understanding.

Jamison's raw emotion. His boldness and disregard for the opinions of others. The thoughtfulness hiding underneath the bravado.

I thought of the Calloway's, and them bringing me into their family. My parents; our road trips and weekly movie nights. Of Montoya and Ryan, and the rest of my hockey team.

When I came back to myself, my chest ached, but it wasn't hollow. They were here with me, *right now*, and they would not be forgotten.

And with a job like Dr. Ward's, I had the chance to do something that made a real difference. Something that could help people. A way to fix things, in a small way.

For the first time in a long while, I could see beyond the next moment. For the first time since I could remember, I looked forward to tomorrow.

And there, in the quiet, in the peace, I smiled.

ACKNOWLEDGMENTS

This book wouldn't have happened without the help of many wonderful people.

Thank you to Meredith Anderson for being my copyeditor. Your enthusiasm for the story and keen eye for detail have helped make this the best novel possible.

To my parents, thank you for supporting my dream and reading those *very* rough first drafts—and being kind enough to say it was good. To Paulina and James W. for your encouragement and excitement surrounding the project. To Annie for helping me come up with crazy plot ideas that never made it into the final version, and for being the one I could always fall back on.

To my early supporters and Beta readers at college when I needed good friends and hardly knew what Beta readers were: Josh, Michael, Emily, Rachel, James R, Christian, and Cleo. And to the final readers who helped me understand this book might actually have a chance in the real world: Jim, Cooper, Jodi, Ella, Tianna, Sasha, and Mitch.

Special thanks to Kyle for those creative days during lockdown that kept me sane during a difficult time. To Trent for never doubting this dream and for your unwavering friendship when I needed it most. And to Rebecca for being one of the first people to truly believe I would publish a book one day. As requested all those years ago, the first copy I sign is for you.

PLAYLIST

#GROWNUPS | FEIN

WE COME RUNNING | YOUNGBLOOD HAWKE

IT'S JUST A LOT | K.FLAY

FUNERAL SINGERS | SYLVAN ESSO

EDEN | NOMBE, GENEVA WHITE

SEARCH PARTY | SAM BRUNO

COASTIN' | ZION I, K.FLAY

STRAIGHT RAZOR | MATT MAESON

DIVE | COAST MODERN

SEDONA | HOUNDMOUTH

HERO | FAMILY OF THE YEAR

UNBELIEVERS | VAMPIRE WEEKEND

BATTERY | RYAN CARAVEO

FIGHTING | SANTS OF VALORY

NATURAL | IMAGINE DRAGONS

STRONGER | THE SCORE

DREAM | BISHOP BRIGGS

WISHING IT WAS YOU | K.FLAY

REASON | MATTHEW CHAIM

NEXT TO ME | IMAGINE DRAGONS

MONSTER | MUMFORD & SONS

WEIGHT OF IT ALL | HANDSOME GHOST

SOMEPLACE BEAUTIFUL | ALFRED HALL

FUN | SIR SLY

SILVER LINING | EVAN WIZE

ABOUT THE AUTHOR

DAVID SLOCUM IS A WRITER AND ARTIST FROM DENVER, COLORADO. SOME OF HIS FAVORITE THINGS INCLUDE: BOOKS, CATS, ICE HOCKEY, THRIFT STORES, AND THE SEASON OF SPRING.

TITLE FONT | ERBAUM
BODY FONT | ADOBE GARAMOND PRO

WORD COUNT | 84,351